BITTER HARVEST

Recent Titles by Anne Goring from Severn House

NO ENEMY BUT WINTER
KATE WEATHERBY

BITTER HARVEST

Anne Goring

This first world edition published in Great Britain 1998 by
SEVERN HOUSE PUBLISHERS LTD of
9–15 High Street, Sutton, Surrey SM1 1DF.
This first world edition published in the U.S.A. 1998 by
SEVERN HOUSE PUBLISHERS INC of
595 Madison Avenue, New York, N.Y. 10022.

Copyright © 1998 by Anne Goring.
All rights reserved.
The moral right of the author has been asserted.

British Library Cataloguing in Publication Data

Goring, Anne
      Bitter harvest
      I. Domestic fiction
      1.Title
      823.9'14 [F]

      ISBN 0-7278-5394-5

All situations in this publication are fictitious and
any resemblance to living persons is purely coincidental.

Typeset by Hewer Text Ltd,
Edinburgh, Scotland.
Printed and bound in Great Britain by
MPG Books Ltd, Bodmin, Cornwall.

The Story So Far

Carrie and Adele Linton have returned from the East Indies to early-Victorian Manchester after the death of their parents. Their widowed Aunt Linnie is happy to take in her sister's children, but then she remarries and this second marriage proves unfortunate for all three. George O'Hara is a scheming bully who treats his wife with contempt and condemns Carrie to the life of a skivvy, threatening a similar fate for the delicate Adele if Carrie does not obey him. Carrie's friendship with carter's lad Jem Walker is one of the few solaces she has as she grows up.

Then, out of the blue, a Mrs Dorothea Sanderson calls to see the girls. She explains that their father had been very kind to her when she was first widowed in Penang some years earlier, and she now feels obliged to see that his daughters are well-provided for. Though Mrs Sanderson has her doubts about George O'Hara and his designs on the girls' inheritance, she has no wish to involve herself any further.

Dorothea and her present husband, Miles Sanderson and their son, Elliot have returned from the Far East to England because of Miles' failing health. Later, while his wife and son are touring the continent, Miles takes up the cause of the Linton sisters. He outmanoeuvres their stepfather, ensures they complete their education and then engages a chaperone to supervise their entry into local society.

In order to keep the family under his eye, Miles Sanderson also arranges for them to move to the lodge of his house, Beech Place, and takes George into his employ as a carpenter.

Carrie's intelligence and courage soon attract the attention of

Anne Goring

philanthropist Edmund Brook. It would be a very good match, but her heart belongs to Jem Walker. Too independent and self-willed to submit meekly to the path Miles Sanderson has marked out for her, Carrie is determined to invest some of her own money trying to improve the dreadful slums she has seen in the heart of the city.

Dorothea Sanderson is displeased when she sees a growing attraction between her son and Adele, even though Elliot has become engaged to Margaret Gordon. In the past Dorothea has been careful to protect her son from unsuitable influences, even ensuring Elliot's childhood friendship with a Malay brother and sister was ruthlessly severed. She determines to be equally ruthless with Adele.

But she is unaware that Mahmood has made his way to England in pursuit of the woman who ruined his life, and that of his sister. George O'Hara too, with the aid of his mistress, Sally Quick, plans vengeance – on the Sanderson family, and on the Linton sisters.

Chapter One

ADELE was sketching in the small herb garden that adjoined the glasshouses. She was sheltered from the gusty breeze by a high hedge of clipped bay laurel, so that she had full advantage of the March sun. From the old stone seat she had a view of the barn where Uncle George had his carpenter's bench, and a glimpse of the stable yard, framed by a gnarled apple tree. Most importantly, she could see clearly along the path that led to the orchid house. It was early and she did not expect Elliot yet, but she had hastened to escape the lodge before Aunt Linnie or Carrie found her some sensible household task to perform. She seemed to have had so little time to herself lately. Mrs Dawes had embarked with them on a relentless round of morning and afternoon calls and even Adele, sociable as she was, had grown a trifle weary of the company of Mrs Dawes's acquaintances. They hardly ever saw Joan or Maud or any of the younger people, and even if they were present it seemed that she was forever called from their company and obliged to wait upon elderly spinsters or widows. And there was not even a ball or musical evening in prospect and her gown of yellow gauze lay unused in the press.

She sighed, frowning. There had been one or two events – a theatre party, an outing to view a new arrival at the menagerie in Broughton Park – but she and Carrie had been excluded. Mrs Dawes had not even mentioned the occasions; they had found out from someone else who had attended. Both outings, they learned, had been lively and the parties had consisted mainly of the younger set.

Anne Goring

Carrie had shrugged it aside. "I had rather not go and peer in at poor frightened beasts confined in little cages. Do you remember that poor old lion, all tattered and filthy, in that travelling menagerie that came to Malvern? I had to box a little boy's ears for throwing sticks at the poor skinny thing. It scarcely had strength – or room – to move from its tormentors."

"I still think it mean of Mrs Dawes not to include us."

"She has no obligation," said Carrie sensibly.

"I think we have offended her in some way," Adele pondered. "Do you not think so? She was so pleasant with us at first, but now she is quite cool."

"Perhaps she has worries," Carrie said mildly.

"Perhaps." Adele was unsure, and she looked at Carrie carefully. Her sister's face was unconcerned and guileless. She was the culprit, Adele guessed. Mrs Dawes's displeasure was due to Mr Brook paying too much attention to Carrie at the ball, when it was expected he would propose to Joan. Mrs Dawes was punishing them both and it was unfair. It was hardly Carrie's fault that Mr Brook had made a set at her.

Carrie just laughed when she mentioned it, then grew red and cross. "Mr Brook is a pleasant gentleman. A friend, no more. Do not dramatise so."

Adele had not spoken of it again because she saw that Carrie was genuinely unaware of having caused any upset, and did not truly care that they were being denied any real social life. She was happy busying herself with dreary things like Mr Brook's housing scheme – fancy Carrie becoming excited because Mr Brook had taken up her idea for buying up and improving old property. "You see, my idea was not so reckless after all," she had cried, her eyes shining. "Mr Brook thinks it has possibilities. He took away the notes I made and thinks he may persuade one or two other gentlemen to set up a committee. And if he does – why he is to invite me to be on it!" Then as though that were not enough, there was this sudden interest in herbal remedies that had her ordering books from the circulating library and brewing evil-smelling concoctions over the kitchen fire. "It would be a

Bitter Harvest

help to you, Aunt Linnie," Carrie said gravely, "if I could know something of the subject. Then, if Mrs Walker were not available, you would not be without someone with experience should you be taken ill."

Adele's lips curved in a mischievous smile. Carrie thought she was being so clever and cautious and she was as transparent as glass. These trips to consult Mrs Walker over the herbs might fool Aunt Linnie but they did not fool her. Carrie was as soft on Jem Walker as he had always been on Carrie. Not that Adele had any intention of ruining Carrie's peace of mind by telling her what she suspected. Let her enjoy her secret, even if Jem was so ordinary, with neither looks nor fortune to recommend him.

She shivered deliciously, thinking of Elliot. She knew, quite simply, that he was everything she had ever dreamed of. The handsome elegance, the courtesy with which he treated her, as though she were delicate porcelain, the warm eyes that never seemed to leave her face and sent ardent, silent messages as he discoursed, so knowledgeably, about his plants. There was nothing coarse or unrefined about him. No clumsy attempts to hold her hand, no boastings or posturings to draw attention to himself. He was as perfect a gentleman as she would have expected of the prince of her dreams, with just a hint of smouldering fires, to spark her own heart to a melting, silent affirmation of love.

And now, of course, she had the poem. It had been days since they had met. That last, precious time a servant had come looking for him as his mamma had unexpected visitors. He had waved the girl away, frowning.

"How tiresome," he said. "We – I – have so little time to attend to my orchids. I had hoped to have a whole uninterrupted afternoon." She lowered her lashes shyly against his glance that spoke of his disappointment in leaving her so soon. "I must go. Forgive me, Miss Adele." At the door he turned and said, diffidently. "There is something on the bench there I should like your opinion of."

She saw the paper and reached for it. "A poem? I am

5

Anne Goring

not an authority but I shall take the greatest pleasure in reading it."

"As I did in the writing, however poor an offering it may seem." He bowed, elaborately casual. "Pray, do keep it, Miss Adele, if you find it engages you at all."

It was now her most treasured possession. Carefully folded it lay wrapped in tissue at the bottom of her handkerchief box, to be brought out when she was alone and read with quickened breathing and a heart bursting with joy and pride. She had no idea whether or not it was good poetry, nor did she care. The dashing lines alluding to Beauty walking alone, radiant, the sunlight reflecting on her gold hair and her eyes the colour of rain-veiled violets were clearly meant to be her. And Love, humbling himself at her feet, eager to reveal his heart to his adored one, was Elliot. Oh, it was so romantic, that each time she read it the lines blurred with tears and she longed to rush out and find him and cast herself into his arms and hear the words from his own lips.

If only he could break beyond the barrier of his gentlemanly reserve.

She heard a voice calling and her pencil stilled, but it was only Uncle George moving with his slow tread up towards the herb garden. "Making a sketch are you then?" he asked pleasantly. "Let me see . . . yes, very pretty." He looked around, breathing deeply of the mild spring air. "Aye, it's a grand morning for being out of doors. I've a mind to repair the barn door. It's been waiting for a day like this."

She patted the bench beside her. "Will you not sit a moment and enjoy the sun with me?"

He shook his head. "Mr Sanderson doesn't pay me to idle my days away," he said gravely and she flushed at the rebuke, feeling suddenly idle and pampered. He stood large and dignified despite his working clothes and she wondered uneasily if the difference in their position was a source of hurt to him.

"I should not be here at all," he went on, "save that the

Bitter Harvest

cat has strayed. I feed it in the barn in the hopes that it will rid me of mice, dratted creatures, but I haven't seen it for some days."

She had seen the fat, black cat several times about the gardens, and carefully avoided its purring advances. "It has not been here this morning," she said, then hesitated as she caught sight of a slender figure – elegant in grey broadcloth, a blue cravat knotted artistically at his neck – strolling up the path to the glasshouses. Her heart began a wild erratic thumping, so loud she was sure Uncle George must hear it. "I . . . I will come and tell you should I see it," she said hurriedly. She put down the sketch pad and drew her shawl round her shoulders with an exaggerated shiver. "I have grown quite chilly sitting here. I must move." Elliot disappeared inside the orchid house and she prayed fervently that Uncle George would remove himself. "Should you perhaps look for the cat in the orchard?" she suggested hopefully.

Uncle George did not answer. He hooked his thumbs into the pockets of his moleskin waistcoat and turned his florid face up to the sun. "It'll doubtless come back when it's hungry." Slowly he swayed backwards and forwards, eyes closed.

Adele replaced her pencil in its box, rattling it in a decided, packing-up manner.

"Did you say you felt cold?" Uncle George murmured. "How very odd, for it seems to me unseasonably warm." He swung his head round, scrutinising her with his light unblinking gaze. "Perhaps, though, your colour is over-hectic. I trust you are not sickening for something. Should you like me to escort you back to the lodge?"

"Oh, no," she said hastily. "That is, I have sat too long and there is a cool breeze from time to time."

"Then might I suggest you move somewhere warmer? Master Elliot has just gone into the glasshouse to inspect his orchids. I know you have found shelter there even in the most inclement weather." He smiled and it was a knowing smile. It alarmed her so, that in a fluster, she stood up and dropped her pencil-box,

Anne Goring

scattering the contents. Her fingers trembled as she gathered them together.

"Allow me," Uncle George said, taking them from her and calmly replacing them in the box. He shook his head. "I fear you are a little excitable this morning. You might do well to go straight home."

"No . . . I . . ." A blackbird burst into a torrent of song from the top of the hedge. She took a breath, steadied herself. "I . . . I think I might take your advice and go into the orchid house for a while. I do have a sketch Mr Sanderson might like to see. Of one of his new acquisitions."

Uncle George nodded. "Yes, yes." Then, slowly, as though the words were wrenched from great depths. "Adele, I should like you to know that you have always had a special place in my affections."

She stared up at him in surprise. "That is kind of you to say so, Uncle George."

He raised his big hand and laid it on her shoulder where she felt its grip, warm and strong and heavy. "Your sister now – well, Caroline and I could never be close. But you were such an engaging child and are grown into a beautiful young woman with the character to go with it. Unspoiled and charming."

He spoke so earnestly that she felt a warm rush of colour to her face.

"Do you remember how I used to buy you pretty things when you were a child?"

"Why, yes," she said. "I had quite forgot. I had a dress of white frills and you brought me blue ribbons for my hair."

He shook his head. "I was not always the villain Carrie would have me be. I did my best. I was so often distraught over your aunt's health that it made me less amenable than I might have been. It was a time when I needed sympathy. Carrie gave me only hostility. But you were warm-hearted and soothed my over-burdened spirit on many occasions. If I was harsh with Caroline –" he raised his arms in a helpless gesture

8

"– it is possible she brought down my wrath upon herself deliberately. In her heart I think she was never agreeable to her aunt marrying at all."

A memory came, of Carrie in candlelight, her small face sharp-boned, frowning, "I hope Aunt Linnie has chosen rightly. I cannot bring myself to like our new uncle too well." And her own sleepy answer. "He seems nice. He has promised me a new doll . . ."

She said, awkwardly, "We had been through hard times, Uncle. Orphaned so far away it meant that Carrie had all the responsibility. I was too young to understand."

He sighed. "She was against me from the start and because I felt her hostility I replied in kind. We started badly and the fault lay as much in me as in her. Yet Carrie has an unforgiving spirit. Even now she is cold towards me – no, do not protest. I sense it, though I've done my best to make up for any harm she thinks I may have done her in the past. If only all could be forgotten and we could make a fresh start."

"But I will speak to her," Adele said. "I am sure she does not realise how you feel. I will explain. Oh, I should be so happy to see us all comfortable with one another."

He smiled sadly. "You are generous, Adele, but too trusting to suppose mere words will influence your sister. Believe me, I have travelled and known adverse times. I know human nature. Caroline is not the kind to forgive and forget. Besides, I have my pride and wouldn't wish you to beg favours on my behalf. So, say nothing, I beg you."

"If you wish it." Her large violet eyes were unhappy. She felt torn between loyalty to her sister and distress at Uncle George's obvious unhappiness. She had never felt the same degree of animosity towards him as Carrie had. She had been so much younger and frailer. Carrie had been the one who protected and comforted and the weight of Uncle George's displeasure had fallen on her. Carrie had suffered and still remembered the old hurts. For Adele, a creature who lived for the present moment, the past was already blurring. There was hardly anything left to

Anne Goring

her of the time in Malaya. The early days in the cottage were dim and confused. She had been ill so much. It was an effort now to recall the poverty and sadness of the days after Uncle George had come to them. They were quite overlaid by more recent memories, the fun, the happiness, of the Malvern years. But whatever the rights and wrongs, she hated to see anyone upset, as Uncle George clearly was. If he had done wrong, he was contrite now.

He had drawn away from her and was staring broodingly across the garden. She went to him and laid a hand timidly on his sleeve. "You have offered your friendship, Uncle George," she said simply, "and now I offer you mine. I shall pray that in time Carrie may be your friend, too."

He smiled then and his pleasure kindled all the warmth of her sunny nature. When he had at last gone, she was able to make her way to the orchid house, glowing with the knowledge that she had made him a little happier.

The silence that held them seemed alive. The close, moist atmosphere of the orchid house, the trailing stems, the still, waxy flowers, hung in a green waiting quiet.

At first he had spoken quickly, almost nervously, overanxious to set her at ease. "My dear Miss Adele – pray take a seat here. See, I have brought a cushion to make the chair more comfortable. That is a splendid angle to view the *Vanda teres*. I fear it is rather too hot. The wretched gardeners repeatedly ignore my instructions. The windows should have been unlatched in this sun. One must do things oneself to have them done properly."

Carelessly he turned back the cuffs of his snowy shirt. She was fascinated by his hands, long and fine, dipping with precision in among the pots; tenderly transferring shoots to new earth prepared for them. He brought elegance even to such a mundane task. Her heart seemed swollen with contained emotion. Her fingers trembled against the sketching paper.

Into the silence she said, "The poem. I read it."

Bitter Harvest

"Oh, that . . ." He waved his hand, dismissing it carelessly. Her breath caught in her throat. "I – I thought it splendid. Perfectly splendid."

For a fraction his hands paused in their task. "Then I am pleased such a trifle was to your liking." His tone was light. She willed him to turn and look at her but he was absorbed. "Pray keep it if you think it worthy."

"I shall treasure it."

"Then that also is pleasing. We are both content." He dusted his hands. "Now you have a small keepsake and I must have one, too."

"Keepsake?"

"For when I am gone. It is not so long now. I shall be leaving for the South at the end of April. I . . . we shall take a house there for a while. But eventually I shall go right away from England and never return. I detest the climate, the damp cold." He laughed airily. "The only place I am comfortable is here, in the orchid house."

Her heart thumped loud and slow. She stared at his averted face and her voice came thick and husky. "Away? You will go away?"

"It is the sun for me. Once I am married."

The word hung oppressively between them. She felt its weight, heavy as lead in her chest.

"But I should like a keepsake. A memento of someone who has shared my interest in these fascinating orchids." His voice faltered, then proceeded briskly, as though he read a set piece. "We have had some agreeable hours. I shall remember them in my future life, when I look at one of your paintings. You will consent to give me a small sketch, Miss Adele? My favourite is the *Cypripedium insigne*. It is so delicate."

Like you, he thought. Like you. He dared not look at her. Her adoring eyes would undermine his resolution. He had known the moment he gave it to her that the poem had been a mistake. He should have kept it secret, to cherish through his life as a reminder of something beautiful and forbidden. It was hard to

Anne Goring

cut down a flower before it had blossomed fully, but he must steel himself and suffer. The alternative was too difficult, too dreadfully complicated. He had tortured himself cruelly at what must be done. Pacing his room he had pictured himself living with Margaret, bearing always the grief of a lost love in his heart. He saw his children at his knee, gazing up at him fondly. "Why do you look so sad, Papa?" and for their sake putting aside his suffering and pretending cheerfulness. This image of suffering borne with quiet dignity sustained him. He would write many great poems and hide them away. And when he and she were dust they would be discovered, hailed as masterpieces, and scholars would argue over who was the mysterious beauty who had been his inspiration.

"I shall have all these orchids moved eventually," he said. "No one here has the knowledge or patience to tend them. Wherever I settle I shall make accommodation for them." He heard her breath rasping the silence. He fussed with a pot of begonias. "But your painting will travel with me, I do assure you." He waited for her answer, some politeness to show that she understood and accepted. Unwillingly, his gaze was drawn to her. His hands stopped their busy, useless movement. "Miss Adele! What – are you ill?"

She leaned forward on the rough chair, her face suffused, beads of perspiration dewing her forehead. "Air," she gasped. "Outside . . . help me!"

He felt her bones, fragile as a bird's under his hands. Supporting her, he led her into the cool, fresh sunlight. Her knees buckled and she fell against him. He held her more tightly, aghast at the strain of her fight for breath. He half carried her to the bench and sat beside her, chafing her hand, calling her name over and over again, feeling impotent and afraid. He partly wished a gardener's boy, a servant – anybody – would come to his aid, yet a deeper sense revelled in her closeness, her dependence, her hand lying frail in his, her head, as the paroxysms eased, falling limp against his shoulder. He stroked her disordered hair. "Oh, my dear," he said. "My dearest, dearest Adele . . .

Bitter Harvest

there, lean against me. You are shivering. Let me wrap your shawl around you."

"It is months since I had an attack. It was so unexpected," she whispered faintly.

"Did I upset you? Was it – was it something I said?"

"A dog, a cat, sometimes sets me breathless. I ... I shall recover myself shortly."

He did not – could not – release her. Tenderness engulfed him. She stirred against his shoulder, raised her white, thick-lashed lids. He gazed into the violet depths of her eyes and, knowing that what he did was folly, he bent his head and lost himself in the wondering innocence of her kisses. And even as he inhaled the fragrance of her skin and welcomed the soft clinging hands that twined about his neck and felt his own body's response, part of his mind still remained aware that he was only making things harder for himself.

After he had gone she sat on in the garden, taking no notice of the freshening breeze, nor the clouds that were concealing the sun. A deep, warm contentment filled her heart. Her lips, her hand, still burned from the hot kisses Elliot had pressed upon them. Those few horrid, dark moments in the orchid house when he had said – when she had believed – that he would leave her, were banished. Forever. He had spoken no more of going away. How could he now? They loved each other. Their destiny was to be together. All would be well. He would see to that.

Presently she arranged her shawl about her head and shoulders. Her throat and chest felt raw still, but it was a minor discomfort. She walked across the herb garden, her skirt brushing against clumps of rosemary, sending sharp gusts of perfume into the air. Only then did she notice the bulky figure standing on the path waiting for her. Her hand flew to her throat. His expression was grave. How long had he been there? What had he seen?

"Uncle George! Are you still looking for your cat?"

He did not move and the frown deepened between his brows.

Anne Goring

"The cat is not important," he said solemnly. "What I have witnessed is of great consequence."

She twisted her hands together, lowering her eyes from his unblinking stare. "It was . . . that is, I was not well. Elliot – Mr Sanderson – he had to help me from the orchid house. I was overcome . . ." She wished she had Carrie's strength of mind, instead of stammering, guilt-ridden, denying the love so golden and precious. She thought, despairingly, now he will tell Aunt Linnie and Carrie and everything will be spoiled.

But, miraculously, Uncle George was laying his hand in that familiar way on her shoulder, saying, "Do not look so distressed. Your secret is safe with me. I've known what it is to be young and in love myself." She turned wondering eyes up to him and he smiled benignly. "Young Master Elliot is a dark horse. I had no idea he had designs on my niece."

"And no one must know," she cried urgently.

He chuckled. "Dear me, I have never seen you look so serious. That young man has truly captured your heart."

"Oh, yes," she breathed, "yes."

He pressed her shoulder. "Lucky fellow," he said then, gravely, "Take care you are not hurt, Adele. He is promised elsewhere, you know. He will be married soon."

"No!" The word came out loud and harsh, paining her throat. "No! We love each other. He will not marry her and go away."

"Ah," he breathed, "you are more foolish – braver – than I supposed."

She quivered underneath his hand like a trapped bird. "You will promise not to say anything?"

"I give you my word. As you must give me yours." His smile was kind, his eyes bright and knowing. "You offered me your friendship earlier. You must promise me that should you need help, or advice, you will come to me. We shall share this secret, you and I. I am not a creature of convention, Adele. I have never taken much heed of rules and propriety. Which is why,

Bitter Harvest

I think, I may have been an uncomfortable companion for your dear aunt, who is a conventional soul and much influenced by the opinion of others." His grip tightened. "I believe everyone should make his own destiny, follow his own instincts. I wish you to be happy and I will do all in my power to help you achieve your heart's desire."

"Oh, Uncle George," she whispered. Her eyes filled with tears. "Thank you."

He watched her trip away with a light step and his smile broadened. He paced slowly to the orchid house and went inside. The fat, sleek cat stretched its paws and yawned largely when he moved the barricade of seed trays and plant pots which he had arranged earlier.

"Lazy bugger," George said grinning, reaching down to lift the limp, boneless weight. The cat arranged itself, purring, on his arm. "You played your part well, old friend." He caressed the silky ears. The cat was often chased from the glasshouses by the gardeners, for it liked the close warmth and was artful at finding a dark, confined place to curl up and doze. Lately George had taken to snuggling the cat down in there when the gardeners were out of the way. Sooner or later, he had surmised, both Adele and the cat would be together in the glasshouse. An interesting combination. And if Master Elliot were there, too ... It had been an outside chance, for the silly little ninny was less prone to the chokes these days. But it had paid off handsomely. The whole touching scene had been played out for his sole amusement. And now, so cunningly, he had her. And through her, that prancing milksop, Elliot Sanderson. His thick fingers bit roughly into the cat's vibrating throat. "You can go back to catching your own breakfasts now," he growled, "you've grown overfat." But he did not begrudge the animal its share in the meaty pastries Mrs Price brought him. Hoisting it up on his shoulder where it lay draped black and silky, a warlock's familiar, he bore it back to the barn to share in his midday repast.

* * *

15

Anne Goring

Dorothea Sanderson stood at the window of her husband's bedroom and watched her son wander up the path from the direction of the kitchen gardens. She was not amused. She had thought him safely up in his room and now here he was, obviously returning from tending those orchids of his. Even from here she could see his disarranged cuffs. Doubtless his hands and nails would be soiled. Ridiculous, when there were gardeners enough to do his bidding. It scarcely seemed the hobby of a gentleman, yet she knew there were other gentlemen who took a scientific interest in botanical subjects. Elliot would be pleased and surprised when he learned of the enquiries she had made on his behalf. She smiled, her good humour restored.

She could not help feeling proud of this son of hers. Even in disarray there was a well-bred air about him. Put him in artisan's clothes and he would stand out from the rest. She had groomed and nurtured this handsome stripling, brought him to this perfection, given him a splendid future. A future in which, sadly, she would perhaps share very little. He would never know the sacrifice that it was to part from him. In anger and pain she had borne him and loved him in spite of – or because of – it. Delivering him to the arms of another woman would be painful; a woman she did not particularly care for, but who had strength and intelligence and would be clever enough, as she had been, to shield him from his own weaknesses and whom he could lean upon without realising that he leaned at all. Ah, she was going to miss him for all that . . .

Behind her, Miles said, "I am not at all sure, Dolly."

She turned quickly. "Charlotte, of course, will do nothing without your permission. But the parties are agreeable."

"Except the child."

She spread her white hands. "You still think of her as a child, but she is not. She is grown – and because we women notice these things where men will remain blind – she is well aware of her own looks. Charlotte has noticed how forward she is become. I myself have seen her flirting outrageously. It would be unseemly if she acquired a reputation of that sort. A good, steadying influence will be the making of her."

Bitter Harvest

"Mrs O'Hara?"

"Will be approached as soon as you give your approval. Charlotte does not see any difficulty there. The matter has already been hinted at."

Dolly felt contrite that she must press him. He looked tired and his skin had a grey-yellow pallor. He sat before the fire in his bedroom, holding his hands to the blaze, a rug draped across his knees. She thought, with a pang, how frail he looked. He was growing old.

She said, "Really, Miles, you are taking the matter too seriously. You have done your duty by these girls. Anything Robert Linton did for me has been repaid in full. Let others take the responsibility now."

He looked at her with his shrewd gaze. "And you, Dolly. What is your honest opinion? Do you not think the age difference too great?"

She met his eyes without flinching. "Do you ever regret our marriage, Miles? Twenty-five years separate us, but I have never thought it of any consequence."

"But you were not a green girl, fresh from the schoolroom. You had been out in the world."

"And had a poor time of it," she said fervently. "Would that I had had the benefit of a parent's wise advice. But I had not and was taken in by a scoundrel. If I had married you instead of Tom at seventeen, I should have saved myself a deal of heartache." Her voice softened and she walked, with that particular grace he loved, across the room, to kneel in a swish of silk skirts at his side. She reached up a hand and smoothed the deep indentations between his grey brows. "It grieves me to see you look so tired, dearest. I should not have bothered you. It could have been left to another time."

"No, no. You did right, Dolly." He eased his back against the chair willing the dull weight of pain in his chest to ease. It was bad today. The doctor's pills did little for it. They merely blurred his mind, making him sleepy and dull. All he wanted was to be allowed to escape back into the half-doze that blunted

Anne Goring

the edge of the pain. He forced himself to smile, gratified to see some of the worry ease from the handsome dark eyes. "I shall trust your judgement. Tell Charlotte that as long as Mrs O'Hara approves – and the girl herself, of course – then I shall give my blessing."

Dorothea closed the door of his bedroom softly and leaned her back against it. She felt the tension drain away. It was done, and more easily than she expected. She was honest enough to admit that Miles's current bout of ill-health had much to do with her victory and when he was recovered he might well be less amenable. But by then everything would be settled. Her quick mind raced over the problems. Charlotte would easily persuade the aunt of the benefits. The girl was a minor and could have no influence once her elders had come upon a decision. The sister might be difficult. Her mouth tightened. She must be kept out of the way while everything was arranged. And she must not see Miles on any account. He was fond of her and took her opinions seriously. She must give strict instructions to the servants that no one must visit Miles without her consent. His illness was excuse enough. Yes . . . yes, it would work out well, she was sure of it. She straightened herself, twitched a crumpled fold on her skirt. She would have a message sent to Charlotte Dawes immediately and then she would summon Elliot. Her expression softened. He, dear boy, would be gratified at the little diversion she had planned.

For the next few days he, too, would be safely out of reach.

A note from Mrs Dawes came for Aunt Linnie early the following morning. Carrie took it in to her aunt and fetched pen and paper at her demand.

"Mrs Dawes is to call upon me this afternoon," she explained. "And Maud Dawes would like you to accompany her to the dressmaker while her mamma is here with me. Joan is engaged elsewhere." Her hand shook as she wrote. "Oh, dear, this is so hurried. The best lace cloth in the wash and the parlour due for a turnout. And we ate the last of the cake yesterday."

18

Bitter Harvest

"Surely Mrs Dawes will understand, if she chooses to call at such short notice."

"Yes, but this occasion . . ."

"Is it something special?"

Aunt Linnie hesitated, shook her head, said plaintively, "I find the prospect of any visitors quite daunting nowadays. It tires me dreadfully to make conversation and it is such a worry watching Jane to ensure that she serves correctly and does not drop anything."

"Then I shall stay and look to things. I need not go to the dressmaker's with Maud."

"Yes, you must," her aunt said sharply. Her glance slid away from Carrie. "Miss Dawes has particularly asked for your company. It would be impolite to refuse. No, we shall manage, Adele and I." She sealed the letter and said, her tone less flustered. "Adele shall arrange the tea table and supervise Jane."

"I am surprised Maud asked for me. She and Adele can rattle on for hours about fashions, whereas I have exhausted the subject in two minutes."

"You are the elder, dear. Perhaps Mrs Dawes thinks it more suitable. Besides, she wished Adele to show her some of her watercolours. Now give the boy the letter and pray, dear, do remove whatever it is you are brewing in the kitchen. The smell pervades the whole house. I would rather you set to making those almond biscuits Mrs Dawes liked and Jane may then be free to polish the parlour."

By the time the Dawes's carriage arrived Carrie was almost glad to be making an escape with Maud Dawes. The impending visit seemed to have stirred Aunt Linnie to an odd mood that swung between tetchiness and a kind of suppressed excitability. She was impatient and critical over everything. The biscuits were not crisp enough. The tablecloth must needs be pressed again. The parlour carpet must be gone over with cold tea-leaves to freshen it and all the brasses redone. And through it all Aunt Linnie wore an expression of extreme long-suffering and

Anne Goring

complained frequently of the effect all this upheaval was having on her nerves.

Yet as Jane closed the lodge door behind them, Carrie was overtaken by an unwillingness to leave. Something deeper than a reluctance to spend an afternoon with a girl with whom she had little in common and engage in activities in which she had no interest. It was as though some instinct was warning her that everything was not as it seemed. That Aunt Linnie's fluster, Mrs Dawes's smug, complacent smile, were outward signs of something hidden. As though she were being sent away so that the ladies could talk of things they did not wish her to hear.

"Come along, do," Maud urged. "Or we shall be late."

Carrie walked slowly from the door. She looked at Maud, already seating herself in the carriage. "Tell me," she said, "Is there some special reason for your mamma to be here this afternoon?"

"Special reason?" Maud's face, round and florid and so like her mother's, bore an expression wholly innocent. "Should there be one? Oh, pray do not stand there, Caroline, there is a great draught blowing in."

Slowly Carrie climbed the steps and settled herself opposite Maud. She stared back at the lodge as the carriage moved away. Her spirits were unaccountably depressed, and with all her heart she wished she did not have to go on this outing. But she would just have to settle to it and hurry Maud through her dressmaking appointment and return to the lodge as quickly as she could.

It was, Carrie discovered, impossible to move Maud Dawes in any way she did not wish to go. Between the fittings for her two new gowns, there were gossipy interludes to be enjoyed with the dressmaker, swatches of material to be picked over and new fashion plates to be discussed. Carrie sat amid the untidy clutter of the dressmaker's workshop and did her best to contain her impatience, as Maud fetched materials for her to see and asked her opinion on the cut of the one gown and the trimming on the other. Then, when they were at last bowed out by the dressmaker, it was to find that they must now deliver

Bitter Harvest

some bonnets for re-trimming. This involved a detour to the other end of the village and yet another lengthy consultation in the milliner's front parlour.

But eventually Maud was satisfied and the carriage was directed back to Beech Place. There, blocking the drive by the lodge, another carriage waited. An ancient, ponderous equipage with a sway-backed nag between the shafts.

Maud leaned across and tapped Carrie on the knee. "There!" she said archly. "Mrs O'Hara did have other visitors this afternoon, but I was sworn to secrecy and I dared not say a word. Mamma was most insistent."

Carrie stared at her, "A secret? What is going on. Why is Mr Prince's carriage here?"

"You will find out quite soon. But I think the best person to ask is Adele." She sighed dramatically. "Mamma thinks she is truly lucky to have such an offer."

Carrie went cold. She said, "Tell me Maud, what it is that you know and I do not. Tell me this minute!"

Maud compressed her lips. "It is not for me to say. Mamma told me —"

"Oh, rot Mamma!"

Maud's face went bright pink. "How dare you speak so!"

"Tell me!"

"Ask her yourself, for I shall never speak to you again, Caroline Linton. Such manners. Of course, one might expect such lowness from a person who was once a scullery maid . . ."

Carrie was already out of the carriage. She ran to the lodge door and flung it open. Mr and Miss Prince stood in the hall donning capes. Both so tall and gaunt, they seemed to fill the small space with dark, musty-smelling garments. Their faces, long and sallow, turned to her. And behind them, Mrs Dawes.

They all wore smiles. Miss Prince's was tight and prim; Mr Prince's wolfish, his long teeth prominent; Mrs Dawes's cool and confident.

"Ah, Miss Linton," Mr Prince said. "A fortuitous meeting, but alas it must be brief. Miss Prince does not like to be out late at this changeable time of the year and there is a look of rain about the sky."

Carrie felt as though she had run a hundred yards. She said, breathlessly, "I did not know that you were to call this afternoon, sir."

Mr Prince wagged a finger in front of her nose. "It was a matter to be discussed privately with your aunt. But it is settled now, to the satisfaction of all parties."

"Settled? What is settled?"

Mrs Dawes said, with a sweetness in her voice that Carrie had not heard for some time, "I think Adele should tell you herself, my dear."

"You should be the first to hear the news from your sister's own lips," Mr Prince said, adding archly, "And I entrust you to take extra care of the dear girl in the coming weeks. Such an excess of excitement may prove an irritation to a delicate constitution. May I recommend a frugal diet and plenty of rest?"

Carrie stared blindly at the three smiling faces. They seemed to float past her in a flutter of dark drapes and nodding bonnets. Their rustling voices pattered at her mind. Then they were gone and she was alone and forcing herself to walk into the parlour.

"Aunt Linnie?"

Her aunt lay on the sofa looking drained and exhausted, but her eyes were calm.

"They have told you?" she asked.

"Nobody has told me a thing, except to hint at some secret! For heaven's sake, Aunt Linnie, explain."

Her aunt's voice was low and clear. "Mr Prince has asked for Adele's hand in marriage. It is a most suitable match. He is a banker and apart from private means is in receipt of an income of over £3,000 a year. Both he and Miss Prince are well connected, and respected in local society. Adele could not do better."

Carrie found her voice. "And Adele? What is her view of this?"

Bitter Harvest

"She has sensibly let herself be advised by Mrs Dawes and myself."

"Mr Sanderson will not allow this!"

"Mr Sanderson gave his approval first. Naturally, I should not have gone against his wishes had he not been in favour."

"But he cannot be," Carrie said wildly. "I must speak to him myself. I will go right away."

"You will not Caroline! Mr Sanderson is a sick man. He has been ordered to rest and Mrs Sanderson has forbidden all visitors."

Carrie struggled for control. "Mr Prince has been married twice before. He is an old man. He could be her grandfather."

"Nonsense. He is not yet fifty. For some men that is the prime of life. He is well preserved for his years."

"Oh, yes. Well preserved. Like his sister, like the house they live in. You have not seen the house, have you Aunt Linnie?" Her voice was icy cold. "It is a dark house because Miss Prince keeps the blinds drawn for fear the sun might fade the carpets. It is chilly because they keep the smallest possible fire in the grate. And have you noticed their clothes? They have bought nothing new for years."

"And how does that signify? Persons of their years do not always wish to keep up with fashion."

"They do not buy because they do not like spending money. It is common knowledge. Living frugally as they do suits them, but can you imagine Adele living in such a house? She is young and pretty. Her life has just begun. It would be like – like sealing her up in a tomb! The Princes will subdue everything that is bright and happy about her – oh, why will you not listen?"

Her aunt had reached for her embroidery and was sorting silks, laying the strands across the work as though the blending of colours was of absorbing interest. "Listen?" She glanced up, her expression bland. "Why should your opinion be of any consequence, dear? It is all settled. And I pray, Caroline, that you will not upset your sister with such nonsensical talk. She is perfectly content with the arrangement."

"Is she?" Carrie asked, bitterly.

"She sees all the advantages. She has not the . . . the indiscipline which, I am sorry to say, is so evident in you, dear. She is willing to be guided by those older and wiser."

Aunt Linnie's voice was quietly triumphant and Carrie hopelessly, helplessly, realised that Adele, so foolish and willing to please, had allowed herself to be persuaded into agreeing to this obscene betrothal.

She said, pleading now, "Aunt, why have you allowed this? You are our guardian. You could have refused. If you must marry off Adele why must it be to the first man who offers for her? A younger man –"

"Would bring no guarantee of happiness. Mr Prince may not live in a grand style, but he will give her security and protection. These are no small matters. And I dislike your expression, Caroline. Marrying off, indeed. You speak as though I were disposing of your sister like a parcel. We all – Mrs Dawes, Mr Sanderson, myself – have only her welfare at heart. She is a lucky, lucky girl to find a husband – and so well placed a husband – so quickly. And mark me, Caroline," she added, as Carrie moved to go, "nothing of these high-flown arguments of yours to your sister. I will not have her upset."

Carrie moved to the door. With her hand on the latch she turned. It seemed to her aunt that the flesh had been pared from her bones. Her face was pale, the bones sharp under the skin. Only her eyes blazed with life in a face shorn of comeliness. "You have done your worst for Adele, but remember that I am of a different mettle. You and Mrs Dawes and Mr Sanderson may think to order my future to suit yourselves but I shall not submit. The man that I marry will be the man I choose because I love him and he loves me. No matter were he the poorest, most ineligible man in the country."

When she had stormed out, Linnie sank back against the cushions, all pretence at choosing embroidery silks abandoned. Her hands trembled and weak tears pressed against her closed eyelids. She had expected – dreaded – a battle with Caroline.

Bitter Harvest

Steeled herself to it. She had remained calm and had felt herself in control. But Carrie's last defiance had shocked her. She was a wicked, wicked girl to speak so. After all that had been done for her. She had not an ounce of gratitude in her body. Oh, this younger generation! Even Adele had proved unduly perverse. She had first taken the news of Mr Prince's intentions to declare himself in a totally frivolous manner. She had laughed as though it was an entertainment put on for her benefit. A joke. Linnie had been worried that Mrs Dawes might take offence and had resorted to a little play of tears in order to give Adele a proper awareness of the seriousness of the situation.

Adele had sobered quickly enough, though she had kept repeating, "But I do not wish to marry Mr Prince. I cannot. I do not love him." In the end Mrs Dawes had had to remind her that respect and submission were all that were necessary on her part. The match was an excellent one for a girl in her position. The decisions were already made. If she chose to be refractory she would offend a great many people, not least those who had gone to a deal of trouble on her behalf. Adele had grown quiet, saying after a while in a small trembling voice, "Is this true, Aunt Linnie? That I have no choice?"

"Dearest child, you must be ruled by your elders and betters. This is a splendid chance for you. You will be a wife, mistress of your own establishment, before your own sister. She should, by rights, be the one to be married first . . ."

"Then let me wait," Adele begged. "I do not wish for an engagement. Time enough when Carrie is married."

"Ah, but Carrie has as yet no prospects," Mrs Dawes told her. "Mr Prince is most eager to press his suit. A man in his position has no need to wait upon convention."

Adele's glance went helplessly from one to the other. "I do not love him," she said again, but her voice was less sure, as though what she saw written on the faces of the two older women already defeated her.

Mrs Dawes, sensing it, smiled encouragingly. She advanced to Adele and put a motherly arm about her shoulders. "Such foolish

Anne Goring

romantic ideas you young girls have," she said. "If every woman waited to meet the man who lived up to some absurd imaginary ideal, there would be scarcely a marriage in the kingdom. It is perfectly sufficient that Mr Prince has a deep regard for you. Indeed, he is quite enamoured. It is truly touching in so mature a gentleman. And you will find, as women do find, that after marriage the respect and trust that you place in your husband will, in the natural way of things, turn to affection and love. Why, I myself am a case in point. I submitted to my parents' choice with great misgivings. Indeed, I shed tears for I felt my heart was given to a young officer of handsome aspect but no prospects. Ah, I see that surprises you, but everyone goes through a heedless springtime of youth when the senses are pliable and given to wild burgeonings of fancy. But with every year that has passed since, I have thanked heaven for the perspicacity of my parents. It saved me from the consequences of my fickle yearnings. Mr Dawes has proved the most amiable, the most agreeable of partners. As for the young officer – why, he ruined himself at the gaming table not two years later. The last I heard of his unfortunate bride, she was forced to take in sewing in order to keep them both."

Adele listened in stunned silence. Against Mrs Dawes's maroon silk-draped stoutness, she looked small and defenceless.

Aunt Linnie's treacherous emotions quivered uneasily. She was so very young, a child still. Was it right that they should force her? *Force.* Her mind shied away from the word. No, of course they were not *forcing* her. It was silly to think that way. Mrs Dawes, Mr Sanderson both thought the match very suitable. She herself felt that the security and status the marriage would bestow upon Adele far outweighed the disadvantage of age. Indeed, the age difference might prove to be in Adele's favour, for she could find herself a widow in time, still young and personable – and rich. If she was so disposed she could remarry whom she wished. She jerked her thoughts away. Her natural anxiety to see the child settled was leading her thoughts astray. There was

Bitter Harvest

no reason why the marriage should not turn out splendidly. Adele was only responding with the sensibility perfectly proper in her situation. It was an overwhelming prospect, but when she was accustomed to the idea, she would accept it with all her natural gaiety.

The sight of Mr Prince somewhat renewed Linnie's doubts. She had hazily imagined a jolly, comfortable man, rather like the banker in Cheshire who had been so helpful over her father's affairs. Mr Prince, entering her parlour in his rusty black frock-coat, looked neither comfortable nor jolly. Even his smile was grave, though his manners were impeccable. He fetched chairs, handed round cups, made civil conversation but, like his dour, straight-backed sister, there was something formidable in his bearing. Linnie could not imagine him ever offering sherry wine and comforting words to a girl suddenly finding herself practically penniless, as old Mr Jackson had. Mr Prince, she felt, would have short shrift with debtors.

But then, Adele was no debtor and he was, undoubtedly, infatuated. He could scarce take his eyes from her and hovered about her chair devotedly. She pushed all doubts aside. It was too late, anyway. It was all moving on, inexorably, past her, like a theatre performance: Mr Prince requesting Adele to take a breath of air with him in the garden, the two of them leaving the room with Adele still in a state of bewilderment so that she drifted out in her pale dress and shawl like a beautiful wraith; Mrs Dawes assuring Miss Prince that Adele's unusual silence was merely the result of girlish nervousness brought on by the solemnity of the occasion. Then, Mr Prince returning with Adele's hand on his arm and his smile wider, asking for their congratulations; Jane moving importantly among them bearing glasses of Madeira; glasses raised in a toast to the happy couple . . . And Adele standing there, head bent, silent, then, slowly, raising her head and staring at Linnie, the gentle eyes that smiled upon the world so gaily, now holding such a wealth of reproach that the wine caught in Linnie's throat, making her choke.

It was quite five minutes before she could bring herself to

Anne Goring

look again at Adele and by then she had gathered together her dislocated thoughts. It was absurd to feel guilty. Guilty! When all she wanted was to see the child comfortably settled. When everyone had gone to so much trouble . . . when she herself, racked as she was with her nerves, had so much to bear.

Indignation was a comfort. It quite bore her up when, after the company had left, Adele slipped from the room without a word, and when Carrie had hurled her accusations in the wildest manner, spoiling things. Turning what should have been a joyful occasion into something miserable. Instead of the gratitude she deserved, all she had received was insult.

Self-pity washed through her. She could hear Jane intoning a hymn as she washed the dishes, but she felt alone and rejected. Her jangled nerves sent quivers of discomfort through her head. She needed the soothing effects of Mrs Walker's cowslip mixture, but she had finished the bottle last night in anticipation of today's disruption. Everything was against her! Tears gathered, she groped for her handkerchief and mistily saw the firelight glinting on the bottle of Madeira that Jane had not yet returned to the cupboard. Another glass of wine, she told herself, would perhaps be soothing. She moved from the sofa with more ease and certainty than she showed when others were in the room. She found a clean glass, poured the wine. Taken in short quick gulps, it glowed warmly if briefly in her stomach. There seemed little harm in taking another to prolong the medicinal effects.

When Jane came in to refresh the fire, she saw that Mrs O'Hara had fallen into a doze. Poor invalid lady, she was quite worn out with the excitement. And such excitement. Miss Adele engaged to be married! Oh, she'd hoped it would have been Miss Carrie first. Not that she'd choose someone like Mr Prince, him being old. No it would be someone young and handsome and very, very rich. Nothing but the best. All the same, it was exciting that there was to be a wedding, even if Miss Adele didn't seem overly agitated about it. She'd peeped at them out there in the garden. Mr Prince had been holding Miss Adele's hand and talking all solemn. Miss Adele had stood there as stiff and pale

Bitter Harvest

as that marble statue that stood in the front hall of the Home, and hadn't even lifted her head. Jane was sure that if anyone ever asked her, she'd grin fit to bust. But then, she weren't no lady and ladies acted different. She heaved the coal scuttle down quietly. The fire was right enough but there was a dirty glass there she'd missed and the wine to be put away. The bottle was almost empty. She wrinkled her nose at the smell of it. The ladies must've liked it to drink so much. She'd once tasted the dregs of a bottle and hated the rough sourness. But ladies was probably bred to enjoying such things, just like they was taught to speak nice and know dance steps and how to behave proper when a gentleman asked you to marry him.

Mrs O'Hara stirred on the sofa and her head fell back among the stuffed cushions. She began to snore gently. Ladies was even ladylike over that, Jane thought, remembering the gigantic roarings of the overseer who slept at the end of the dormitory at the Home. She tiptoed to the cupboard and replaced the depleted bottle within, gathered the dirty glass and crept to the door. Mrs O'Hara snored on gently.

A wedding in the house. Bound to be lots of comings and goings, visitors and such. Lots of extra work, too, of course, but she didn't care two pins about that. It would be worth it to see smart company in the parlour, the ladies in grand frocks and bonnets. Her heart skipped inside her bony chest. P'raps there might be somethin' new for her. Even, mebbe, a uniform, like them uppity maids at the big house wore, with a skirt that swished, and an apron with frills on.

She clasped her red-knuckled fingers round the wine glass, her eyes shining. Oh, it would be lovely to have a weddin' in the house. She drifted into the kitchen lost in a dream of black and white starched splendour.

Carrie went straight up to the bedroom, but Adele was not there. She had fled. Away from the lodge, away from the garden where *he* had touched her hand with his moist fingers. So hatefully had his fingers lingered. The repulsion of it had shivered up

Anne Goring

her arm. It had taken every bit of willpower not to snatch her hand away. She had imagined wildly, in the moment that he stood over her like a great black shadow, what it must be like to have his body, his elderly wrinkled flesh, pressing against her, sharing her bed.

Mrs Clare, of the Malvern school, had been a woman to whom the duties of the marriage bed had come as a profound shock. She had been kept in complete ignorance by her own mamma but she was determined that the girls within her care, most of them far from their own families, would benefit from a sensible talking to when they were of an age to understand. Each girl in the term before she left was called privately into her parlour, given tea, cake and a little homily on marriage and motherhood. In her kind, firm way she spoke as plainly as she was able. She repeated several times that it was all perfectly. natural and that this was the way that the human species had reproduced itself since Adam and Eve, that a loving husband would be patient and considerate with his bride. She laid much emphasis on the pleasures of motherhood knowing, sadly, that for many of them motherhood would be the only consolation. Then she turned the subject deftly to other matters, until pale cheeks had gained colour, scarlet ones lost their flush and incipient giggles had been dispelled.

Adele, stumbling through the grounds, thought on a sob that it might have been better not to have known what to expect. She could not bear even his smallest touch, so what fresh horrors were in store after the wedding – in the night – in his bed. Oh, what had they done to her, Mrs Dawes and Aunt Linnie, who should have understood? It had been like pleading with two stone statues, who neither heard nor cared. *They* had made the decision, *they* must be obeyed. Her feelings were of no account. She must submit. She had thought she was in a nightmare and must soon wake. But it was not a nightmare and reality was a sickly wavering in the pit of her stomach. It had taken all her strength to stand on her feet. Her mind had gone slow and thick with a strange chill, as though the warm, real person she was

Bitter Harvest

had shrunk away, very small, and she watched from far off as she went through the ritual imposed upon her. She wanted to cry out, stop, stop! I will not do it! I love another! I love Elliot! But that could not be spoken of.

She had tried to explain to Mr Prince. "Sir, I did not realise that you had expectations of marriage. I do not feel myself ready for such a step . . ."

"Such innocence," he had breathed. "Such artlessness. It is an adorable trait and so sadly lacking in more worldly young women."

The fervour in his voice frightened her. "I . . . I do not love you, sir," she said, tremulously.

"I have love enough for two, dear child." His fingers pressed into the bones of her hand. His nails were thick and ridged, like horn. "Now, shall we return and give the glad news to our dear ones? Come, take my arm."

With the little piece of her mind that still functioned, she thought, I am no one, nothing. He does not care that I have not consented. He has not listened. He has taken me as his possession.

When it was all over, her first instinct was to find Elliot, so she had stumbled outside, her shawl thrown carelessly about her head and shoulders. He must be in the orchid house. He must! He would make it right. He would stroke her hair and kiss her and tell her that of course it was all a mistake. She must not marry Mr Prince . . .

"No, Miss. He isn't here." The smallest garden boy knuckled his forehead respectfully.

"Has he been here this afternoon? Is he to come later?"

"Gone away, miss."

"Away?" Her voice was a horrified whisper. "Where, oh, where?"

"Dunno, Miss. Left orders wi' Mr Emms about his flowers. Would you like me to ask?"

"Yes," she cried, then, "No. Never mind." Outside her distress Adele was aware of the boy's curious eyes. She must not cause

Anne Goring

talk. She had to be calm. She tried, painfully, to smile. "It is of no consequence."

The boy went back to his hoeing. She forced herself to step slowly away. Overhead the thick cloud let fly a scattering of fat raindrops. She felt them against her face, chill as betrayal, as she walked along the gravelly paths, aimless now, for there was nowhere to go, no one to turn to.

She did not know quite where she wandered. Once, she found herself standing on the hill behind the house, staring down at its tall chimneys, remembering the first time she had walked here with Elliot on a wild, cold winter's day. Later, she came to in the herb garden, by the seat where she had leaned against him, circled by his arms, dazed by his kisses. Then her feet carried her on, slow and purposeless, and the rain began to seep down, wetting the hair that escaped from the shawl, sleeking it in dark blonde tendrils to her cheeks. She looked about, blinking. The shower would pass but she should find shelter. The stables, perhaps, or Uncle George's workshop.

The door stood ajar; there was the rich smell of sawn wood. Uncle George was at his bench and she stood inside the door gazing blankly at the pieces of furniture awaiting repair, at the baulks of wood, at the tools ranged neatly on hooks against one wall.

The sawing halted abruptly as he saw her. "Why, this is an unexpected pleasure," he began, then seeing her expression, "Is aught the matter? And you're wet. Take off that shawl and come through here." Another room, small, cosy in spite of the stone walls and cobwebbed beams. A small fire in a wide hearth, an old sagging chair, unworthy of repair, and a low table. He took her shawl and spread it before the heat to dry, pushed her unresisting down into the chair, drew up a three-legged stool, and regarded her earnestly, sadly. "They came, then," he said. "The visitors. The banker and his sister."

"You knew?" she whispered.

"Aye. Your aunt said it was all settled, bar putting it to you. All arranged by his lordship." He jerked his head in the direction

Bitter Harvest

of the house. "Highly suitable they tell me, though you don't look none too happy."

She shuddered. "I cannot marry him. I cannot! I came to find Elliot, to tell him, but he has gone away." Her eyes were luminous, tragic. "Do you know where, Uncle George?"

"Not far, I believe. Gone to visit some nob as collects orchids, with his mamma."

"Then he will be back?"

"Aye, in a day or two."

He saw her stiff shoulders sag with relief. "I thought . . . I thought he had gone to . . . to London, earlier than expected."

"Oh, no," he said heartily. "The housekeeper told me. It was all done in haste. The invitation came unexpected-like."

She sat in silence, looking into the small red glow of the fire, digesting the information, taking fresh heart from it. After a few moments she glanced at her uncle.

"Could – could you speak for me?" she asked timidly. "To Aunt Linnie. Explain that I do not wish to marry Mr Prince. You, alone, Uncle, know where my . . . my feelings lie."

He appeared to consider this, then said gravely, "I fear I have no influence. None at all. Your aunt and Mr Sanderson made it clear when you went away to school that I was to have no say in your affairs. Did you not speak up for yourself?"

"I tried. They did not listen."

He saw the hope wash out of her face, leaned forward and pressed his hand on her shoulder. "Do not despair," he said earnestly. "You aren't yet married to the gentleman. Elliot Sanderson is still free. We may yet be able to do something, if we tread quietly, carefully and above all, in secret."

She started to cry, all the emotion of the afternoon dissolving in a river of tears.

Uncle George passed her his handkerchief, holding back his satisfied smile, and when the storm of tears was passed began, in his benevolent voice, to tell her precisely how he might be able to help.

33

Chapter Two

ADELE was unreachable.

Carrie longed to offer comfort. Had Adele wished, Carrie would have defied them all. She would have taken on Mrs Dawes, the Princes, even Mr Sanderson whom she liked and respected. She would have battled single-handed for her sister had Adele broken down, reached out for sympathy, hinted at her distress. But Adele said in a flat, unrecognisable voice, "I do not wish to talk of it." It was as though she had pulled down an invisible shutter between them, blocking communication, checking any compassionate gesture. Behind this self-imposed barrier, Adele held herself with frozen dignity, a girl shocked into adulthood in a matter of hours.

If Adele would not speak, then Mr Sanderson must. Carrie went to the house, begged for an interview. The housekeeper, summoned by the maid, took some satisfaction in repeating the mistress's instructions. No visitors.

"Then a message," Carrie begged. "I have a letter, if you would pass it to him."

"I'm sorry. Mr Sanderson must not be disturbed in any way." She was not in the slightest bit sorry. For anyone else, she might – just might – have been moved. After all, the master had been a creaking gate for years and had pulled round after all his bad bouts. He was merely feeling his age, a tired old man who must be cosseted in order to face the journey to London for his son's wedding. But this girl was the niece of that ailing, clinging woman at the lodge. Dear George's wife. Mrs Price knew that in other circumstances dear George would have declared himself and *she*

Anne Goring

would now be installed in the lodge. The admiration in his eyes was obvious. A woman's instincts never failed in these matters. Her secret adoration was returned. Only the bounds of honour kept them apart, tied as he was to an invalid wife. Hours of burning sleeplessness had given Mrs Price the opportunity to burnish her resentment against the woman who stood between her and George. She was a burden, a millstone. But for her he would be free to marry. Resentment, soured by frustration, was a living ache that spread its tentacles to encompass the two upstart nieces who had been a trial and worry to dear George from the beginning. So why should this impudent girl expect special treatment?

"Surely it will not upset him to read a short note?" Carrie pleaded.

Mrs Price's black bombazine skirts almost crackled with authority. "It is quite out of the question. I have my orders. Mr Sanderson is not to be troubled. When Mrs Sanderson returns she will doubtless be able to attend to whatever little problem you have."

"And when will that be?"

"A few days, I understand."

A few days which spread to a week and more. A few days in which March turned to blue and gold April and Adele celebrated her eighteenth birthday by becoming the possessor of Mr Prince's family betrothal ring. The great bloodstone surrounded by pearls sat heavily upon her slim finger, weighing down her small hand.

A few days in which time Miss Prince, now assuming the role Mrs Dawes had once played, took her brother's new fiancée on a round of calls to show her off. Adele, docile and pale, seemed content to go, dutifully recounting later to Aunt Linnie, who had been there, what they were wearing, what they had said. Aunt Linnie seemed not to notice that these accounts were less light-hearted than they had once been. Indeed, she did not care to notice. She was relieved that Adele went without protest and seemed to have become adjusted to her newly-engaged state.

36

Bitter Harvest

A few days in which time Carrie had appealed to Mr Brook and he, maddeningly reasonable, had failed to take issue with it. He had sent the carriage for her. The inaugural meeting of the proposed Society for the Improvement of Housing for the Respectable Poor was to be held at his house. She was to meet the three other gentlemen Mr Brook had recruited, but she was the first to arrive and she poured out her story hurriedly.

He listened gravely, then said, "I am sorry you are so distressed. It must have been a shock. But if, as you say, Adele is resigned . . ."

"Resigned!" Her eyes blazed at him, angry green lights glinting in the grey. "Surely Adele deserves to take more than resignation to her marriage. This match is indecent."

"Come Miss Linton, that is an exaggeration."

"He is thirty years older if he is a day. He has been married twice before."

Edmund looked uncomfortable, wanting to push this unexpected complication aside. He had looked forward eagerly to this meeting, the precursor, he hoped, of many. He had expected smiles and gratitude because he had set in motion a cause dear to Miss Caroline's heart. He had wanted to show her off as a young woman of intelligence and charm, and here she was tight-lipped, upset, wanting him to interfere with something that did not really concern him. Indeed, at this delicate stage, he would not wish to offend her aunt. It could make things awkward later.

"Forgive me, Miss Linton, but this is a family matter, surely. It would be unseemly of me to interfere, even though I do not care to see you distraught and would wish to do what I could."

She swallowed back her anger. "It is I who should ask forgiveness. I was too outspoken. It is just that I feel so helpless." She managed to smile, a faint shadow of the one he longed to see. "Adele has been bullied into submission. That is why I was despatched out of the way so that I could not speak up in her defence. Mrs Dawes, my aunt, they both bullied her."

He said, reasonably, "From what I know of Mrs O'Hara I

37

Anne Goring

fail to see her in the role of bully. On the contrary, she seems a retiring person, of some sensibility. Charlotte Dawes, now, can be overbearing, but she would do nothing, I am sure, without Miles Sanderson's agreement."

"If I could speak to Mr Sanderson. Oh, I am sure he does not fully understand Adele's predicament, shut away as he is, and ailing. If he did, the engagement could at least be deferred until Adele is older . . ."

"It would be unlike him to do anything without careful consideration. If he has given the match his blessing, you may be sure he has examined all aspects."

"Except Adele's happiness."

"Naturally you are distressed that you are to be separated from a dear sister, but she will be living quite near to you and you will still be friends and confidantes." Edmund saw the protest rise to Carrie's lips and added, placatingly, "However, once Mr Sanderson has recovered – and I could not dream of intruding upon him at this time, it would be most discourteous – I shall mention the subject. We sometimes take luncheon together at our club. In such an informal atmosphere matters may be touched upon that might be delicate in other surroundings." But it might be weeks, he thought, by which time Miss Linton would have come to terms with her sister's forthcoming marriage. He saw the flicker of hope in Carrie's eyes and smiled encouragingly. A somewhat devious notion crept into his mind that perhaps Prince as a brother-in-law might be an advantage anyway. He was too old for the girl, that was obvious; old, narrow-minded, devoted to his health and the making and keeping of money. But related by marriage, a useful ally. There were always improvements to be made to the factory and to his workers' houses and it was not prudent to tie up too much capital. He smoothed the thought away. Later . . . later. Now he wanted to concentrate all his thoughts upon Miss Linton . . . Caroline.

He does not really understand, Carrie thought despairingly, for all he seems such a kindly man. But she tried to compose herself in view of the coming meeting.

Bitter Harvest

"Come now," Edmund said, "the other people will be here any moment. Allow me to escort you to the drawing room. My housekeeper will be in attendance, no other lady as yet being on this committee. It is a pity Miss Adele is not now free to accompany you. I shall, in future, send a maid in the carriage.

He is more concerned, she contemplated wryly, that I have travelled alone in his carriage, than that my sister's whole future is at stake. But it had been foolish of her to expect him to do more than he had offered. Though every instinct cried out that with each day of delay Adele's future lay more securely in Mr Prince's hands, she must accept that Mr Brook could do no more. He had been her last, faint hope of influence. There was no one else to turn to. She must stifle her disappointment and be grateful that he would approach Mr Sanderson when he was recovered.

Mr Brook was giving a short description of the gentlemen who would be coming. ". . . I can foresee no problems except, perhaps with Mr Arthur Wharton. A good-hearted fellow but inclined to bluster if he cannot get his own way. Do not let his manner upset you, it conceals a generous nature . . ."

The gentlemen arrived and grouped themselves around the small table laid out with blotters and pens and clean sheets of paper. It was a relief for Carrie to turn her mind to something practical. The gentlemen read the notes she had prepared and Mr Wharton offered congratulations to Edmund Brook on the conciseness and clarity of his report.

"This is Miss Linton's work," he answered, wishing to give due credit.

"The deuce it is!" Arthur Wharton had been a trifle put out that a woman – and a very young one at that – should attend this meeting. Women, he felt, could offer nothing but a frivolous distraction, their minds being by nature unable to compete with the logic and reason of men's.

He glanced through the report again, failed to find fault with it, and stared fiercely at the quiet, brown-haired girl sitting opposite. She did not quiver or blush or fiddle with her handkerchief or

Anne Goring

dissolve into tears. All annoying habits of his wife and daughters when he fixed them with his critical eye. Her cool glance met his without flinching. He blew through his moustaches, thinking her a forward minx and young Brook a schemer for forcing the girl to seem responsible for a philanthropic cause of his own.

As the meeting continued his opinion wavered and he began, wistfully, to imagine what it would have been like if one of his own daughters had turned out to have a sensible head on her shoulders like Miss Linton. Why, he might, just might, have encouraged her to take an interest in his two smallwares mills. He had longed for a son to take up the reins after him and all he had got was a set of plain-faced wenches, looking set to be spinsters and caring not a fig for anything but that they had money to spend on bonnets and frocks. Ah, for a girl like Miss Linton. One who could give clear intelligent answers to a plainly-put question and had pertinent questions of her own to ask. One in whom a man might confide. What a difference it would have made to his life.

Resolutely ignoring the fact that he had crushed any sign of individuality in his daughters and allowed only the minimum of education, deeming female blue-stockings a form of creature unnatural in the extreme, he gallantly offered clever Miss Linton his arm as the small party went across the garden between the lines of poplars that screened the dye works from the house, to view the new cottages young Brook had had built.

By the end of the afternoon the new society was formed, its aims drawn up, a subscription list opened and an appointment made for the committee to view the house in Ancoats. Mr Wharton demurred at the last item. "Surely, Miss Linton, there is no need for you to attend. Such a low neighbourhood, most unelevating."

"Should I have cause to worry in such stout company?" Carrie asked demurely. "I think not – and I have not yet had the chance to look over the property. It would be impossible to envisage any improvement scheme without seeing it for myself. Besides, as a woman, I may have an eye for some small domestic

Bitter Harvest

improvement that you gentlemen might overlook in your concern for the larger issue." She refrained from saying that there were women and children having to live and work in the slums of the town in conditions so appalling that his only thought should be to relieve their suffering, not quibble about whether a well-fed female might have her sensibilities offended. Maintaining the same air of sweet reasonableness, she added, "I did think, too, that Jem Walker might be invited to meet the committee – perhaps when we visit the house, for if we meet at midday he could, I dare say, arrange to join us in his dinner-hour. He has been a great help to me and he may be useful to the society in the future, travelling about the town as he does. Other suitable properties might come to his notice."

"A splendid idea," Mr Brook said and the others agreed.

She carefully drew on her gloves with fingers that trembled slightly. Another little victory! Another opportunity seized to see Jem. As she bade Mr Brook goodbye he said, warmly, "We have made an excellent start, Miss Linton." Then, diffidently, "Are you pleased at the outcome?"

"Indeed yes. And I must thank you, Mr Brook, for supporting me. Without your aid my idea would have come to nothing."

His heart stirred. Her gloved hand lay quiescent in his. He pressed it, whispering conspiratorially, "You handled Wharton perfectly." She had diplomacy and tact and he felt that she had come through some sort of test. That this meeting, her conduct, the impression she had made on men whose opinion he valued, had supported his judgement that he had chosen well. "Until next week, then," he said, reluctantly releasing her hand.

"If I may, Mr Brook, I will make a detour and leave a message for Jem at his home."

"Of course. My carriage is at your disposal."

He watched the carriage go and turned back into the house. He should go into the works, there were some estimates to go over with his chief clerk, but the thought of the noise and bustle deterred him. He walked through the quiet house to the music room, riffled idly through the sheet music on the stand, selected

Anne Goring

a piece and sat down at the piano. Beethoven played forte suited his mood exactly. He played almost without reference to the music, which was as well, for as the theme of the *Appassionata* rang out, his whole mind was joyfully occupied with pictures of dear Caroline.

Mrs Walker was engaged with a client in the scullery. She had let Carrie in, motioned her to a chair and whispered that she wouldn't be a minute.

Carrie sat in the small kitchen. Everything spoke of slender means and pride. The care with which each mismatched item of crockery was ranged, shining, along the dresser shelves, the high polish on the brass poker, the scrubbed whiteness of the big table that took up most of the space, the neat way the herbs were hung in dry bunches along one whitewashed wall. Carrie sniffed the aromatic tang of them. She thought, in a cottage like this, poor and plain as it is, Jem and I could be so happy.

The dark thoughts she had been repressing all afternoon came flooding back. She saw Adele's hand weighted down with the great bloodstone ring that would soon be matched by a gold wedding band, and despite the bright fire in the hearth she shivered. She felt so useless. It had proved easier to put in motion a society to help poor people she did not even know, than to rescue her sister from a marriage that would wreck her life. She stood up restlessly and walked to the window. Down below the river swirled, discoloured from the wastes poured into it from Mr Brook's dye works less than a mile away. On the opposite bank the grass was springing fresh and green. Soon the primroses would be out and the hedges bursting with leaf. She and Jem had once wandered along these banks on her half-days from Miss Tucker's. She clenched her fists. Whatever happened, whatever opposition she had to face, she would know the freedom to walk those paths with Jem again. She would not submit humbly to whatever scheme her aunt thought suitable. She was not like Adele, pliable, too eager to please . . .

42

Bitter Harvest

She turned from the window as Mrs Walker came from the scullery with her visitor. Carrie caught a glimpse of a thin, tear-reddened face before the girl pulled her frayed shawl over her head and slipped like a shadow from the house.

"Poor lass," said Mrs Walker shutting the front door and sighing. "Nothing I can do for her. It's too late and there'll be another mouth to feed come summer. Such a pretty lass she was and now look at her. Scarce twenty, with three little wenches at her skirts and another on the way – and her husband with an injured shoulder and turned off from the pit in consequence. Eh, dear, these youngsters hurry to be wed and think nowt to the future." She studied Carrie's face, reading it with an eye practised in other people's troubles. "There's no help for Miss Adele then?"

Carrie shook her head. "I do not know what to do now," she admitted.

"Then perhaps it'd be better to let things lie as they are, love." Mrs Walker laid her large work-scoured hand on Carrie's arm. " 'Tis a shameful thing that she should be pushed too young into marriage, but then a woman's lot in this world is never easy. That lass as has just left would testify to that – and many another I know of too, rich and poor, for I've looked to women in grand houses as well as hovels. But it's easier to make the best of things when you've a warm bed to lie on and good food set before you three times a day and no landlord hammering at the door for the rent."

Carrie looked into the wise eyes set into the strong-boned, plain face and knew the truth of it. Yet the body might be fed and content, but what of the mind, the spirit? But she knew Mrs Walker understood – she and Jem were the only ones who did. Frustrated in her attempts to see Mr Sanderson she had hurried down to the cottage by the Irk and found in Mrs Walker someone who would listen quietly and sympathise. Carrie had poured out all her outrage and gone away calmer. Later, in one of those snatched, precious times when she and Jem were alone, he had held her so hard she had felt her bones

43

Anne Goring

would break. They stood in the lane, in the dusk, two darker shadows against the sombre trees. He was still in his working clothes and the roughness of his horse-smelling jacket rubbed at her cheek.

"Oh, God, Carrie," he said harshly, "how can they do it to her?"

His grip tightened fiercely and she knew he was not thinking of Adele at all, but of their own circumstance.

"They will not serve me so," she said. "If they locked me in and starved me, I would find a way to get out. To get to you, Jem."

"If they locked you in, my little lass," he whispered, "I'd get a cleaver and break down the door myself."

They clung together and despite the brave words there was a desperation in their hungry kisses as though, Carrie thought with a shiver, Adele's plight was casting its shadow across their own lives. Which was foolish, for she was not Adele, to be forced into such a situation. She and Jem were young and strong and prepared to fight.

Yes, Jem and his mother understood and cared. But neither, sadly, had a jot of influence.

Mrs Walker said, "Set you down and take tea with me. Kettle's boiling."

"Thank you but I cannot stay. Mr Brook's carriage is waiting to take me home."

She gave the message for Jem and Mrs Walker stood at the door and watched the carriage clatter smartly down Hendham Vale. Billy Walsh's May was at her doorstep goggling at the shining equipage. Mrs Walker nodded to her. She had thought a while back that May had caught Jem's eye, but she'd heard since that she was walking out with a lad from Rochdale Road. In the last few weeks since young Carrie had taken to calling, on account of her sudden interest in herbs, she'd been startled into realising where his true feelings lay. Not that he'd say anything. Close as an oyster, he was. But once, by coincidence – or so it seemed – Jem had come in while Carrie was here. True, he did

Bitter Harvest

occasionally call home if he was delivering close by, but this time he'd come a fair distance out of his way and he'd dawdled overlong until she'd reminded him, sharply, that Carter Smith would be docking his wages if he didn't get off. All the while he'd been in the kitchen he and Carrie scarcely spoke. She was engrossed in writing out some recipes; he, apparently, was only interested in the glass of ale and hunk of new bread he was downing. In fact, it was in Mrs Walker's mind to speak to him later, for she'd brought neither of hers up to be ill-mannered. Poor they might be but courtesy cost nowt.

But then, when he gathered himself to go, Carrie, strangely clumsy, knocked her notebook to the floor. Jem picked it up and handed it to her and he, too, seemed overawkward, for the book almost went from his fingers and in retrieving it their hands met, the book lying between her palms and his hands cupping hers. For a moment they remained so. Mrs Walker stared at them, startled and they looked at each other and small, secret smiles lay in their eyes and touched their lips before Jem, slowly, let his hands fall. Then he was gone and Carrie was bent once more over her notebook and everything was quite ordinary again. Only Mrs Walker knew that there was nothing ordinary about what she had observed.

She had regarded Carrie with new eyes after that, seeing her as someone who loved and was loved by her son. It moved her strangely. She had always liked the girl, admired her courage in those bad times after her simple, foolish aunt had brought that wicked man to live in the cottage, when anyone with an eye to see and an ear to listen to his silver tongue, could tell him for a rogue and a rascal. She had been grateful that Carrie had taught Jem his letters. For that alone she would have put herself out to visit Mrs O'Hara while the girls were away at school, and heaven knows it had been an inconvenience at times, having to listen to an endless list of aches and pains, given in such a plaintive voice. Of course the woman had suffered. Of course her health was bad. But Mrs O'Hara had, Mrs Walker guessed, submitted meekly through her life to whatever circumstance overtook her,

Anne Goring

just as she now submitted to ill-health. With an ounce of spirit and determination Mrs O'Hara could have forced herself to do more and so gained strength and vitality. Many a time she had offered to take her on a turn around the garden or in the grounds, but always there had been a headache or a backache or a dizzy spell to prevent it. Mrs O'Hara had taken to her couch and slipped comfortably into the role of permanent invalid.

Aye, she liked Carrie, recognised in her something familiar. A thread of will and strength. The mark of a fighter. The lass had needed it sorely in the past – and would need it again.

The carriage turned the bend and was gone from view. Carrie Linton was a good lass. Honest, intelligent, kind. She would make a good wife for someone. But for her Jem? Her strong brows came down. She couldn't wish for a better prospect for him, a girl of good background with dowry enough to set him up in business on his own account. And a love match, at that. Ah, if it were only that simple. If only that wide invisible gulf didn't exist. The gulf that divided rich from poor; the quality folk from the humble artisan.

Slowly she went into the cottage and stared about. Its shabbiness, its spareness struck at her painfully. In her work she visited many a grand house to attend at a lying-in or a deathbed. It had never occurred to her to envy those who lived with servants scuttling to do their bidding, with rooms full of fine furniture and draperies and seven courses for dinner served on silver dishes. She accepted, unquestioningly that the world was a divided place and that poverty must exist side by side with opulence. The years had told her that peace of mind came from accepting the limits of your station in life; of striving to better yourself within those limits. Her sole ambition had been to lift her family away from the threat of the poorhouse. Through dogged determination and hard work she had done that, living from day to day, every farthing and ha'penny she earned spent with scrupulous care until she had edged them all away from destitution.

For the first time she realised how pitifully small had been

Bitter Harvest

her victory. For Jem she had wanted nothing more than he should grow to manhood dignified by the knowledge that the true virtues of integrity, honour and compassion were not bought with money; that a labouring man working diligently at his trade might be as proud of his achievements as the master who had command of a hundred men. She had seen her hopes fulfilled, though her compliments were sparing. "Our Jem's got a steady head on his shoulders", was the limit of her praise, but her inward satisfaction was great. She rejoiced that he was in regular work in a respectable trade and well thought of by his master. But now . . .

She looked down at her rough hands, the skin coarse, the knuckles getting knobbly with rheumatism. A poor woman's hands speaking silently of toil and hardship. She was suddenly, shockingly, ashamed of them. Ashamed that her horizons had been so limited. Grieved that the material things in life were not hers to heap onto her son. Fine clothes, golden sovereigns to be spent carelessly, the things that impressed the worldly, that gave a man power to make others do his bidding, to win and woo whichever lass took his eye.

Bitterness swelled up. She leaned back against the door, struggling against the unfamiliar surge of envy of all those moneyed women whom she had vaguely scorned because they had nothing to do but fill their days with idle amusements and gossip. But they were the ones who could send *their* sons out into the world comfortable in the knowledge that money would smooth their path . . .

It was a while before common sense reasserted itself; before she could straighten her shoulders and say aloud in her normal practical tones, "Eh, Lizzie Walker, you're daft . . . daft. Your brain's running on afore your feet. Like as not it's just a passing fancy they have for each other. No use worrying ahead of time . . ."

But it troubled her that she had given way too easily to foolish feelings she had no business harbouring for a minute. And it troubled her, too, that despite her sensible words, the

Anne Goring

conviction remained that the attraction between her son and Carrie Linton was not to be dismissed so lightly. If that was the case then theirs would not be an easy road, but one of great difficulty. And well might she have cause to worry over them.

As a child, Adele had once been frightened by the story of lost souls abandoned for eternity in a limbo between heaven and hell, forever doomed to wander in a grey nothingness. It seemed to her far worse than having to face the fires of hell and all those rows of grinning imps holding toasting forks. At least if you went to hell, you knew it was because you had done wrong in this life. Into limbo were sent the truly innocent – like the souls of poor unbaptised infants. It was so terrifyingly unfair.

It seemed, in her distress, that she had been consigned to a kind of limbo. All her pleas for rescue had fallen upon deaf ears. She felt as if she were shrouded in grey, gloomy fog in which she moved, walked, talked, even smiled. As though her body belonged to someone else, obediently going about its daily affairs under the approving eyes of those who had brought this terrible punishment down upon her. And all the while the terror and confusion were locked up in a small corner of her mind and only in her dreams did the terror unfold and spread and cause her to start out of nightmares with tears running down her cheeks.

Once or twice she had come close to confiding in Carrie but Uncle George's cautions would come to her. "If the slightest word got out of your . . . your friendship with Elliot Sanderson, it would be the end of all your hopes. You realise that, don't you, dear girl? Elliot's mamma would remove him from here instantly and place him far out of your reach. No, we must lie low, play cunning. You must speak of our little scheme to no one. Not even to Carrie. *Especially* not to Carrie. She has an impulsive nature and might, out of a misguided desire to help, speak out of turn – to her friend, Mr Sanderson, or even, in defiance, to Mrs Dawes." He had paused, staring at her gravely, compelling her to nod in agreement, for she knew, understanding

Bitter Harvest

as her sister might be, that Carrie would quite likely make a fuss in her determination to help. And that would spoil everything, beyond all hope. "It is far better that we hold the secret between the two of us," Uncle George went on. "And that you appear to comply with your aunt's wishes in the matter of Mr Prince. Speed and secrecy must be our watchword."

She had said, sadly, "You mean to be kind, but I think you are building castles in the air. The one who is most concerned, Elliot, is not even here and if he were he might not wish . . . might not care enough . . ."

"No, no, no!" His face was shocked. "You must not think like that or we are defeated before we begin."

"It is hard to have hope when it all seems so difficult."

There was a pause and she wondered, uneasily, if she had offended her uncle, his expression went so dark, but his voice was as smooth as ever as he said, "I have already put forward enquiries, dear girl. It seems that all can be arranged with the utmost facility and discretion."

"But Elliot . . ."

"You forget I have seen young Master Elliot in your company. I have seen the way he has gazed upon you. He is a man deeply enamoured. He will not, I am sure, be so faithless as you believe him to be."

"But I did not . . ."

"You must have trust. In him. In me. My deep desire is to see you out of this unhappy predicament. If you think my help is of no consequence, then you must speak now."

She drooped her golden head, a flower bending to the gust of a cruel wind. "I did not mean to impress you so," she said miserably. "If Elliot were here perhaps I should have more courage."

"He'll come. Have faith you silly girl. You will have your heart's desire. Promise me you won't harbour doubts."

"I will try," she breathed. She wanted to believe. More than anything in the world she wanted the comfort of believing that Uncle George would miraculously make everything all right.

49

Anne Goring

When she was listening to him it all did seem quite possible. She slipped away as often as she could to visit him in his workshop, anxious for his persuasive words to drive away the dark fears that constantly hounded her. She found herself paying him little attentions when he was at home. Fetching him his slippers, his tobacco, lighting the taper for his pipe, as she had done as a child, as though by pleasing him with these small rituals it was a kind of talisman.

Away from him, certainty dropped away, leaving her defenceless, lost. The worst times of all were when she was in Mr Prince's house. The high, dark rooms suffocated her, the old heavy furniture enclosed her, a prisoner. She sat stiffly in the parlour amid Miss Prince's collection of bric-à-brac that cluttered every flat surface. Figurines, pottery vases, pictures in velvet frames, cases of stuffed birds, seashells, embroidered pincushions . . . they seemed to flow towards her in an overpowering wave.

They drank weak tea from fragile cups, nibbled bread, wafer-thin and sparely buttered, and tiny portions of dry seedcake, served by a pinch-nosed maid who looked as withered as the dried poppy heads and dessicated grasses bunched into vases on the mantelpiece.

Everything in this house seemed drained of its juices. The house itself was shrunk in upon itself, activity within it limited to a few rooms, the rest shuttered, draped in dust sheets, sprinkled with camphor and lavender against moth, the air still and damp and stale.

Mr Prince had brought two wives here. If their youth had ever made an impression on these rooms, there was no evidence of it. They had died, one of a decline, one in childbed, their brief sojourn as transient as a candle flame in a draught. Only Mr Prince and Miss Prince remained and it was hard to believe that they had ever been young. They might have existed for all their years greying, frugal, preserved like the stuffed birds in the glass cases.

Sometimes Mr Prince was present, standing straddle-legged before the small fire, discoursing strongly upon some subject

50

Bitter Harvest

that interested him – the charge upon the rates of the shiftless poor, the frivolity of women's fashions, the low moral tone of the current theatre productions and the equally low morals of everyone connected with it, as he knew to his cost having, in his earlier days, listened to a plausible rascal who had wheedled a loan for the setting-up of a new theatre and had absconded with the money, leaving behind a pack of creditors . . .

"I hope," he had said, fixing her with his steely eye, "you do not hanker after theatre parties, Miss Adele. Mrs Dawes, I feel, was slightly irresponsible in introducing you to such doubtful pleasures." His discoloured teeth gleamed. "But there are many modest enjoyments a young married woman may undertake in her own abode. My sister will guide you in your housewifely duties and then you have your sketching and painting. There will be calls to make and visitors to entertain – not," he added hastily, "that we make a great show. That would be unseemly and a tax on my dear sister's health. I take business associates to my club to dine so you may have your little feminine parties in peace."

The mask that was her face twitched into its automatic smile and her thoughts cowered back. Was it possible that for the rest of her life she must listen to that voice dictating what she had to do, how she had to think? That she must bear, as she bore now, his hand taking hers, the brush of his moist lips on her forehead?

But if Uncle George's plan did not come to fruition, it would not matter. She would be cold and dead inside. Elliot would go and take her heart and her life, leaving only a husk to exist in this chill house, with these loveless old people, until she shrivelled and withered and became one with them.

Adele was out making afternoon calls with Miss Prince when Elliot and his mamma returned to Beech Place.

Aunt Linnie mentioned it, fretfully, as she rearranged the cushions at her aunt's back, then half drew the blinds to shut

Anne Goring

out the sun that was slanting into the room, before she went upstairs to take off her bonnet and cape.

"Such a trying afternoon. I had a bad headache and it made me feel quite faint. I felt obliged to have a glass of wine." With a plump, limp hand her aunt indicated the glass and bottle on the table by the sofa. "I know Jane is entitled to her half day off, but she must have it in future only on a day when one of you girls is at home. Caroline is hardly in the house these days – off on errands of her own and quite oblivious to my needs. Indeed. she was extremely trying after you were gone, quite pert, in fact." She dabbed at her flushed cheeks with a scrap of lace handkerchief. "She told me, so very defiantly, that she has the intention to visit some Sunday School in the town. To teach poor children their letters, or some such scheme. I told her straight, I forbid any such thing. It is bad enough Mr Brook taking her into town slums, even if she is chaperoned and in the company of several respectable gentlemen, but this . . . this Sunday School business is quite out of the question. But would she listen? She just put her nose in the air and declared that with or without my consent she would go, and that Jem Walker was as good as any gentleman to escort her there and back – better even, for he had been brought up to look after himself and spent his working days travelling about the town." Aunt Linnie gave an enormous, sobbing sigh. "I had never thought to live to see such ingratitude. When I think of how I took you both in, two orphaned lambs, and am rewarded by defiance and impertinence . . ." The plaintive voice wailed on.

Adele said, "Oh, dear", and "Pray, aunt, do not upset yourself", and "I am sure Carrie did not mean you to be upset", only half listening, vaguely sorry for her aunt, vaguely admiring Carrie for taking such a stand, but encompassed as she was by her own troubles, only wishing to escape to her bedroom.

"And just as I had closed my eyes, such a clattering and rattling. That coachman should be told not to take the corner so wild. I thought him to be driving the carriage straight through

Bitter Harvest

the parlour. Mrs Sanderson must have been shook to pieces, poor woman."

Adele held herself very still. "He . . . they are returned then? Mrs Sanderson and Mr Elliot?"

"And a good day for travelling. I declare, had I been a well woman I should like to have taken the air myself. I always enjoyed the spring weather when I had my health. Ah, you do not know how lucky you are, Adele, to be young and strong. Now hurry upstairs with your bonnet, child, and then make me some tea."

Her instinct was to rush to the orchid house. He would be bound to go there as soon as he could, but she must be careful. Very careful. She went upstairs on shaking legs. The trembling coursed right through her, a mingling of joy and relief. She could scarcely undo her bonnet strings or remove her cloak. She lay on the bed staring at the ceiling. He had returned. Soon she would know. And now that the time was close, fear hung dark amid the sparkling happiness that quickened her heartbeat.

He rode past the lodge next morning. Adele was dressing. She had had a restless night, falling into a heavy sleep at dawn and Carrie, out of kindness, had not roused her.

She sprang to the window at the sound of hoofbeats crunching on gravel. He passed below her on his lively bay mare. He looked neither to right nor left. Her fingers trembled as she let the blind fall back into place and buttoned herself quickly into her dress. After the days of dreaming, the reality was almost too much to bear, yet her mind was clear and sharp, as it had not been since the dreadful day when Mr Prince had claimed her. Elliot would ride down the lane and take the stretch of common land at a gallop. Sometimes he would ride as far as the river, sometimes only to the village, but always he returned along the bridle path through the woods. Often when he took his morning ride she would contrive to be idling in the garden when he returned so that they might exchange a few words, but today she must find a more private place.

Anne Goring

She forced herself to eat a little breakfast, then rose from the table, saying casually, "It is so sunny that I shall take advantage of the light and sketch the primroses in the lane."

Aunt Linnie was not yet downstairs and Carrie was too busy discussing with Jane the day's menus to do more than call a casual warning that the breeze was cool and she should wrap up well. It was so simple.

Clutching her sketching pad Adele was quickly out into the sunshine. It had rained in the night and the sun fired a rainbow off every dew-hung twig. The blood sang in her veins as her feet carried her across the lane and into the wood. She could smell violets and the rich scent of wet earth. Her cloak was soon blotched with damp as she brushed past the long pink buds thrusting out from the beech saplings, and the new green hawthorn leaves. She did not pause until she came to the far side of the spinney and could look down the sweep of the hill. There was no rider in sight. She stood still, breathing fast, her eyes fixed upon the path, her thoughts winging away, willing him to know she was waiting for him, willing him to turn and head for home.

She had been standing there for some moments when the crack of a twig alerted her. She started guiltily, fumbling with the sketching pad, making a hasty attempt to look as though she was working. Nobody came. She glanced back. The trees hung close, shadowed, in sharp contrast with the sunlit hillside ahead. She was aware of uneasiness. There was no one about, not even a child picking stones in the field below, no one to hear if she called. All the stories she had heard about tramps and vagrants suddenly loomed large. Miss Prince's friends had, this winter, been particularly troubled by tinkers knocking at the door and frightening the maids. The newspapers were full of tales of threatening beggars moving out into respectable districts to seek riper pickings. Even Jane had come in last week with some tale of a disreputable character seen hanging about the lane, who had run off when the gardeners had been called.

Now, the realisation of her isolation prickled her spine. She

Bitter Harvest

edged from the shelter of the trees out into the warm glance of sunlight as, somewhere amid a tangled thicket of hazel and briar, a shadow moved and a rustling came to her ears. The wind, she told herself nervously, merely the wind. And, seemingly, it was true, for when her eyes found the spot again, there was nothing there but the budding branches moving gently in the breeze.

Then she forgot her fears, for a horse and rider were coming up the hill and a great bubble of happiness caught her up as she watched that slender, grey-coated figure coming closer. At first he did not see her. He stared idly about him, his hands easy on the reins, letting the horse pick her way over the rough path. His pale aristocratic face under the fashionable beaver hat was calm, composed. Too composed. He had been away, and in that time her whole life had erupted horribly. If he loved her, surely he could not ride out on a spring morning looking as if he did not have a care in the world.

He caught sight of her and shaded his eyes. He smiled, then, and waved. Was that smile a touch guarded? The wave a little diffident? A surge of fear came rushing back.

"This is a pleasant surprise," he said as he reined in beside her. He swept off his hat and the breeze tugged at the dark locks that curled so romantically about his ears. "Meeting you quite sets the seal on a delightful ride. Such a morning! Though I fear the clouds are building. We shall have rain later. But that is true April weather. You have been sketching? I have some splendid new specimens for you to view. It has been a most interesting visit. You shall hear all about it – and about my new acquisitions. The gentleman we visited – the friend of an acquaintance of my mother's – has made a speciality of the *Cattleyas* of South America. He has generously given to me some fine examples." Was his voice a little high? His words, perhaps, too hurried? His glance merely touching her face before flickering away, as though fearing to linger?

"How . . . how nice," she said faintly.

"There was this magnificent *Percivaliana* still in bloom – a purple blotched with yellow. I was deeply impressed. His hot and temperate houses are models. Models." He stared over her head, his eyes as brilliant as they had been when he had taken her in his arms that day in the garden. "When I have my own establishment, I shall have orchid houses built on the principles he outlined to me . . ."

"Elliot . . . Elliot, have you not heard?" Her voice was thready. She was unaware that she used his given name out loud.

"Heard? What should I have heard?" His gaze refocused upon her.

"That I . . . that Mr Prince . . ." She closed her lips against the choke that rose in her throat. But she could not hide the tears springing to her eyes. All the anguish of the last days rose up in a great sob. She half turned away, her body shaking with the effort of trying to suppress the heartache.

There was the jingle of harness, the creak of leather as he swung down from the mare yet, for a moment, he did not touch her. She heard him repeating, "Tell me, pray, what distresses you so." And above the sounds of her own torment she recognised that he spoke differently now, his voice less certain.

She knuckled her eyes childishly with her fists. Tears spilled over the pale kid of her gloves. She could not bring herself to look at him as the words came gasping out in broken phrases, and the telling seemed to bring the reality into focus. She thought, it will happen, of course it will happen. Elliot does not love me and I shall go to Mr Prince and be shut up in his dark house and never, never know happiness again. I was wrong to let Uncle George persuade me otherwise.

She heard a stifled intake of breath, felt a tentative touch upon her arm.

"I . . . I cannot believe it. You and that dreadful old man. It is impossible!"

"It is the truth." The racking sobs broke out afresh.

"Oh, do not cry. Women's tears have always undermined me. And yours – my dear Adele – are particularly painful, for you know my regard for you is a tender one."

The words spilled out almost of their own volition. As

Bitter Harvest

uncontrolled, as instinctive, was his action in reaching out to draw her close. All his careful reasoning against tangling himself further in an impossible situation fled under the unbearable poignancy of her sorrow. She lay pliant in his arms, her slight body shaking, and he found himself moved and strangely excited by her helplessness, just as he had that other time in the garden. Later, he knew, there would be recriminations. He would have his conscience to torment him. Exquisite pain to deal with. But now it was so much easier to submit to the sensuous pleasure that lapped him, to give way to delicious imaginings of what it might be like to be possessed of such beauty, such tenderness, such childlike dependence.

Elliot's fingers sought the yellow curls escaping from her slipping bonnet, brushed the warm flesh of her cheek. The surge of desire that went through him blotted out the last guilty thoughts of Margaret, even now deep in preparations for their wedding. Her image, the memory of the sharp green eyes, were quite banished.

His lips moved against her forehead, pressed the silky hair at her temple, whispered endearments. Wanton phrases that could never, never have been spoken in his decorous courtship of Margaret. To Margaret he had talked of affection, respect. To Adele, whose arms crept so warmly and joyously around his neck, whose eyes – magnificent eyes like drowned violets – regarded him as they might some young god, he spoke recklessly of love.

Her tears were ones of happiness; her mouth quivered to a smile of aching sweetness. Shyly, she said, "I hoped . . . I longed for your return. I knew that if . . . if you loved me, everything would be well again. You would make everything right."

He stroked her cheek. "My little dove," he murmured, "how you have suffered."

"Nobody would listen to me when I said I could not marry Mr Prince. It was so frightening. As though I was nothing . . . of no importance. Just an object to be passed from hand to hand."

"Speak no more of it." Pity ground his stomach; anger against

Anne Goring

those who would marry this helpless girl to a foul old man. "You need have no more fear." He would speak, of course, to Mamma. It would not be easy. He should have to employ the greatest tact. But she was the one. She arranged everything so beautifully. She had influence everywhere. Papa, ailing as he was, would bow to her strength.

A crusader's spirit fired him. Under that adoring regard he felt capable of fighting giants. He felt as strong and powerful as he had once, so long ago, wandering in the tropical forest with Mahmood and Fatimah, swimming in the surf with a slim brown girl's laughter echoing in his ears. Mahmood and Fatimah. Those simple friends of childhood. They, too, had thought him a young god. He had grown up in the warmth of their undemanding admiration. They had vanished from his life and taken his childhood and youth with them. He had been sick to his soul. No one, not even Mamma who had always striven to give him everything he wanted, had understood the depths of his grief. He had mourned long for those dear friends. Mahmood, who had been his brother. Fatimah, who had stirred the first feelings of manhood, a faint echo, he realised now, of the magnetism Adele had for him. Though the two had no superficial resemblance – Fatimah musky-dark with all the sensuous grace of her race, Adele rich in the golden-skinned beauty of cooler climes – there was a similarity. It was a quality of ingenuousness. An absence of artifice, of sophistication. It shone, open-hearted, unreserved, from a pair of long black eyes set above broad cheekbones and from the violet ones that gazed up at him adoringly now.

"You will not be forced to marry anyone against your own wishes," he said boldly. "I shall not allow it." And, borne up by the strong tide of his emotions, by the naked trust in her face, he felt it to be nothing less than the truth.

"Oh, Elliot," she murmured. Her mouth tasted salt from her tears, but her voice was a happy onrush of words, phrases, tumbling haphazardly between the breathy silences their kisses imposed. It took some time before the import of her words penetrated his excited senses. Her breath was warm against his

Bitter Harvest

skin. "At first, when Uncle George explained it to me, I could not think it would ever happen . . . but now you are here and we are together it all seems quite possible . . ."

He raised his head. His glance took in the clouds moving across the sky, slowly swallowing up the blue of a morning that was too brilliant to last. Cloud shadows darkened the valley, and the breeze, rising, stirred the whip-like branches of a sapling birch, causing it to tap against his shoulder like a cautionary finger.

Carefully Elliot said, "Adele, you know that I have spoken to you of love. I do not regret that for one instant . . ." He hesitated. The alarm that flared in her eyes filled him with anguish. Guilt quenched the fire of his own exultation and faces he had sought to forget, now rose accusingly in his mind. His mother's strong, dominating, fondness turning to shock and rage as he imagined her reaction to this scene he played out with Adele. From Margaret, what? Tears perhaps? More likely he would feel the whiplash of her acid tongue rather than vapours and frets. And both women would turn together the full weight of their scorn and contempt upon this sensitive, helpless child whose only crime was to love unwisely. As he did himself.

For a few heady seconds he thought of this wild plan Adele's uncle had concocted and how it might be made to work. To make his life with Adele! To submit to his instincts and emotions, rather than to logic and common sense.

But even in those few seconds he knew it was not possible. He had part of his inheritance, true, but the best part would come to him on marriage. The right marriage. Mamma would scarcely consider an orphan, with little to recommend her but beauty, a suitable match. He knew the strength of her ambition. He had watched, sometimes amused, sometimes rebellious, mostly respectful, the way she threaded through the maze of intrigue, gossip, manoeuvrings, that characterised polite society, always carrying him along with her driving ambition to see him married – not merely well, but into the class of persons where the possession of a comfortable fortune obtained through commerce might be

59

Anne Goring

considered an obstacle rather than an asset. Where parentage and pedigree were of prime importance and any unseemly hint of common trade might cause the right doors to be firmly closed in one's face.

For him, because of Mamma's skill, the right doors had stayed open. Invitations had flooded in and when he grew bored or restive, there were always the fashionable clubs to which he had entrée. There were times when rowdy male company suited his mood. Perhaps he needed this outlet from his mother's domination, but even then she was indulgent when he came home mildly the worse for drink or having lost too great a sum at the gaming table. Indeed, she was proud that he mingled in smart society with ease, even if it did mean adopting some of its coarser ways. He had gone along lazily with Mamma's plans. Was it weakness? He dismissed the idea. No, not weakness. Expediency. Once he had his full inheritance, once he was married, the bond would be severed. He would use his money as he wished. Retreat to some villa in the sun to grow his orchids and write poetry, returning to society as and when he chose.

And there were aspects of society that gratified him. The pleasure in knowing himself to be the pride of his tailor; awareness of his own good looks emphasised by the exquisite cut of a coat and expensive barbering. He had enjoyed the flirtations with coquettish misses, matters of fluttering glances, stolen embraces, pouts and sighs and giggles. And one thing he had learned was that such escapades by no means ceased upon marriage. Indeed it was quite the thing for a married man, once his wife was breeding, to let his glance wander elsewhere.

The thoughts went through his mind in a flash. So much at stake. The important marriage. The respect of society. The comfortable life. Above all the esteem, the support, of his mother. Against all that the tug on his heart of a pretty face, a pair of yearning violet eyes. Oh, they could be happy, so happy, together. It needed one word. An affirmation. He strove for the strength to say that word, but his throat was

Bitter Harvest

closed to it. All he could see was his mamma's face, proud as she looked at him, and he quailed at the thought of her wrath. How could he deceive her? How could he let her down in her time of triumph? Her whole spirit was bent on his marriage.

The colour rose and fell in Adele's face. Her lashes lowered. "I – I have been too bold," she whispered. "I should not have spoken out."

"My dear one." Elliot gripped her hands between his. "Do not look so. I am not shocked. I love you so much."

"Then you will take me away? Oh, we shall be so happy."

He made his laugh light. "Not so fast. All this – well, it has come sudden, you understand. You realise how I am committed elsewhere. I must think how best to resolve it all."

A child's simple trust glowed in her face and a creeping sickness seemed to invade his heart. He must dash all that light from her eyes, betray her faith. And he had not the strength to do it. For a few clear seconds he hated himself, knew disgust for his cowardice, before the careful reasoning of self-interest hazed the painful edges.

"We must be discreet."

"But I may tell Uncle George? He will wish to make the arrangements. He has turned out to be a real friend. I always knew he had a good side."

"Wait a little," he said hastily. "A day or so." His face felt stiff as he smiled. "Let us share this secret a while longer. It will make us feel . . . closer, having this bond." The treacherous words fell so easily from his lips. Because he could not meet the joy in her eyes, he closed his and pressed a kiss upon her forehead. A judas kiss. When he was away from her, when he could think clearly, he would pen a letter. It would be a kind letter, a persuasive letter, the message masked in fine phrases and loving words, telling her why an elopement was impossible.

After she had gone he remounted and turned the mare's head away from the house. Scarcely knowing where he went he let the horse take him while he set his jumbled thoughts in order. By the time he had attained some kind of calmness the clouds

Anne Goring

had massed up, spreading soft and grey across the sky and as he turned into the lane that would take him home, the first drops of rain fell. He did not hurry the mare. The burden of guilt weighed him down and it was almost as though it dragged at the heels of the tiring mare.

A gust of wind set the tree branches clashing. A ragged edge of black scudding cloud spread over the reaching branches. Soon it would be raining in earnest and he shivered. A hellish climate. The sooner he was away from the cold and damp the better. As soon as the inheritance was his he would buy that villa in Italy where people laughed in the sunshine and took life at the same slow rural pace of their ancestors and did not hurry about, tight-lipped and frowning in grey, dirty cities.

Italy with Margaret. But how much better it would have been with Adele.

Confound it, why did he have to make such a choice? He should have been born a Muhammadan, worshipping Allah and allowed many wives. Then he could have married Margaret for her intelligence and good breeding and Adele for love and no one would have condemned him.

He smelled violets. In the undergrowth, under the thorn hedges the flowers were secretly lifting their heads. Primroses starred the woods. Spring was here. Time was moving on. Angrily he wished time would race ahead . . . that it was next year, the year after, with this awful decision behind him and Adele reconciled. Adele, he cried silently, forgive me. Adele, my heart . . .

"Great God in heaven!" The mare shied, almost unseating him. He fought to keep his balance and to steady the startled beast. "What the devil do you think you're doing, springing out like that. Have you no sense?"

The tattered figure, broad-brimmed hat pulled low, had stepped out almost under the nose of the horse.

"I was almost thrown, dammit!"

The man did not duck his head or sing out an apology or slink back against the hedge. He stood his ground. Then, as the horse cast an apprehensive eye at him he lifted his

Bitter Harvest

hand and ran it over the soft muzzle before catching hold of the bridle.

Then he raised his head and looked straight at Elliot.

There was no instant recognition, only a terrible premonition of being on the brink of some awful revelation, so that the gentle tapping of the rain on the rutted ground, the creaking of the beech branches, the fluttering of some disturbed bird filled the silence like alarm calls.

Elliot saw, under the uplifted brim of the hat, the great black patch concealing the eye socket and part of the scar that crawled from the hairline down to the chin, lumpy and pink and puckering one side of the mouth so that it stretched upwards in a permanent sneer. Against that obscene deformity, the sallow skin, smooth against the thrust of the broad cheekbone and the dark glistening eye on the undamaged side of the face, came as a shock.

For an instant Elliot saw him as a stranger – one of the verminous pitiful ghosts who haunted the back alleys of the town, emerging only to beg a coin from a passer-by before sinking back into the shadows. He lifted his arm as though to strike with his riding crop. But something held him back. As he stared in sick fascination at the ugly wretch, the twisted mouth opened to reveal jagged stumps of teeth and the creature said, softly, "I have travelled a long way to find you, young master."

Then he knew.

"Mahmood?" His voice was a horrified croak. "Mahmood? But it cannot be – for pity's sake what has happened to you! How have you come here?"

The dark eye stared back at him, unblinking.

"I have come to speak with you. There is much you should know."

"But you must come back with me," Elliot began shakily. "My dear friend, to find you here like this – why it is what I have dreamed of. But your injury . . . forgive me, but I am shocked beyond belief. You must tell me everything when you are warm and fed and out of those appalling rags."

Anne Goring

Mahmood shook his head. He did not smile and Elliot recoiled at the unfathomable chill in that unblinking gaze.

"Why ever not? Mamma . . . Papa . . . they will be delighted to see you. To give you the help that you need."

"I think not," Mahmood said.

The rain was falling steadily now. Mahmood's slow voice went on and on. Expressionless, relentless, it related the tale he had waited so long to tell.

Elliot listened, the reins slack in his cold hands. He watched the raindrops falling in small glistening diamonds upon the sleeves of his coat. As his mind took in the sense of Mahmood's words, the drops of water sank into the cloth, losing all their silvery brightness.

Presently, as Mahmood finished speaking, the damp speckles ran together in spreading blotches, spoiling and distorting the pale broadcloth of his new coat.

Chapter Three

SALLY Quick pushed herself off the pillows. "What are you up to, you sly fox?" she asked.

George smiled up at her and ran a finger up the soft inner flesh of her arm. "I've a mind, Sal, to have a bit of fun."

She lightly slapped his hand away. "Don't do that. Makes me go goosey, like as if someone walked on me grave."

She got up from the tangled bedclothes, yawned and stretched. Her sturdy limbs, the black silk of her loosened hair, glowed with vigour and life, exotic in the frowsty room. Dress her up, he thought, as he often did, in silks and satins and ostrich plumes and she'd knock those high-nosed society women into cocked hats. Give her a fresh start in a new country and she'd ape her betters and no one would be the wiser.

Sally pulled on her shift, covering the full rich curves of breast and hip. He leaned back contentedly, hands behind his head, admiring. She played to him, grinning knowingly as she dressed, lacing her bodice slow and tight, taking her time putting on her stockings, aware from long familiarity how he enjoyed the performance.

"What are you up to?" she repeated. "What little mischief are you planning for poor Carter Smith, then?"

George reached for his coat thrown across a broken-backed chair close to the bed. He drew a rolled piece of paper from the pocket and tossed it to her.

She frowned at the handbill, her lips moving as she slowly spelled out the words. Presently she looked at him. "Australia?" she said, puzzled. "This is about a ship leaving for Australia."

Anne Goring

"Fancy it, do you? Just you and me?"

She dropped to the bed as though her knees had buckled, her face agape with astonishment.

"It's something when I render Sally Quick speechless," he mocked.

But she did not rise to the bait as she usually did. She merely sat looking from his face to the handbill and back again.

He hoisted himself upwards and gripped her knee, feeling the muscle and flesh under the coarse cotton skirt. "I mean it, Sal. I've money put by. I've heard that there's opportunities for a man with sovereigns in his pocket. We can make a proper go of it, you and me. No need for a handle to your name or fine connections out there. It's a new land, with towns and cities springing up out of the wilderness. It's a place where fortunes can be made."

"But . . . but it's where they send 'em from the dock. Worse than hanging being sent out there, I've heard. There's heat and diseases and wild animals and man-eating heathens – if you live through the voyage, that is. Bodies is tossed over the side all the time."

"Criminals," he said softly. "Criminals all of 'em. Packed like cattle into the holds of leaky ships. Sent to labour in the cruellest parts of the country where no right-minded person would go of his own accord. It's no wonder they give up and die. But not us. We shall travel like the quality we shall profess to be, in a sound ship with a cabin to ourselves, Sal, and good food, a trunkful of handsome clothes . . ."

"Eh, come on, is it a joke or what? Where's the brass to come from all of a sudden?"

"No joke. I've money saved." His grip tightened on her knee as though willing her to believe and understand. "Bit by bit I've saved it. All my little – er – investments," he winked knowingly, "have fruited to a tidy harvest. It'd surprise you to know how much I've put aside for you and me and our future together – and there'll be more in the kitty before we go."

"And her?" She jerked her head so that her black hair

Bitter Harvest

swung sharply about her face. "Her you're married to? What of her?"

"I've been tied to that whining bitch for too long," he said bitterly. "Let that sour-faced niece of hers take her on."

"So you're upping and leaving her and proposin' to have me by you permanent-like."

"A fresh start, Sal. A new country. Opportunities."

"But you couldn't never marry me legal."

"What's a bit of paper to us? Nobody'll ever know in Australia. I'll buy you a gold ring. We can have a fresh name. You can choose it. What do you fancy? Smith? Brown? Jones?"

For once she did not respond to his cajoling. She broke his grip and went to stand at the window. She pulled aside the grimy curtain and stared through the cracked panes at the alley below.

"It isn't much I got here," she said. Her husky voice that could be so strident was quiet, flat. "I got me room, me friends, me old gran. Not much, but it's all I know. Me ma was a travelling woman, going from fair to fair about the country. She was here at Knott Mill when I was born. She died of childbed fever within the week. Me gran didn't know who me father was for sure, but thought he might have been a foreign sailor met up with when they was at Liverpool. Anyways, Gran had took up with a local man and left the fair, taking me with her. And I've been here in Manchester ever since. Never been no further than Kersal Moor, once, for the races."

"Then just think of it," he said. "The places you'll see. The sights. The adventure of it all."

"I dunno George. Me gran goes on all the time about her travelling. Specially since the rheumatics has her tied in knots and she can't hardly get over her front step. But me, I've never felt the need of it. If me pa was a sailor from foreign parts and me ma had itchy feet, they've passed none of it on to me."

"We'll be together, man and wife, as good as."

"Will we, George?" Sally did not turn round when he came up behind her and took her by the shoulders. She said, "We get

67

Anne Goring

along well, you and me. We knows each other. We understands each other. P'raps . . . P'raps I hoped as one day – sometime – you'd be a free man and we'd have a few words said over us by a parson and set up house proper. Well . . . I've never met anyone else I'd have a particular fancy to set up with, I'll say that."

"I've sprung it on you too sudden." He nuzzled his face into her hair. "Once you've thought about it, you'll know why I think it's a fine chance for us."

"Mebbe. But what if it don't work out? What if you get tired of me? There'll be nowt to hold us together. You can up and leave and I'll have no friends in that heathen place."

"Course you will." He swung her round and shook her urgently. "You'll make friends, easy as winking. And besides, who's talking of splitting up before we've even started out together." He ran his hands up her arms and cupped his palms around the firm flesh of her neck. "Without you, the adventure won't be worth a candle. Think of it as a challenge. You'll be acting the part of a lady – and you can do it, you play act often enough for me."

"It isn't that George. That'd be the easy bit . . . the fun. Oh, we'd have fun all right. It's just . . . just, I dunno, I've a funny feeling about leaving this place, about going off. Like when you touched me just now and it was like someone going over me grave."

"I never thought you were the fanciful sort, Sal."

"I'm not. Usually. Like you said, you sprung this on me sudden." She managed an imitation of her usual saucy smile. "If you're really set on it – if you want me to go . . ."

"If I want you!" He made to banish her fears in the way they best enjoyed. She responded ferociously and he felt satisfaction that he had won her round. And relief. For that instinct that had been his friend so long was pressing him, now, to get away. He was getting more restless with each day that passed. Besides, her unexpected reaction had piqued him. He had expected enthusiasm, laughter, excitement, not wariness. But even this

Bitter Harvest

added a certain spice to the moment, gave an extra zest to his caresses, until she thrust him away, gasping and protesting.

"You're mucking up me frock!" Then, mischievously, she fluttered her lashes, shook out her crumpled skirts and added in a high, genteel whine, "And you are taking me out to dine, sir, this evening?"

"Of course, my lady," he cried. "How say you to a mutton pie and a glass of porter?"

"Admirable," she said, mincing across the room in sharp parody of the many third-rate actresses she'd watched from the pits of the more disreputable theatres. "Providing you make no more assaults on my virtue."

He slapped his thigh. "By God, Sal, with you at my side I can't fail. You'll make a grand ladyship."

She swung round, pointing. "Ah, but Carter Smith. You've not told me about him, yet. Where does he fit in with this plan of yours?"

"Oh, him. Just a joke," he said easily. "I've a mind to settle a few old scores before I go."

"What you got against him – except that he'd give all his horses and wagons in exchange for an hour between the sheets along of me? Bleedin' old hypocrite, an' him a pillar of the church."

"His weakness is you and your like, Sal, my pretty. What about teaching him a lesson for ogling you like he does? Shall we give him a fright – and earn a few extra sovereigns into the bargain?"

She listened, grinning. His explanation was bawdy, deliberately aimed to appeal to her earthy sense of humour. He did not lie to her. He rarely lied to Sal. He merely omitted the true reason for wanting to compromise the estimable carter. She had surprised him once today with her reaction. He did not want any unexpected scruples to come between him and his intention to give Caroline Linton a nasty turnabout. Oh, yes, that superior miss had some turbulent times ahead of her. They all had, up in their smug fastness at Crumpsall. They were blind and innocent, but soon the first

Anne Goring

stone would be cast and some very unpleasant tremors would upset them all.

It had gone so very well, better than he ever could have hoped. He had been right to wait. His instinct for timing had not let him down. The inner voice that had kept him cautious these last years, was growing stronger and more insistent. Once these few rough ends were neatly tied and justice served on those who had wronged him, he and Sal would leave the grime of this stinking town behind.

He had tasted the delight of success the moment when Elliot Sanderson had silently come into his workshop and stood, an alien, peacock figure, uncaring that his glossy boots trod among sawdust and woodshavings.

"Good morning, sir," he had said, amiably, wiping his hands on his apron and advancing slow and humble. "What an unexpected pleasure. What may I do for you?"

The boy, he saw with deep relish, was white-faced, his soft, sulky mouth quivering. Such an ordeal for the poor young man, going against his mamma and papa. Making a decision for himself for once in his spoilt life. And so quickly on his return from his trip too.

"There is something I can do for you, young sir?" he enquired again, innocently. "A small item of furniture for your room? A repair of some kind?"

There was genuine anguish on Elliot's face, as though he fought some inner battle, or almost, from his pallor and the tremor in the hand that held the riding crop, as if he had received a mortal shock. The poor weak fool. Unable even to take a step from the apron strings without looking as though his guts were being wrenched out.

"You know why I am here," he said hoarsely.

"Indeed no," George said, anxious to prolong Elliot's distress."

A nerve twitched along the tense jawline. "It is ... Miss Adele Linton. I ... she ... that is, she told me I should speak with you."

Bitter Harvest

"What of, sir? Is it some small commission the dear child requires?"

"You know, man. You have her confidence." The words burst out. "Do not play cat and mouse with me. You have offered your help in the matter of . . . of an elopment."

With exaggerated care George advanced to the door, closed it cautiously and beckoned Elliot to the inner room. "I had to be careful, you understand," he explained in a stage whisper. "Pray do not raise your voice, sir. One never knows who may be close by, and secrecy is of the essence, is it not? Will you take a seat?" George waved a fawning hand to the chair in which Adele had sat and wept and listened to his comforting. Elliot shook his head stiffly. "I must not linger – if anyone should see . . ."

"Why, sir," George said, smiling. "It is merely that you come to ask if I could execute a carving of one of your orchids." As if he were a conjuror, he produced from his apron pocket a block of wood half formed to the shape of flowers and leaves. "A trifle I amuse myself with. It will serve as an excuse."

The boy's eyes flickered nervously over the carving, but there was no interest or awareness there. Other matters were more pressing.

George did most of the talking. The boy put in a question or two, but seemed too unstrung to take much note of the answers. All he was concerned with was speed. "I must get away soon . . . soon," he repeated. "Why should we delay?"

Because, George thought, the time must be right for me, you poor sod. Aloud, he said, "A few days, merely. I shall need that time to arrange the travelling and the preacher. All must go smoothly."

Elliot passed his hand over his eyes. "Perhaps it would be best if we went now. The waiting will be unbearable."

"Ah, love is impatient, I know. I have been young and in love myself."

The hand paused, shielding the eyes. "Love," he said in an odd, bewildered voice. "Yes. Love is impatient. And strange. And cruel." Then he dropped his hand. "As you wish," he sighed. "I will trust your judgement." His shoulders sagged. He looked spent and sickly, but calmer. "It is not long and I must bear the waiting." George bowed him to the door where Elliot paused and said, "Three of us will travel. I shall be taking a servant with me."

"Do you think that wise?" George's eyes narrowed. A servant. His thoughts ran through the house staff. A potential babbler. "Your valet, perhaps? I would beg you to consider –"

"You do not know him." For the first time the boy's voice held authority. "He will travel with us. There is nowhere else for him, but with me. Make such arrangements as may be necessary."

It had given George great satisfaction to do so.

Sal burst out laughing, bringing his mind back to the present, and Carter Smith. Her throaty roar was infectious. "I can just see the old lecher's face," she gasped, mopping her eyes. "Caught with his breeches down. It'll do me heart good. You're a one Georgie. It's nearly as good as pretending to your missus that you spend your time in Manchester with Samuel Quick."

George let laughter take him. His great shout contained all the satisfaction, the optimism, of one who knows luck is on his side. It was the cry of the gambler as the dice falls in his favour, of the cockrel standing triumphant over the bloody spill of feathers and flesh that had challenged it . . .

"God, it'll be a sight to see," he choked presently. "What a picture to take with us. We'll be laughing about it for years – when we're lounging about in our grand house in Australia with servants running at our call. We shall think then of this room and Carter Smith bare-arsed in it."

Another paroxysm shook him. He did not notice that Sally had sobered. Tears of laughter still smudged her rosy cheeks, her mouth still quivered, then, silently, formed the word, "Australia." And, suddenly, the tears might have been from some unknown sorrow.

"You're sure, Georgie?" she asked in a hoarse whisper. "You're sure about this travellin' – that it'll be for the best?"

Bitter Harvest

"Take my word on it!" he roared. "Harbour no doubts, my girl. We're set to take the place by storm, I feel it in my bones."

She picked up her shawl and swung it round her shoulders, then lifted her chin as though accepting a challenge and said, "Right, if you say so, I'm game. Now, how about that hot pie. You've fair worn me out with your carryings-on, you great lout. I need feeding up."

Arm in arm they went from the room. She kept him laughing with a crude joke she had heard from a flower-seller that morning. But even when the low sun, striking over the broken roofs and leaning chimneys, lit their faces as they emerged from the dark maw of the alley, her eyes remained shadowed and full of apprehension.

The dove, released, circled above Carrie's head, made as though to alight on her shoulder, then fluttered up and settled on the branch of a cherry tree. It cocked its eye at her, then at the strutting fantails around the dovecot.

Carrie called to it and scattered a handful of corn on the lawn. The fantails flew to her feet in a smother of white feathers and after a few moments the dove fluttered down to join them.

Jem thought that the picture would stay in his mind to be treasured forever. Carrie in the green garden, the sunlight catching the curling tendrils of hair escaping from her bonnet and the birds jostling at the skirts of her blue dress. It stirred a recollection of another time and place. Of a young girl with hawthorn petals in her hair waiting at a gate in the early morning and a blackbird singing. He had loved her and worried over her then, when she was still a child with harrassed eyes and work-roughened hands. He loved her now, a woman grown. He would love her as long as he breathed and his body ached with contained tenderness and desire.

She emptied the last of the corn around the dovecot and folded the muslin bag. Then, moving gently so as not to disturb the birds, she came to his side and put the bag in the lidded basket that had held the bird on its journey from Beech Place.

Anne Goring

"A happy ending to the story," Jem observed.

"Where there's food it'll settle, the pretty thing," the old lady said. She helped out at the mission school, a kind, wrinkled, nut-brown lady, whose small garden housed a collection of stray animals. She had shut her several dogs and her crippled jackdaw, that followed her like a little dog itself, into the cottage while the bird was introduced to the flock, so it would not be startled. "Ah, but you've a kind heart to think of rescuing a scrap of life like that. Life that's held cheap. I don't hold with the notion that animals are things without feelings, to be cruelly used and maltreated as though they were bits of wood and stone." She tilted her head to one side, almost like a little grey bird herself, her starched white cap like a feathery topknot. "I've even heard parsons preach that animals have no souls, but when the Lord calls us I reckon heaven will be full of all these creatures. If it isn't," she added stoutly, "I shall want to know the reason why."

Jem could imagine the redoubtable old lady tackling St Peter himself if she'd a mind to it. Carrie laughed. "Miss Blackshaw, if I had any doubts about leaving the bird, I have none now."

"You can rest assured that it won't end up as pigeon pie, Miss Linton. Now a glass of my gooseberry wine, before you go. It's a tidy walk to Crumpsall and a warm day, like summer almost, though I dare say it won't last. Sit you down on the bench there. I won't be a minute."

She bustled away and Carrie slipped her hand into Jem's. He pressed her fingers and drew her on to the bench. It was a moment that needed no words. It was enough that they were together and had one more precious hour before they must part. Church bells rang, rising and fading as the breeze eddied, counterpoint to the birdsong pouring like liquid gold from the high hedge round the garden and the grounds of Strangeways Hall beyond. His arm slid round her waist. Carrie's head rested against his shoulder, her gold-tipped lashes made faint shadows on the curve of her cheek.

"Oh if we could only stay here," she said dreamily after a while. "Just the two of us in this dear little cottage. The

Bitter Harvest

garden is like an enchanted place, so peaceful, so loved and cared for."

"We shall have a cottage like this in time, sweetheart. I swear to you."

"It is hard to believe that the town is so close. We might be miles from its noise and grime."

"Don't think of it. Think about me . . . us."

She said, simply, "I think of you always Jem. You are part of my heart."

They sat in golden silence until Miss Blackshaw returned with a tray. They drank the sweet, cold wine that tasted of summer and nibbled sugary biscuits. The old lady told them of the animals and birds and Carrie's eyes smiled over the rim of her glass and Jem wished that this time could go on and on. The sunshine, the birdsong, the sound of bells and Carrie at his side.

They walked home unhurriedly, though they had dawdled overlong. At every stile, at every gate, at every bend in every lane, they paused to laugh over nothing, to kiss, to cling together; the tall, spare young working man in his good Sunday clothes, the neat plain young woman with the slow and brilliant smile that made her beautiful.

The Sunday quiet lay over warm fields and woods and cottages and Jem looked ahead and rejoiced that there would be other days like this one.

He could not know that, for them, this was already summer's ending.

Mahmood saw them return. From the shelter of a ruined wall he watched impassively as the two figures clung together then parted to go their separate ways. He saw the girl pat her hair, her clothes, putting on a new brisk aspect that quickened her steps as she walked alone down the lane towards the lodge.

He eased himself back into the undergrowth. He had spent the morning, as he spent most of his days, watching the comings and goings about the house. Fixing in his mind the pattern in

Anne Goring

the lives of those who lived there, and those whose business it was to wait upon them and tend the gardens and horses. When he made the final move there must be no bungling. He knew the girl in the blue dress was the sister of the one the young *tuan* loved, and much foolishness there was in this idea of a runaway marriage. It ill became a man of position to dishonour himself in this manner.

Mahmood had listened phlegmatically to the *tuan's* disjointed outpourings when he had brought food and clothing to the tumbledown, ivy-grown shepherd's hut that was his temporary resting place. He had squatted there silently, his back to the mossy stones, while *tuan* Elliot crunched dead bracken and twigs underfoot as he paced the small enclosure, talking, talking. Thoughts, feelings, plans poured out, much of it incomprehensible, as though the *tuan* spoke aloud merely to clarify his own intentions. Occasionally he paused to dart a question about Mahmood's experiences. Mahmood answered him calmly and watched the anguish flicker in the handsome young face.

Elliot's distress did not touch him. Once, they had been brothers and friends. Too much lay between them now. Disaster, death had riven the bonds that had once linked them. Mahmood could look at this young man, with his youth, his health, his beauty, and feel nothing put a pale and distant sadness, an echo of nostalgia for a lost way of life. Sunlight, a green island, a house on a hillside, smiling faces, a slow and ordered existence that had seemed unchanging . . . It seemed strange, even, that Elliot should feel a responsibility for what had happened. For the wickedness of one who shared his blood. "I will make it up to you, Mahmood. You will come away with me. You should not be sleeping in the open like this. Good food will put flesh on your bones. I will look after you. Perhaps one day you will – we will – return to the East Indies, but I have plans to go to Italy. You will like it there." Mahmood had shaken his head. Elliot barely noticed. "The sun is strong and the Mediterranean coast beautiful. I will rent a villa and

Bitter Harvest

grow my orchids. We – the three of us – will find peace and happiness . . ."

He had gone away, then, unheeding of Mahmood's silence, totally bound up in his own problems.

Now Mahmood moved easily, despite his uneven gait, back into the shelter of the trees. He would not, could not, go with *tuan* Elliot. His way lay down a different path. One he must tread alone, however dark and bloody, to wreak the vengeance that would heal the knotted hurt in his heart.

Carter Smith felt agreeably at one with the world as he came out of church that evening. Above the slate rooftops of St Ann's Square the sunset flared pink in a sky of deepening turquoise and the air even now had a balmy tang after the pleasant day. He inhaled deeply the familiar town smell of sun-warmed dust and horse-muck and soot, set his beaver at an angle his wife would have frowned on as rakish, stowed his prayer book in the pocket of his frock-coat and set off at a brisk trot, rolling slightly on his bowed legs across the flags. The carriage bearing the last churchgoer homewards bowled past him and the Sunday quiet settled back over the pigeons and sparrows that made supper from blown chaff in the gutters, and the hackneys drowsing in hope of a late customer.

He paused at the Exchange, a complacent smile flitting across his narrow features. It was not often he was out alone of a Sunday evening, but his wife was taken with a megrim and his two elder girls were at home fussing over the last of the packing before the great move to Higher Broughton. He had been nagged at for getting in the way and was glad to escape to evening service for once.

"And I might go and have a bite of supper with Joe Arnold," he'd called into the turmoil of boxes and hampers and tea chests. The women had barely time to bid him goodbye and he hugged his little white lie to himself and later begged forgiveness on his knees in church, for Joe Arnold was off visiting somewhere and he had given himself a few spare hours for solitary enjoyment.

77

Anne Goring

The evening stretched agreeably ahead. No sedate walk back to the Meadow and incarceration in a stiff-backed chair behind closed curtains while his wife worked at her tatting and criticised the sermon, the parson, and the bonnet of every woman in the congregation. No, the evening was his to do as he pleased.

His stomach gurgled gently, reminding him that dinner had been a scrappy meal. A nice chop or two with boiled onions and a wedge of apple pie to follow would do him nicely. He'd wander up to The Royal for an appetiser of brandy and water, then to his favourite chophouse in the Shambles. Maybe later he'd have a game of skittles or then again he might content himself with a stroll about the town. The thought came to his mind that he might spy a few ladies of the night displaying their wares on the shadier side of the well-known thoroughfares. Ladies to stimulate the imagination. He reminded himself that he, a pew-holder, had just attended divine service at St Ann's. Reluctantly he pressed the tempting thought aside.

But he could not subdue the buoyancy of his spirits. He felt a positively youthful surge of well-being. The fine spring evening, the appreciation of himself as a person of some standing in the town – why, it had taken him all his time to acknowledge the greetings and bows from other members of the congregation before and after the service, not to mention the kind enquiries about Mrs Smith's absence – the satisfactory conclusion to a business deal he had been negotiating all winter, the contract to be signed tomorrow, all combined to a most agreeable sensation of contentment.

He had to admit, too, that the prospect of the villa at Higher Broughton in no small measure added to his satisfaction. He had cavilled at first – and still did loud and long to his wife – at the expense. The rental alone was more than fifty guineas per annum, not to mention the new pieces of furniture his wife insisted were absolutely necessary and the extra staff to run the house and garden. He'd be lucky to come out of the business less than £200 the poorer.

Nevertheless, when he had stood amid the builder's rubble

Bitter Harvest

before the glossy mahogany of his new front door, staring up at the sound red-brick façade, the bays and gables ornamented in creamy stone, his heart had swelled. An address to be proud of. He glanced left and right. Similar villas flanked the short cul-de-sac, set square in pieces of rough land, some already lawned and planted with shrubs. Solid citizens lived here and were, the agent had boasted, snapping up the leases. "So convenient for town, yet smell the air, sir, fresh as if you were miles out in the country. As healthy a spot as ever you'd wish to settle in . . ."

From habit he had frowned, made a disparaging remark or two about the quality of the building, the extortionate rental. He stumped about the new floorboards, his footsteps echoing noisily, while his wife calculated aloud the amount of materials needed for blinds and curtains and the agent tripped anxiously in their wake.

The place felt right. He could see himself at the head of the table in the dining room, flanked by guests. Then the ladies retiring to the parlour – no, drawing room – while he handed round cigars and port to the influential businessmen he'd be asking to dinner. People he'd never have contemplated inviting to the house in the Meadow. The men with the factories and small mills who'd need a good reliable delivery service. Aye, for a man with expansion on his mind the new house would be an asset. He had to agree with Alice. For once she had been right. It behove an ambitious man to have a good address. An expense, surely, but an investment with hidden benefits.

Times were good and the future had a rosy tinge, and he'd no qualms now about living away from the yard. Young Jem Walker was shaping up even better than he'd anticipated. He had a quick mind and a pleasant manner. Already he had the measure of old Spencer who'd been surly when the lad had picked him up on one or two errors in his books. Jem had spoken civilly, but he'd been firm. Carter Smith had heard him and suppressed a dour chuckle as Spencer began his usual whining excuses and Jem neatly cut him short. There'd been mutters among the men,

Anne Goring

too, when they'd learned the way of things. But somehow, Jem had steered a diplomatic course, staying his usual quiet self, not becoming boastful or overbearing.

In fact, as the weeks passed, and he continued to pull his weight in the yard, not shirking any of the dirtier tasks yet staying after hours to learn the mysteries of the files and ledgers in Master's office, they began to see that Jem's position might be of use to them. One by one, the requests had come in. "P'raps now you have Master's ear, Jem, you'd mention the matter of me lad needing work. He's good wi' hosses." "How do you reckon this trace? On it's last legs, eh? Speak to Master about it, would you? He takes note on you." And Jem had spoken to him. Straight up and with no hesitation and not shirking to give his own opinion or to argue.

Carter Smith had been secretly amused, though his narrow face had shown only its usual frowning melancholy. "Getting above yourself, aren't you?" he'd growled. "You'll be telling me my business next."

"I don't aim to do that, sir." Jem's straight gaze did not waver. "But you've entrusted me with responsibility for the yard in your absence and I don't want things going wrong. That trace is getting worn beyond repair."

"Very well, you see to it. And let the order be a ha'penny more than I think is the right price, then I shall dock it from your wages." Or, "Let the lad start and if he proves useless I shall want to know the reason why."

He'd chosen well, there. Jem was proving to be worth his salt. He'd promised him a rise of two shillings a week starting next week after the move. He was almost inclined to cap it with an extra sixpence, but withdrew such an extravagant gesture prudently. Later on perhaps. Jem was benefiting enough from the free lodging at the yard.

"Thinking of getting wed?" he'd joked. "Make a fine set of rooms for a pair of newly-weds, the top floor of the old house."

He'd noted how the blue eyes became wary. "No, sir, I'm not thinking of it yet."

Bitter Harvest

"Courting, perhaps, eh?"

A hesitation. "Not courting, sir."

"But an eye on some good-looking wench, I'll be bound. And a fine catch you'll make for some lucky lass."

"Not for a few years yet." His voice was firm, dismissive.

Young men were notoriously secretive about their lady loves and he'd bet that there was a petticoat somewhere in the offing. Come to think of it, Jem had had a spring in his step for some time and a light in his eye that was perhaps not all to do with the way he was thriving on the responsibility showered on him at work. He was different from the peaked, quiet worker he'd been in the winter. Here was a young man with purpose and ambition. Doubtless a pretty face had something to do with it. Not a bad thing, either. A woman to work for gave a man stability.

He'd been a bit of a lad himself. He refreshed himself now and again with the recollection of the times long past when he'd spent all his energy in pursuit of saucy smiles and flashing ankles. When all his ambition had centred on exploring the mysterious and exciting territory that lay under a woman's skirts. He'd gone about with a rough and ribald crowd of lads. All scattered now. Turned into sober and conscientious citizens, strict with their daughters and tough on their sons, as though they'd never had a lewd thought in their lives.

His other interest had been the acquisition of money. He never felt better than when his pocket was full and his dad was not predisposed to fill it unless he pulled his weight at the yard. Slowly he began to see that there were possibilities in the carrying trade. The town was booming. Factories and warehouses were springing up everywhere. Men with enterprise were making fortunes. Perhaps the carrying trade would not make him a fortune but it could quite well keep him in comfort all his life.

His dad lacked the capital to buy more wagons and horses, and capital they needed. So, coolly casting his eye over the young women of his acquaintance, his glance came to rest on Alice

Anne Goring

Sedgemoor. She was plain and lanky and primly respectable. Her overwhelming asset was the fact that she was the sheltered only child of a draper in the wholesale trade. He courted her carefully, treating her as he might a nervous horse. She shied from all but the most restrained demonstrations of emotion and was inclined to do a great deal of praying. Instead of roistering with his mates he was obliged to attend church three times of a Sunday and innumerable weekday Bible classes and prayer meetings. Sometimes he wondered if the effort was worth it. Then he thought of the dowry the draper had promised to bestow upon his daughter, and his resolution strengthened. Once married, he would show her that there was more to life than praying and timid hand-holding. A few lusty infant sons would knock the primness out of her.

He was wrong in that. The primness was ingrained. She tolerated his lovemaking in rigid silence and prayed with even more fervour afterwards, which did nothing to improve his temper. The sons he had envisaged following him in the trade were all daughters. Nevertheless, the dowry was his and, later, Alice had inherited the whole of the draper's estate and he was able to build up his business to its present flourishing state – even with the girls to marry off. Expensively. Alice had seen to that, though it had been like drawing blood to spend on such frivolity.

The disappointment he had felt in having only daughters was somewhat relieved now that the girls were, in their turn, breeding. Already he had two fine grandsons and, though infants yet, one or other of them might take an interest, given time. He liked the thought of that. Continuity. These grandsons of his would be better educated, better off, than he'd been. He himself had had a rough and ready kind of upbringing, but at least he could read and write and number which was more than his dad could do. The old man would be proud indeed if he saw the yard now, not to mention the house at Higher Broughton and the pew at St Ann's. And just as he had built on the foundations his dad had laid down,

Bitter Harvest

so the grandsons would bring their own talents and ideas to expand trade.

Carter Smith had downed his fourth brandy and water without realising it. The fumes rose heady and warm to his brain, bringing roseate visions. He saw the spanking lines of wagons – painted green, his favourite colour – with his name in bold in great curling letters on the side. He saw the big glossy horses, the workers doffing their caps at his approach, the tall young men, vaguely featured, who were his grandsons grown up, bringing their problems to him, deferring to his age and experience. He saw yards, depots, all over the town emblazoned with his name.

He made his way out of the smoky taproom. Dusk had closed in over Market Street and the air, cool now, made him dizzy, so that he had to pick his way carefully over the setts. A nice chop, now, and perhaps one more brandy to round off the evening. Then he would walk home the long way round, let himself in by the back door, and settle himself for the night in the spare room. Alice would be too busy nurturing her headache to scold him for being late. She would probably think he was considerate in leaving her in peace.

Yes, it was a very satisfactory sort of evening.

The chops were succulent, melting in a pond of hot gravy, the onions fat and juicy. He followed the apple pie with a wedge of prime Stilton. He sat back replete. The low-beamed ceiling sent back a warm fug of the savoury steam rising from the tureens the waiters carried to the tables, and the tobacco smoke curling from the pipes of customers who dawdled over brimming glasses. A man alone at the next table caught his eye and nodded. A vaguely familiar face, ruddy, smiling. A customer perhaps? No. Someone seen somewhere. In the Meadow? A respectable looking man, rising now and coming to speak to him.

A full stomach and a general feeling of bonhomie caused him to acknowledge the man's greeting more warmly than he might ordinarily have done. He did not quite recollect asking the man to sit, but there he was opposite, calling for more brandy, telling him how pleased he was to have this opportunity to

Anne Goring

speak, being well-acquainted with Jem Walker through his niece who was walking out with the lad, and how grateful everyone was to Carter Smith for his generosity in improving the lad's prospects . . .

The agreeable words washed warmly into his ears. He found himself talking to this good-natured stranger as if he had known him for years. When the man had excused himself after shaking him by the hand and expressing such gratitude for the treatment of young Jem that Carter Smith could readily believe himself a philanthropist of the first order, he realised that he had not enquired the gentleman's name. No matter, he could find out from Jem. He rose unsteadily from the table. Those last brandies had been unwise. He negotiated the tables with extreme care and on the threshold stood swaying, taking his bearings, before he set off in the direction of Long Millgate. It was getting late. Alice would be fast asleep and the daughters returned home. He would slip to bed safely unobserved.

A few roisterers swept noisily past, almost setting him off balance. He smiled foolishly at their retreating backs. Young lads. Such as he'd been himself. Nice to see 'em enjoying themselves. He moved on, taking the familiar streets by instinct rather than observance, taking short cuts through narrow entries that he might have avoided in more sober mood, vaguely aware of the raucous nightlife of the Meadow. People overflowing from beerhouses, sitting on house steps, gathered in knots in the shadows.

"Good evening, to you, Carter Smith, sir."

He came to a swaying halt, catching hold of a crumbling iron railing to steady himself.

"My, but you're out late, sir – and taking a risk. They're not wholesome parts for gentlemen such as yourself to be seen in." The warm husky voice was like a caress.

She stood in a patch of guttering lamplight falling from a broken shutter, her black hair loose about her shoulders, her red skirt hitched high above her ankles. She was smiling, her head tilted to one side.

Bitter Harvest

He blinked owlishly. Hazed in the flickering light she looked, for all her sturdiness, an insubstantial figure. A dream woman come to taunt him out of brandy-borne visions.

"You look, sir, a man in need of a bit of help." She stepped closer, disengaged his hand from the railing and placed it on her shoulder. "There, that better? Lean on me, do."

"No . . . no." His voice was hoarse. He tried to move his hand, but somehow she had fastened her arm around his waist. His eyes now fixed themselves on the creamy, juddering globes of flesh bulging from her bodice. They closed upon him, pressing soft and warm into his chest. Her musky smell filled his head.

"Come along wi' me sir, do," she murmured. She moved slowly against him, grinning, her tongue flickering behind her white teeth. "We'll have a good time, you an' me."

"I can't. Leave me be, Sally Quick," he said weakly. He wanted to move his hand from her shoulder but it seemed to have rooted itself there, drawing up warmth from the skin so close under the thin bodice. "You're wicked," he slurred. "A wicked woman. A Jezebel." His head was swimming. Everything seemed to be happening very slowly. The way she wrapped her free hand round his neck, the way her face – the open, red mouth – came closer and closer to his.

"A Jezebel, am I?" she said. "Tell you that in church, do they?"

He tried to summon up the face of the rector. Jeremiah Smith. A man of God who carried his own name. He would have banished this . . . this harlot with a word. But the rector's features swam away. Only Sally Quick's face was real, human, tempting.

"Who's to know?" she whispered. Her teeth nibbled at his earlobe. Her breath was damp on his cheek. She took his hand from her shoulder, moved it downwards. "Come wi' me. Me room's close by."

He groaned. "I'm a respectable citizen . . ."

"We're all respectable citizens, sir. Only some of us is less fortunate. I only know how to please gentlemen such as yourself.

85

Anne Goring

As I shall show you. This way, now. Just a few steps. That's it . . . hold on to me. Oh, you saucy dog, you. I can see we shall have fine games."

The stairs were steep and dark. He tripped on broken treads and she pulled him upwards. He heard her laughter, low and cajoling. Blindly he went on until he stood in a dim room lit by a single candle. There was time yet. Time to retreat. Time to beat back his body's responses to the feel, the smell of her. But he did not want to, God forgive him. He felt himself gawping, heard his breath quickening as, in the dimness, she flung off her shawl, kicked off her slippers, drew her red skirts high, then dropped them with a laugh. She whirled around him, her nimble hands undoing buttons, pulling at his arms and legs.

He found himself sitting upon the bed without his boots and breeches. He was trembling with anticipation and apprehension. The bed creaked as she flung herself beside him, drawing him down on top of her. His hands scrabbled at her bodice.

Then a voice. A voice with a smile in it. A man's voice, pleasant, hearty. "Well, well, what have we here? Not our estimable Carter Smith, a man of the church, consorting with a known whore?"

The light had strengthened. The man held a candle above him. A drop of hot grease fell on his bared thigh.

Silence. Frozen, stunned silence. Then Sally Quick laughed. She threw back her head in gusty abandon, twisting from under him, pushing up from the bed, falling against the man in a paroxysm.

"His face!" she screamed. "Just see 'is face."

"Not to mention other points of interest," the man said, pleasantly. "Not a pretty picture, Sal, eh?"

"Christ," Carter Smith whispered. "Christ! It was her. All her doing."

"And you hadn't a sinful thought in your head, had you? Dear, dear, that will never do. I took you to be a perfect gentleman when we were talking less than an hour ago. Not a whoremonger."

Bitter Harvest

"Who . . . who the devil are you?"

"A friend. A friend who has your interests at heart."

Carter Smith summoned what scraps of respectability he had left. Dragging the grubby coverlet around his legs, he sat up. His head was throbbing. His brain moved with terrible sluggishness. All he knew was that some dreadful calamity was happening to him in which this smiling man had a part. And that bitch Sally Quick.

"I was lured here," he said. He tried for lofty dignity, but his voice came out thin and reedy. "I shall leave this instant."

"Without your breeches?" said the man, holding them up in his free hand.

"Or your boots, Carter Smith, dearie," Sally Quick cried, waltzing them round the room. "You'll have to come and fetch 'em then."

"Give them to me," he hissed.

"In time," the man said.

"What is it you want. Money? I'm not a rich man. I have but half a sovereign upon me."

"That is not the way you were talking earlier, sir. I had thought you had a flourishing trade. Tut tut. Men without means do not move to Higher Broughton."

"If you do not give me my breeches I'll call a constable. I shall say I was dragged here against my will."

"Dear, dear, that won't do at all. Think again, sir. I have several people's word already that you were seen making through the Meadow less than sober. You solicited the attentions of this poor girl here, forced your abominable attentions upon her until she screamed for my assistance. Do you think your good wife would like to hear such a tale? Or all your respectable church-going friends?"

"How much?" The words were ground out between clenched teeth. The shock was sobering him rapidly. Money. All his years of endeavour would be bled into the pockets of these pair of rogues. He saw it all with horrible clarity.

"Just a small contribution. Say fifty guineas. That is a small

87

Anne Goring

payment, I think you will agree, for so grave a misdemeanour as you have committed this evening."

"Fifty guineas!" He gagged.

"In gold, of course. One cannot trust to paper money with banks so unstable. By tomorrow morning shall we say? The package to be delivered here, in person, by your good self."

Carter Smith closed his eyes. Fifty guineas. Well he could find it without much difficulty. It could have been worse. Much worse.

"And you need not think we shall be pressing you for a further payment," the man said, as though reading his mind. "Sal and I will be leaving the district when the money is in our hands."

"How can I trust you?"

The man shrugged amiably. "We shall trust each other. I shall, of course, keep a small security to make sure you keep your side of the bargain." He held aloft the breeches. "These, sir."

"But how can I get home! I can't go naked."

"It's only a short way," George answered reasonably. "Pull down your shirt-tails and keep to the shadows."

Sally giggled. "Shall I let him have his boots, George?"

"Tomorrow."

"They're my new ones," he wailed.

"All the more reason for you to hurry the money round to us, then you'll have them back again. And your breeches. Before your wife finds out. And remember that we have witnesses prepared to swear to your perfidy on setting about this poor girl, tonight. Pray do not dream up any fancy tales of your own."

Carter Smith stood up. The man was bigger, bulkier, and despite the smile his eyes were cold and calculating. There was no pity there, only a chilling hardness. Any vague idea of outwitting him died.

"I think," George went on, "I would be a poor host if I did not see you to your door. I might even lend you a long coat to cover your shame. You seem a little shaken. There is no need to be. This little matter will be cleared up tomorrow if you act sensibly. If you do not, well, I fear once the mud

Bitter Harvest

has been thrown it will cling for a long time." The door of the room closed behind him as Carter Smith was propelled down the rickety stairs. Fresh air hit him like a blow. He shuddered. "You will feel the cold without your breeches," George said, "we had best hurry." A strong hand gripped his arm. For a big man he moved silently among the shadows. "You will not be troubled if you do all that you are asked. And that includes one other small request."

Fresh anxiety stirred Carter Smith's bowels. Blackmailers never stopped at one demand. Oh, God, that this nightmare was over. Here he was in a black entry, half-naked, with a pitiless scoundrel, when a short time ago he had been so happy.

"I am not a wealthy man," he quavered.

"It is not money. It is a favour. Regarding Jem Walker."

"I have already given him advancement. You know that . . ."

"Not advancement." George chuckled. It had an unpleasant ring that set Carter Smith's bowed white shanks trembling. "Not advancement. I should not like to see the lad get above himself." His grip numbed Carter Smith's arm. His voice was low and chilling. "You will get your breeches back tomorrow, dear sir, but not before you have put into practice a small plan of mine."

Chapter Four

CARRIE woke to the drumming of rain on the roof. She came up out of a deep contented sleep. She had been far away in a green landscape. Jem had been there and she had been with him, a child again. Even as she thought of it the dream evaded her, slipping away so that she could not catch it. She lay still, hearing the rain, and the soft sounds that told her Adele was up. She did not want to move. It felt very early.

"What time is it?" she asked sleepily.

The little sounds stopped suddenly. "I did not mean to wake you."

Carrie opened her eyes. "But you're dressed already!"

"I . . . I couldn't sleep. I thought I would turn out my painting things." She sat at the chest of drawers, the bag in which she carried her paints and her pencil-box propped open. The top of the chest was strewn with the contents.

"Were you feeling ill, Adele?" Carrie pushed herself up on the pillows.

"Not at all. I feel very well." She glanced quickly at Carrie, then away. Sleepily, Carrie realised that Adele did look different. For so long she had gone about the house quiet and wan, or meekly off in the wake of Miss Prince, that it was becoming hard to remember how light-hearted, how smiling and bright a creature she had always been. Now, this grey dull morning, there was colour in her cheeks and animation in her movements.

As though sensing Carrie's surprise, Adele said. "The sun yesterday . . . summer coming . . . I feel refreshed. As if nice things were going to happen." A small pause. "Spring-cleaning,

91

Anne Goring

that is what I am doing. Discarding all the old paints and pencils. I shall buy a new set."

Carrie smiled. "It hardly seems necessary to put on your new dress to sort drawing materials. Take care you do not mark it."

Adele's hand strayed to the moss-pink flounces of her new afternoon gown. She said, carelessly, "Miss Prince thinks this colour too frivolous for day wear, but I like it. So I shall wear it to cheer up this dreary morning."

"Oh, my dear," Carrie said softly.

Adele laughed lightly. "Pray do not speak in that tone, Carrie. So sepulchral. I am to be married, you know. Not buried."

"And – and you are reconciled to it?"

"Oh, yes," she said. "Yes, I am quite reconciled to my fate." There was a faint unreadable undertone, quickly gone. "You must not worry about me, Carrie."

"I have not been able to help it."

"And I have not been communicative. I have not wanted to talk and we have always been friends. It is not always the case with sisters, is it? Do you remember the Cole twins at school? They were forever arguing. It seems a long time since we were in Malvern." She sighed nostalgically. "Happy days. But there will be happier ones to come."

Carrie clasped her arms around her knees. She did not know whether to be delighted or even more anxious at this sudden optimism. But she certainly did not wish to spoil this sudden return to their old intimacy. She said, cautiously, "There will be happier days for all of us, I hope. But promise me, Adele dear, that if you are in the least, well, disappointed in your married life, you will not . . . that is, I should not like to think of you burdened with unhappiness. I . . . I would always be ready to listen, to help . . ."

The hands, so busy with pencils and brushes, stilled. After a moment Adele said, "I appreciate that, Carrie. Truly. I am only sorry that I have not spoken before. It was not possible. You will understand in time. I still cannot . . . you

Bitter Harvest

must believe me when I say that I am making the right decision."

She had turned on the dressing stool so that she stared from the window, over the grassy swell of lawn, to the house standing amid the dripping trees. Carrie could not see her expression, only the tumbled, uncombed hair rioting in a golden mass about her cheeks and down her back.

"Mr Prince," said Carrie gently, "is, I know, much respected. It is just that I have felt the age difference too great."

Adele swung round suddenly, laughing, teasing, "Well, you shall not have that difficulty. Jem Walker's age is just right!"

Carrie jerked upright. "How did you . . . ? What do you mean? I never heard such nonsense."

"Aha! You are as red as fire. Do not try to bluff it out. He has always been sweet on you, do not deny it. And now that sentiment is returned, is it not?"

"Ssh!" Carrie cried. "The whole house will hear!"

Adele slipped from the stool and sat on the bed. She took Carrie's hand. "I do not mean to tease," she told her, solemn now. "I know you wish it to be a secret."

"But if you have found out, must not others, too? Aunt Linnie . . ."

"You have been the soul of discretion. Aunt Linnie, I am sure, notices nothing beyond her own comfort." For the first time there was bitterness in her voice. "No, if you are careful, you will have your Jem. On the other hand, should you come to consider Mr Brook, he is a fine gentleman, cultured and well-off and I think Mr Sanderson would like that match for you, despite Mrs Dawes wanting him for her Joan."

"Adele! Mr Brook is a friend, no more."

Adele laughed. "You are unworldly in some ways, for all you are the clever one. Mr Brook looks at you in a different manner entirely from the way he looks at Joan Dawes. However, keep your sights on Jem if you love him. Do not let others sway you."

Carrie had the strangest feeling. As though she and Adele had

Anne Goring

changed places. As though she were the younger and Adele was old in experience. Which was quite, quite, ridiculous.

Adele stood up. "I shall put my things away now and go downstairs and help Jane. And you will have to get up soon, Carrie. Is not Mr Brook to call to take you into town?" She wrinkled her nose. "Such a day to go poking about in slums."

"The house is not a slum," Carrie protested. "The builders are making a fine job of it and it is on a perfectly respectable street. Indeed, the society is thinking of taking another property on the same thoroughfare."

As Carrie washed and dressed Adele busied herself with her art holdall, finally replacing it in the corner by her side of the bed. "I have a whole morning to myself," she said. Miss Prince will not call until this afternoon. Do you think the rain will clear? I should like to take a walk, but no matter, I can always occupy myself in the orchid house. It is so warm and comfortable for sketching." Then she was gone, leaving Carrie to finish dressing, her thoughts tumbling over the fact that Adele had guessed her secret, and trying to come to terms with the new light shed upon her relationship with Mr Brook. Surely Adele was mistaken. He was courteous, true, and attentive. But no more than he was to anyone else. Of course, this interest in the housing society did throw them together but then he knew and understood her urge to do something useful with her life. He was a friend. No more.

And yet, she thought uneasily, she had no wish for their relationship to be misconstrued by others. Or even by Mr Brook himself. He was she had come to realise, a somewhat lonely man and he might come to depend a little too much on her for female companionship. Perhaps, after today, she should insist on not making these trips with him. Oh, dear, it was all so difficult, for she valued his friendship.

So, busy with her thoughts, Carrie failed to take regard of the bag Adele had pushed into the corner, though she passed it several times. Only much later was she to recall how it had

Bitter Harvest

appeared unusually bulky and that a scrap of lace, such as adorned Adele's best nightgown, poked from the clasp.

And then it was far too late for the bitter recriminations at her own lack of observation.

By ten o'clock Mr Brook had borne Carrie away in his carriage. At a little after the hour, in the easing drizzle, Mr Elliot Sanderson rode his horse out through the gates.

"Such a morning to go riding," Aunt Linnie commented, catching a glimpse of him, erect and pale, staring neither to right nor left. "It is a wonder his mamma does not insist he stays at home. . . . Ah, that is better." She sank onto the sofa. "My rheumatism is troublesome this morning. I think I shall take a glass of sherry wine, if you would be good enough to pour it, Adele. I find it very beneficial. And call Jane to stoke the fire . . . Really, dear, what are you doing with that gown on. It is most unsuitable for morning wear and as for going outdoors at all in this weather, I forbid it entirely. Miss Prince would think me an uncaring relative if I allowed you to go abroad on such a damp day."

"I will change my dress if you wish it," Adele said meekly. "However, I did promise Mr Prince that I would give him a drawing of one of the new *Cattleyas* which I have, unfortunately, left in the orchid house. He is most interested in seeing it. I shall slip out in a moment, aunt, and I shall wrap up carefully, I do assure you. I should hate to disappoint Mr Prince."

Aunt Linnie frowned. "Well, if you must," she said. "But do not linger. Run and change, now. That dress will soil so easily."

Adele had not known she could lie so fluently. The words had tripped from her tongue as effortlessly as if she had never, all her life, been schooled to tell the truth. Her composed outer self, practised through all the uncertain days, then went to the kitchen to see that Jane was occupied busily, spoke a few words, then, sedately, climbed the stairs to the bedroom.

Her hands trembled but slightly as she donned her heavy

95

Anne Goring

cloak, fully concealing the frivolous pink dress. Her wedding dress. She pulled the hood over her hair, and picked up her bag. She was taking little to her wedding. Within a few hours Elliot would be her husband. He would see to everything. He would soothe his angry parents for, sadly, they were bound to be upset. But not for long, she thought with a surge of joy. Nobody could possibly be cross with Elliot for long. Aunt Linnie, certainly, would succumb to his charm. And as for Carrie, well, she would be delighted to know that she would never be Mrs Prince. Horrible, horrible Mr Prince. She need never think of him again. She looked down at her hands. The ugly bloodstone of her engagement ring glinted dully, like an evil eye. She removed it and thrust it into the dresser drawer. Thank heaven she need not wear it again.

With a smile she propped up the note she had written for Carrie on her pillow. Once over her first surprise, she would understand. Oh, she had longed to say something this morning, but she dared not risk any chance of upsetting Uncle George's careful plans at the last minute.

Adele looked at herself in the mirror. Her cheeks were flushed, her eyes sparkling. Her wedding day. *Her wedding day.*

She went downstairs and called, sweetly, "I shall not be too long, Aunt Linnie", before letting herself out of the front door. There she paused for a moment. The drive was empty; no one to observe her strange behaviour as she ducked under the parlour window, keeping, in her best kid boots, to the grass verge. Swiftly she passed through the gates, leaped across the puddled ruts in the lane and took to the footpath through the woods. Then, abandoning caution, she ran, careless of the cascading dampness dislodged from trees and bushes as she brushed their leaves.

She saw him standing by his grazing horse. He turned towards her, his face pale and strained, but dissolving into a smile as he saw her. She ran to him falling, breathless, into his arms. Her hood fell back and he buried his face in her golden hair, clinging to her as though gathering strength from the contact.

96

Bitter Harvest

· It was a moment before she realised they were not alone. She caught her breath at the sight of the figure clad in brown and grey rags that blended with the dun colouring of the tree trunks. As she looked, he rose silently from where he had been squatting near Elliot's horse. A wide-brimmed hat shadowed his face, but as he turned to speak she saw the deformity of his face. A wash of revulsion caused her to look away. Yet Elliot was talking to this strange creature in a language that touched a chord of memory. A dream of arms that had held her close, of brown hands that had soothed away childish tears, a murmuring voice crooning in a language then understood, now forgotten. There had been a monkey chattering on the end of a chain, dancing along a balcony rail and red and purple flowers cascading to an emerald lawn . . .

"I shall not go, *tuan*."

"But you must, Mahmood. It is arranged."

"Our paths are separate now. You have made your choice. I have made mine."

"But what will you do?"

"Go where fate wills."

"Let me give you money. At least that. We shall go to Italy later. You may change your mind. You could join us there."

"No." One word. Final. Contemptuous.

Elliot looked into the ruined face, raised now so that the light fell full upon it, and saw for the first time the burning, shrivelling hate that shone naked in the dark eye. Hatred that wrenched at his guts. Mahmood hated him because he was the son of his mother. His beautiful mother whom he loved. His beautiful, arrogant, strong mamma who had done this vile thing. Who had spoiled innocence, ravaged beauty. Who had killed and maimed out of a misplaced wish to protect him. Was it love or jealously or fear that had driven her? A mingling of all three? Whatever it was, it was foul. And now, retribution. He was glad he had this way to punish her. Glad he could find his true happiness with Adele and feel no conscience about ruining her extravagant plans for him.

97

Anne Goring

Adele ventured, timidly, "Elliot, what is it? Why are you so upset. Who is this person and what is he saying?"

He swallowed. "I knew him once. In my childhood. I thought . . . I thought he might wish to go with me as a servant. It is of no consequence. No consequence at all." His voice strengthened. His grip tightened about her shoulders. "We are better alone. We have each other."

"Oh, yes," she whispered. "Oh, yes. And we must not linger." She glanced out of the corner of her eye at the weird figure. Then, bolder, looked at him fully. A clear brown eye regarded her. The hat tilted its shadow over half his face. The revealed side showed smooth, unmarked skin. It was even more shocking to think that he was young and must have once perhaps been handsome. Revulsion softened to pity. "Poor soul," she said timidly. "What happened to him, to be so desperately disfigured?"

"It is a story that belongs to long ago," Mahmood said.

Adele's hand flew to her mouth. "Forgive me. I did not realise you understood English."

The eye was unblinking, fixed upon her. Strangely it did not frighten her at all now.

He said, softly, "I had a sister. She had beauty. She was as you are now. Innocent. Missy, take care. You are a babe and the world is cruel."

"I shall look after her," Elliot said. "When we are man and wife nothing will be able to touch her."

Mahmood's head twisted, snakelike. In Malay, he hissed, "Guard her well, then, friend of my childhood. Guard her with your life, or those who mistake hate for love will bring tragedy upon her. Upon you both. I hope for her sake and for your own you will find the courage and spirit to protect her."

He turned on his heel. His feet made no sound on the leaf mould. He went, limping, hunched. The silver and greens and greys of the woods took his broken form and swallowed it up, as though taking back one of their own.

"What did he say?" Adele asked.

For a moment Elliot stared into the trees with haggard eyes.

Bitter Harvest

Then, abruptly, he said. "No matter. We shall think nothing more of the past."

"Such a strange sad person."

He pulled her round to face him, gripped her arms tightly. "How can he matter to us, now?" he cried. "All that is behind us. We have a future together. Oh, my dearest Adele, do you mind that we must run off together like fugitives? Shall we . . . should we go back and face them all?" Uncertainty trembled in his voice. "You deserve jewels, a fine wedding gown, a choir singing . . ."

She reached up and touched his cold lips with her own. "I need none of these things. Only you. If we went back now they would separate us. They are too strong, all of them."

He held her close. "Yes. Yes, you are right. Once all is accomplished – then it will be time to face Mamma. Defy them all."

"Uncle George will be waiting. Come Elliot."

Hand in hand they took the path to the quiet place where the carriage awaited them, leaving the horse to stare after them incuriously before returning to cropping the new grass in the clearing.

Jem talked softly and flicked the reins lightly over the solid black haunches of the horse. It needed no bidding. It was close to home and the lure of the stable quickened its pace so that the great hooves struck sparks off the cobbles and the iron cartwheels clanged echoes off the peeling house walls.

Jem wondered what urgent business Master wanted to see him about that had necessitated the disruption of the morning's work. He had been set for Ashton today with a load of barrels, but as he'd been hitching the horse, Carter Smith had stalked across the yard and told him to switch with one of the others.

"You do the Ducie Bridge job," he'd growled, barely civil. "Put Laidlaw on the Ashton run. I want you back here as soon as you've done."

"Is it for anything special?" he'd asked, surprised.

99

Anne Goring

"I'll tell you that when you're here. Now, do as you're bid." Then he'd marched off into the office and banged the door.

"Brandy's his tipple, isn't it?" one of the men guffawed when he'd gone. "Too much on it last night, I reckon."

"Or his missus giving him 'ell over this move."

"About all she can give. Dried up old faggot wi' a face as sour as a pickled onion. Imagine beddin' that bag o' vinegar."

Jem heard the ribald talk with half an ear. Carter Smith's face bobbed palely behind the distorting glass of the office door, then dodged away as though, uncharacteristically, he did not wish to be seen watching them. Something had upset him. Maybe the two daughters who'd been in and out for several days, calling on the men imperiously whenever there was a box to be lifted or a piece of furniture to be moved. Master had grumbled about that as he grumbled about everything.

Well, another day and it would be over. Tomorrow two of the carts were destined to be put at Mrs Smith's disposal, in order to take the furniture to Broughton. That hadn't pleased Carter Smith either. "It's a loss to me, this move is," he'd said. "In every way. New house to please her ladyship. My men called upon to assist when they should be doing other tasks. Now even the cart's losing a day's good business."

Yet behind it all Jem had sensed that he was not as put out as he made out. Once or twice he'd even become expansive. "I've seen a good nag I might buy and there's this gig. Belonged to an elderly man who didn't go out much. His widow's selling it off. Sound as a bell, it is. Needs but a lick of paint. I shall beat her down to my price, never fear, for she's eager for cash. Creditors at her doorstep. Of course, Mrs Smith has a fancy for a carriage so she can queen it over her friends. But that's a needless expense. A nice light gig's all I need to get me back and forth to the yard and to take her to church of a Sunday. If she's a need to go visiting there's nowt wrong with Shank's pony." He'd laughed at his own joke.

Another time he'd outlined his plans for the old house, so soon to be empty. "All that bottom floor I shall turn into an

100

Bitter Harvest

office. I shall have a private room at the back so I can speak to customers without Spencer hanging on to every word. He can have a corner with his ledgers where I can keep an eye on him. As for the old office, I'm considering gutting it. Use it for storage, maybe, or even another stable. As for the top floor of the house, well, that's yours lad. Mrs Smith's leaving you a few bits and bobs we're not needing, to start you off, like."

"That's good of you, sir."

"I'm lookin' to you, Jem Walker. You're taking on a responsibility. My second in command. Once them gates is shut at night, the welfare of this yard is entirely in your hands. Any mischief or thievin' or little lads climbing in and unsettling the horses – then it's you as'll be called to account and don't you forget it." He'd thrust his head on its thin neck towards Jem, lowering his voice. "But do well in this, lad, and there'll mayhap be other opportunities. I'm thinkin' in terms of expansion." He tapped the side of his long nose. "This is between you and me and the gatepost and I wouldn't be telling you if I didn't trust you to say nowt to nobody. Not even, especially not even, Mrs Smith."

"Of course not," Jem said hastily, seeing some comment was expected. "It seems a good moment – though aren't railways now the coming thing?"

"I've thought of that. I reckon in time most of the business carried by the canals will be taken over by railways. But it'll be them little distances between station and factory, between one end of town and the other, where no railway lines will run. Oh, I know, the railway companies will have their own drivers and carts, but there'll still be room for the specialist. For the man with willingness, the right equipment and contacts, such as I've got. With that in view," he paused significantly, "I've taken an option on an old warehouse at Knott Mill. Only an option mind. I've a month to decide. By then all this harrassment will be over. I shall be more settled in me mind."

"Is it for stabling?"

"Aye, there's plenty of room for that. But the warehouse

Anne Goring

is another venture. I was thinking, d'you see, there's many a manufacturer with smallish premises that might be glad of us to store his excess goods. By the day, the week or the month. I've been thinking along these lines for a bit, now. Diversification lad. Collect the goods. Store 'em. Deliver 'em as the client wishes. How about that?"

"Could be interesting."

"Glad you think so. I'll take you down with me the next time I go to look at the place. See what you think. You're young and your eyes are sharp. You may see a snag I've overlooked. Might get a pound or two knocked off the rent. When these upheavals are over, of course. By, I'll be a poor man at the end of this lot."

Jem controlled his smile. Carter Smith was known to be narrow with his money and he was shrewd. Rumour had it that he sat up late at night counting gold sovereigns out of a coffer up in the attic of his house. Jem didn't think he'd be so daft. People who accumulated money made more by investing in other enterprises. Carter Smith must be doing well. Men like him didn't spend unwisely. This new enterprise must have been chewed over for a long time. He wouldn't risk his money lightly.

Jem hoarded this scrap of information. It was another small brick in the wall of his security. Slowly, steadily, it seemed the wall grew. Looking back, he could see how the foundations had grown out of his thirst for education. Starting with those lessons, so long ago, in Mrs O'Hara's kitchen, the need to prove himself had grown. It hadn't been easy. There were many nights when, dog-tired, it had been torture not to let his eyelids droop as the lecturer at the Institute droned on and the symbols chalked on the board blurred into an incomprehensible haze. Yet at other times eagerness overcame fatigue and his brain soaked up all the information it was given and his hand flew across the slate, working out problems, taking notes. And on those nights, he could almost feel the boundaries of his world expanding. Taking him beyond the rigid lines of work and sleep. Taking him beyond fatigue.

Bitter Harvest

Timeless seams of poetry and prose took him back into history, rich with romance and adventure ... the magic of numbers advanced him into a world of logic and order ... knowledge of other continents, other races, led him to look even beyond this planet towards the stars.

The men at the yard had mocked him. 'Eh, lad, what's the use o' filling your head wi' rubbish. You don't need eddication to clear out 'oss shit.' He'd taken their ribbing in good part – even once when they'd hidden his slate in the midden and he'd had to dig it out and sluice it under the pump. The stink had lingered on it for days, but he'd kept a rein on his temper. They'd played the trick from ignorance and rough though they were they were also good-hearted in many ways. They covered for each other in times of sickness, shared out their bread and cheese if anyone was a bit hard pressed before pay day, and were devoted to their horses, proud to see them smartly groomed and healthy.

As the months and years passed, the joking stopped. Bit by bit their attitude changed. They began to consult him. A letter to be written to a daughter in service, one to be deciphered from a son who'd taken the King's shilling and gone to foreign parts; a dispute over rent, an ailing relative seeking an infirmary bed. He'd written their letters, spoken out for them. In the everyday arguments that flared up he'd be called upon for an opinion. And because he'd listen carefully to both sides, weigh the evidence and give his reasoning fairly, they came to trust him as a mediator. Sometimes an old newspaper found its way into the yard and he'd be commanded to read it aloud, while they hung on every word. For days after he'd be asked to read and reread the more lurid paragraphs, so that they could guffaw or shake their heads, gaining every scrap of enjoyment until the newsprint became indecipherable from handling.

Small bricks. Yet each was solid. Because he had the learning, he had been chosen as overseer. Because he had earned the men's respect there was less envious grumbling than there might have been at his advancement. "Well, lad, you're young for responsibility," one had said glumly, "an I'll not say I wasn't

Anne Goring

a bit put out at first. But then, you can read and number as good as any master. That's beyond me, lad, and I'm too old to be starting such nonsense. I'll stick to 'osses, like I've always done and live and die a poor man. I can see you're set for better things. There's many a self-made Manchester man had a worse start than you. But think on it, don't put on fancy airs and graces. Remember us old 'uns 'as taught you all you know about the cartin' trade. We know it an' you know it." Then with a grin and a slap on the shoulder. "Good luck to thee, lad."

It seemed to be the general attitude in the yard and it warmed Jem. He liked these rough, good-natured men. He privately vowed to do everything he could to improve their lot. They worked long hours, abroad in all weathers. Steady work, true, month in, month out and low wages in consequence. Carter Smith, being the man he was, was more concerned for the welfare of his horses. They were his capital. The men were expendable. If one left his job there were a dozen others eager to take his place. Men could be – had been – dismissed for upsetting Carter Smith in the matter of pressing for an improvement in wages or a loan to tide them over a bad patch.

Well, they could bring their troubles to him now. He'd face Carter Smith. He wasn't afraid of him. He knew that Master had a grudging respect for his book-learning, for sticking to his classes, for going of a Sunday to teach at the mission school. He wouldn't dismiss his new overseer for standing up to him. In fact, Jem thought, Carter Smith appreciated plain talking and a straight attitude. Look at poor Spencer who fawned and cringed and was prepared almost to lick Master's boots and was treated with unconcealed contempt. The man had not an ounce of pride and lived in daily fear of dismissal. Jem pitied him, though he could not like him. He was too old and incompetent to find other work. Well, he'd look to Spencer, too. The man had been a loyal worker. That counted for something. Perhaps when Carter Smith was busy with his new plans, he wouldn't have time to be breathing continually down Spencer's neck and reducing him to jellied incompetency.

104

Bitter Harvest

Yes, when he, Jem, was in charge, there'd be a few changes. In charge.

The cart rumbled under the arch and into the yard.

In charge. The words had a triumphant ring. He glanced up at the top floor of what was still Carter Smith's house. He'd have his rooms up there. His own place. Not much, but give him time. One day, he swore to himself, he'd be moving out like Carter Smith. Moving somewhere fit to take Carrie. Someday he'd be his own man. All this learning would come to something. With Carrie at his side anything was possible. This was just the first step.

She'd said once, discussing the future, "I . . . I will have my own income remember, dear Jem. When we are married that will be yours."

"I'm not marrying you for your money, lass."

She'd looked up quickly, her grey eyes glinting under the long lashes, and smiled in relief when she saw his teasing expression. "I never, never want you to feel that it in any way sets me above you," she had said, almost fiercely. "This money, I mean. I would rather give it away to the Mission if I thought it made any difference."

He'd laughed outright then, set his big hands at her waist and swung her up onto the stile so that her face was level with his.

"Oh, aye," he'd said. "I've always known you were a cut above me, and I've asked you to marry me because by so doing I'll be bettering myself." Her eyes smiled straight into his. She put her hands gently either side of his face. "That's just how I guessed it," she mocked softly.

Her mouth was soft and pliant. The warm curves of her body pressed into his. He crushed her hard against him, feeling the surge of desire and sensing her own response. After a moment, he said, huskily, "You can tell it's only your money I'm after." And she had flicked her lashes along his cheekbone sending shivers through him.

Later, when he could think more sanely he could recognise

Anne Goring

the anxiety behind her words. She knew him too well. Knew his pride. And by God he would work to match that money of hers, shilling for shilling, pound for pound. He would take all the extra duties and responsibilities Carter Smith cared to heap upon him. He would watch the yard – and the books – like a hawk, ready to pounce should he see any extravagance or any way in which work could be done more efficiently. That would please Master. But Master would have to learn that loyalty deserved its reward. He'd not be treated like old Spencer.

Jem climbed down from the wagon and gave the horse his nosebag. The yard was empty. The door to the office stood open, so he crossed the cobbles, his clogs ringing loudly, and paused in the doorway. Unexpectedly, the cramped room held strangers.

"Sorry, sir. I didn't wish to interrupt."

Four faces turned towards him. His first thought was that Carter Smith was ill. His narrow features were grey and a rime of sweat stood out on his forehead. Then he realised that the two men were constables and that Spencer's eyes were goggling and he thought, by heaven, Master's in trouble.

"Come inside," Carter Smith said hoarsely.

"This is Walker, is it?" one of the burly men asked.

Carter Smith swallowed. His voice came out strangled. "That's him. That's Jem Walker."

"Don't distress yourself, sir," the constable said kindly. "These things are always an upset. Particularly when it's someone you've held as trustworthy." Then, his voice hardening, he turned to Jem. "This yours?" he asked. He held out the old canvas smock Jem kept to wear for dirty jobs about the yard.

"Yes," he said. "Master knows it's mine. Why?"

"I'm asking the questions . . ."

"But I –"

"And these, what do you know about these?" The constable put his big hand into the sagging pocket of the smock. Jem stared in disbelief at what lay in the open palm.

106

Bitter Harvest

He shook his head. "Nothing. Why should I?"

Both big men laughed. It was a cold, cynical sound.

"You know nowt about it? Three gold sovereigns? A fob watch with your Master's initials on it? Come now, speak up."

"You found these in my smock?"

"And not for the first time. It seems you have a kindly Master, Walker. He has withheld his suspicion before this, not wishing to believe such perfidy of a trusted man . . ."

"What the devil are you talking about? You can't be accusing me of theft!" He fought an impulse to laugh. It was a joke. Some charade dreamed up to test him. His glance went from the dull glitter of gold in the constable's calloused palm to Carter Smith's face, and the laughter was throttled in its infancy. "Tell them, sir. Tell them. I'm to be overseer here. I'd never do such a thing. You've known me all these years."

"I . . . I must believe . . . the evidence of my eyes." He half swallowed the words, his Adam's apple bobbing above the knot of his red neckerchief. His eyes looked wildly about as though he sought escape, but his bowed legs held him rooted to the dusty floorboards. "Spencer . . . he was with me when . . . when we found . . . when we looked in your pocket and found . . ." He passed his hand over his sweating face, swaying.

"Sit down, sir," The constable was solicitous. "This has been a shock. Shall your clerk fetch you a glass of water?"

Spencer tittered nervously. He peered over his high desk, his face full of malicious curiosity.

"I shall be well in a moment." Carter Smith leaned against a stool. "Just do what you have to and go."

The constables closed about Jem. One took a grip on his arm. Angrily, Jem shook him off. "This is daft," he shouted. "I've never stolen anything in all my life. It's a mistake."

"I've heard that tale too often to be moved by it. I'm arresting you now for theft from your master. Are you to come easy and quietly, or will you make a fight of it?" A burly fist pressed into Jem's ribs. "It'll go the worse for you if you do."

"Easy and quietly! Good Christ, man, you arrest a man on

Anne Goring

some trumped-up charge and expect him to go easy and quietly! What manner of man do you suppose me to be?"

"A sensible one to be sure." The constable's voice was smooth, faintly bored. "You'll have your chance to speak before the justice in good time."

They closed about him again, solid men who knew their job. He broke away, appealing to Carter Smith. "You know I wouldn't do a thing like this. Speak for me, for God's sake!" The constable took him roughly by the collar, choking him.

"I shan't tell you again. You come quietly or it'll go against you. I'm a patient man, but my patience is wearing thin."

Jem clawed at his throat but the other man was quicker and twisted his arms up his back, dragging him into the yard. Against the pain of cruelly twisted muscles, he fought to turn his head. Carter Smith clung, ashy-faced, to the doorknob. His eyes looked hunted. It almost seemed that there was a plea for forgiveness in his face before he swung the door closed, slamming it hard against the sight of Jem being yanked across the cobbles and through the archway where the constable delivered several salutary blows to the pit of Jem's stomach while the other held him.

Gagging, Jem was bundled into a small covered wagon in the street. A crowd of urchins had gathered. Through mists of sickness he heard their jeers. A lump of filth splattered against his face before he fell against the greasy floorboards of the cart.

Presently his breathing eased, his head cleared and he saw that he was not alone. An old woman, sourly reeking of gin swayed to the jolting of the wagon, grumbling softly to herself beside him. Two ragged lads grinned broken-toothed smiles. A bloody-nosed man vomited over a bundle of rags that moved and cried and fell to snoring again.

He was travelling with the scum of the town. Where? Somewhere to be charged, locked up as though he was a criminal. The injustice of it seared his mind. It couldn't be happening! He'd wake up soon and find he'd nodded off over his dinner. But the pain in his gut, his shoulders, his throat, denied his reasoning.

Bitter Harvest

Jem tensed his muscles. If he could make the flapping leather curtain at the back of the wagon he could escape. Be away into the maze of Angel Meadow. Lose himself in the warren of alleys. He must think. Think. Carefully he eased himself up and, as though still in pain, fell to a crouch against the greasy wooden side of the wagon, bowing his head to his knees.

His bewildered thoughts ran round and round. How the devil had this happened? Less than an hour ago he had been a happy man with a future. Now he was being carted off. Where? The New Bailey? More than likely. The thought of that grim battlemented building on the Salford side of the river, washed through him with horror. If he got in there, would he ever get out? Would anyone listen to his pleas that he was innocent? Carter Smith hadn't. Carter Smith, who had known him all these years, who had trusted and confided in him, had turned his back. Condemned him without a hearing. No, like as not, it would be the hulks for him. Transportation even. Years of degradation. Separation from his family. And Carrie.

He gritted his teeth. By God, no! He wouldn't let it happen.

Without moving his head he watched the constables. They had their heads together, talking low. One glanced his way, jerked his head, as though they were discussing him. Then he drew the canvas back to see where they were and rattled his staff on the wagon's side.

It jolted to a halt. The constable stuck his head out and signalled to someone outside. Some other poor devil was to be picked up no doubt and put to the grim processes of the law. But the constable was looking at him, beckoning, and the other man had him by the arm and was urging him out. "This is as far as you go, lad," he whispered, nastily. His eyes glinted. Jem allowed himself to be half dragged to the wagon's tail then he did not hesitate.

He hurled himself forward, catching the constable behind the knees. Together they fell to the street outside. He caught a glimpse of tall, blank walls, the back of a factory, then he was on his feet and running. The constable was bellowing in the mud. There were footsteps thundering behind him.

109

Anne Goring

Jem glanced over his shoulder. Christ! There were three men in pursuit.

The street narrowed past a scrap of gritty waste ground where a child leading a pig on a string looked up in amazement. The factory wall went on and on. He searched frantically for an alley. The pain in his gut where the constable had hit him seared him with every breath, but he dared not stop. The men were gaining.

The street took a sharp turn to the right. He hurled himself round the corner, and skidded to a halt. Hell, a dead end. The factory wall rose high and unbroken.

He turned, weaving as the first man turned the corner. The man was older, slower. He dodged past him, swinging out with his fist, feeling the crunch of bone under his knuckles as the man buckled and went down.

But the other two, panting, bulky, something ominously purposeful in their stance, blocked his way. No time to think. He charged between them, head down, desperation giving him strength and fleetness.

He might have made it. The men were knocked off balance. But one of them carried a stick and, as he staggered, he hooked it between Jem's ankles, felling him. Winded, a sharp pain wrenching through his knee, he yet twisted half to his feet, but they were upon him.

The odds were too great. He fought ferociously, but these were rough men from the stews. Men who had been educated with blows from fist and boot. They set with a will about the task they had been well paid for and presently they hoisted their bloodied bundle into a handcart fetched for the purpose, covering it with dirty straw to conceal their handiwork.

Then they set off briskly towards the destination they had been given.

Mr Brook said, "Yes, indeed, a satisfactory morning. The work goes better than I expected. And now that the first suspicions

Bitter Harvest

are past, the tenants are full of gratitude despite the temporary inconvenience they are put to."

The carriage rattled smartly towards Cheetham. Carrie watched fields and houses flash past and was reminded of that wet, wintry day when she and Adele had returned from school. It was the same sort of weather. Grey and lowering, promising more rain, the carriage wheels sending out rainbow arcs of spray in the fitful sunlight. But a different journey this. The hedges and fields were no longer locked in winter duns, but green with spring. The trim gardens to the villas were bright with daffodils and narcissi and she herself was a world away from the girl she had been then. She was in love. She was loved in return. She hugged her secret tightly to her heart.

"The old lady, Mrs Cramp, was it not? She seemed excessively taken with you, Miss Linton."

"Mrs Cramp? Yes, she thought I had a resemblance to her granddaughter."

The wizened old lady had taken her hand and pulled her into the curtained alcove below the stairs where she was encamped while her attic room was repaired. Bright eyes peered out of a mass of tear-stained wrinkles.

"'Tis a miracle," she said, over and over. "The windows was broke and now they're all mended. They've put shelves up and swept me chimbley an' whitewashed me walls. It's a proper palace. An' here's me thinkin' not a month ago that no one cared if the place fell about us ears. Y'see, I've no one left now. All gone." Absently she stroked the cuff of Carrie's dress. "It's been a parky winter, lass. Not that you'd know anythin' of that – and when they said the 'ouse was to be took over by gentry, I thought it was the poorhouse for me. But now they tell me the rent is still to be sixpence. It is true, Miss, is it? I'm afeared to ask the grand gentlemen?"

"It is true, Mrs Cramp," Carrie said gently.

"Then I shall offer a prayer on me knees at t'owd church this very day. For you an' all of the gentlemen."

Embarrassed, Carrie withdrew her hand. She had done so

Anne Goring

little and the task was so huge. Each time she came into town the eyes of the poor children playing in the gutters seem to turn on her in accusation. Much as anyone did it was little compared to the great mass of poverty and ignorance and exploitation to be fought.

"Nay, don't be shy of me, lovey," the old lady said. "Tears come easy when you're old and 'ave spent a hard life. And no one left to see me at rest in me old age."

"You have no family at all, Mrs Cramp?"

"Nay lass. I 'ad a good husband once. He were a handloom weaver. We had a little cot outside o' Rochdale wi' an acre to keep a cow and a pig. Good days, though the work was hard. But we all worked together, childer an' all, at the weavin' and in the field. But at our own pace. The children were bonny then. They was brought up to fear the Lord and to learn their trade and never to let an idle minute go by." She shook her thin white locks. "Then the factories come and it was the end of us . . ."

It was a familiar story. No work for the father, the children fed to the factories to tend the great machines, the children sickening from the harsh labour, the family becoming poorer by the year and, finally, the abandonment of the cottage and the move to the town to seek a better life. Only to plumb the depths of misery and poverty. One by one, by disease and accident, the family was decimated. Only the old lady, worn to bone, clung to life, eking out her existence by a little rough sewing or baby minding.

"Ah, but I has one granddaughter," she said proudly. "She was lucky to be taken into service at a good place. She married a farmer's lad and they've gone to seek their fortune in Americky. She got a reverend to write to me once. I hope she's still happy out in that heathen place. But she had a good 'usband and likely now a brood o' young ones. It gives me comfort to think of 'em." She fell quiet, then her rheumy eyes brightened. "You reminds me of her, lovely. She 'ad your colourin', just, and the sort o' smile that makes you feel better for the glance of it." The small twisted claw sought Carrie's. "There'll be them as'll never be

Bitter Harvest

grateful for what's done for 'em. Why there's folks in this house as'll take all what's done for 'em and more besides and laugh at the gentlemen behind their backs for bein' soft touches. But I wants you to know that you've give one old woman back a bit o' faith in the goodness o' human nature."

Carrie had been touched. But guilt remained like a prickly grass seed caught in a stocking, irritating the skin at every step. If only she had a vast fortune at her disposal, there was so much that could be done.

"Yes," said Mr Brook, "I think we may congratulate ourselves on the way things progress. And, in particular Miss Linton, you must accept my deep admiration for instigating the work of our society, which will bring benefit to the labouring classes."

She replied, a touch impatiently, "We merely scrape the fringe of the problem. For every one we help a thousand others dwell in insanitary hovels and cellars."

He placed his pale-gloved hands on the silver-topped cane and leaned towards her. His understanding smile fed a small spring of irritation. She would not meet his gentle eyes.

"I forget sometimes," he told her, "that you are so young. Youth burns with enthusiasm and impatience. One thing life teaches you is that the world is not to be changed in a night. It is a slow and tedious process. One must do what one can. It is not always possible to do everything one wishes."

"Do you patronise me, sir?"

"Never. I think too highly of your intelligence."

"There is so much to do! I sometimes wish that I were a man, with freedom to take up a profession . . . to use such talents as I have to the full!"

"Ah, but it is not always easy for a man to do as he wishes. We, too, have duties and responsibilities that may take our lives in directions we do not entirely care for."

Two spots of colour burned in her cheeks. He saw the flecks of green that sparked in her eyes when she was roused to anger or indignation. They stared at him now, afire. The fine-boned face that could look so plain in repose had

Anne Goring

beauty in its animation. How he admired her enthusiasm, her vigour.

She said heatedly, "But Mr Linton, you must confess that we women have no choice at all. If we are lucky enough and rich enough to get an education at all, it is of the skimpiest. We are taught to curtsey and dance and play a little music and paint a pretty picture. If we long to use our brains, if we are the slightest bit bookish we are considered freaks. We are taught to be submissive to father, brother, husband. Indeed, to catch a husband is thought to be the only suitable ambition for a girl out of the schoolroom . . ."

He laughed. "I think you will not be too submissive to the man fortunate enough to be your husband, Miss Linton." She coloured and he added, "In retaliation, I lay my own example before you."

"Your music?"

"No, indeed," he said, dryly mocking. "My talent for the pianoforte is slight. My ability to make money with the dye works, perhaps a little more developed. But my real ambition lay elsewhere." He looked down at the neatly gloved hands upon the walking stick. "I wished, as a young man, to be a doctor. A healer I thought then – I still think – is the most noble of occupations. Unfortunately my father thought otherwise."

"But why did you not follow your instincts?" Carrie burst out.

"Why did I not defy my father? Go out into the world and seek my fortune?" He paused, that dry smile of self-mockery again curving his lips. "Oh, but I did. I apprenticed myself to a country physician at Hyde and lived happily with boils and bunions and coughs and agues for nearly a year, and planned later to walk the wards of a London hospital. My only reading was great tomes on medical matters. I knew I had found my vocation."

Carrie looked at him in astonishment. She could scarcely imagine this dapper, rather dandified gentleman involving himself in such earthy labours.

Bitter Harvest

"My parents were distressed, of course," he went on, "but not so unreasonable as to wrench me from my course. Perhaps they thought I should soon tire of poulticing carbuncles and learning to mix noxious draughts. They were wrong.

"But then my father was taken suddenly of an apoplexy. I was an only child. I had been accustomed from an early age to work alongside Papa – when school was finished, during holidays, and so forth. I knew all the processes, the routine – and above all, the men who laboured at the factory. Men who relied upon the employment offered by a smooth-running, profitable concern. With the master stricken and fastened to his bed there was only one answer. My father could not speak but he pleaded with his eyes. Mamma did not beg me to come home, but her tears were as eloquent as any verbal plea. So, I played the dutiful son."

He paused and there was sadness behind his smile. "I was twenty and felt my life was blighted. All that marvellous excitement and enthusiasm I had felt for doctoring had to be suppressed. I took the path of duty and it was not easy. Many a morning I went through the factory doors and it was like entering a prison. The walls closed me inside, and outside was the life I truly wanted."

"Your father recovered?"

"He made a partial recovery but he was never the same man again. He died five years later and my mother soon afterwards. By then I had married and my wife was not strong. I could not have upset her by taking up such an outlandish occupation. Besides, I had come to terms with my disappointment. One does, you know, or one becomes embittered and inward looking. I did not wish that. And again, I had grown to be proud of my achievements at the factory. It has expanded greatly since my father's time. My men have good wages and shorter hours – I'll have none working above eleven hours in the day. Then there is the new housing. It pleases me to see hard-working parents bringing up their families in decent surroundings, and none of their offspring are allowed into the works before they are ten, and then only half time. I should like next to concentrate on schooling. I am considering employing someone to teach the children and to encourage the adults to attend classes of an evening."

Carrie was contrite. "Sir, I owe you an apology for my sharp manner. It is just that I am overwhelmed when I see the poverty in the town and so little seems to be done about it."

"I understand. Believe me, I understand."

She saw that he did, and realised with surprise that she had all along underestimated him. She had regarded, almost unconsciously, his patience and diffidence and kindness as weakness and now she saw his strength. Here was a man who would still, persistently and in his own way, be fighting small battles, making steady advances in the causes of humanity when many a firebrand had fizzled into obscurity. She felt oddly humbled by his story, and very young and naïve.

"Come now," he said cheerfully, seeing her expression. "No need to look so rueful. I did not wish to depress you with my words. Why, it is a lifetime away and I am content as I am. I wished just to illustrate my argument that men are not always the free agents you believe."

"I have been presumptuous," she said. "Nevertheless, I do believe it is true in general."

"That is better! I like to see you with the light of battle in your eye. It pleases me immensely that you are not one of these milksop misses who agree breathily with every male opinion. Nor so waspishly defensive of your arguments that you offend unnecessarily." Edmund's look was so open, his good humour so evident, that she could not be embarrassed. "We complement each other well, I think, Miss Linton", he went on. "We shall make good partners in this society we have founded. And in the future we may see ways in which we may combine together on other worthy projects."

"That would be most satisfying," she agreed, returning his smile.

"We shall relieve the world's troubles between us, eh?" he

Bitter Harvest

joked. Then, suddenly serious, he fell silent, looking at her fixedly, then said, slowly, almost painfully, "We should, I feel, make excellent partners in marriage. Would that, do you think, please you also Miss Linton?"

Despite the rattle and creak and jingle of the carriage, the silence seemed excruciating. Unable to meet his eyes she frantically sought for the right words. She admired him, she liked him and she must honestly say so. But she must say nothing of how her heart was already given. So what excuse? What reason? Oh, why had Mr Brook chosen to propose! She was totally unprepared . . . why had she not heeded Adele's warnings?

"Sir, I am . . . I am deeply aware of the honour you do me." She fixed her eyes on his gloved hands, noting against the agitation of her breathing how tight a grip they had on the handle. Poor man, she thought wildly. How I wish I did not have to disappoint him. "Yet I cannot think of marriage." She could not add, *with you*. It was too hurtful. The words hung unspoken. "I . . . I am sorry," she said lamely. "I had not supposed you had any such intentions towards me."

She saw the hands relax. One lifted itself, hovered as though it might reach to her, but fell to his knee and rested there lightly. "It seems," he said, "my day for upsetting you." His tone, to her relief was neither ardent nor brusque. It was calm, amused, even. "I have been precipitate. I have taken you by surprise. It is my turn to beg forgiveness."

"Think no more of it," she whispered.

"There, I think, I shall not be able to do your bidding."

The beginnings of relief melted away.

"And I hope you, too, Miss Linton – Caroline. . ." his voice lingered on her name, "will not put my proposal entirely from your mind. I appreciate your position, my dear. You have scarcely tasted life and you have been upset by your sister's engagement. I would not wish to hurry you to a decision that will affect the rest of your life."

"But—"

Anne Goring

He raised his hand. "No, do not say anything more. Not yet. Some time in the future, in a more suitable location," once more the touch of dry humour in his tone, "I shall ask you again. In the meantime, all I ask is that you do not dismiss the idea of marriage to me out of hand. Now," he went on briskly, "shall we speak of other matters?"

There was little left of the journey. Mr Brook kept up a flow of inconsequential talk, so that by the time they reached the lodge her composure was almost restored.

He handed her down from the carriage. He did not attempt to hold her hand longer than necessary, nor did he prolong his farewells. He was his usual gentlemanly self. The disquieting proposal might never have happened.

But she knew he would keep his word. She watched the carriage go, then turned slowly to go into the lodge. Yes, he would choose his moment and propose to her again. But next time she would be prepared. She would have her rejection rehearsed a suitable and inarguable excuse ready.

For the moment, she supposed, he would maintain his friendship and she had to admit that if he withdrew that now, she would miss it.

She sighed. How contrary life was. If only it were Jem who owned a factory, who was rich and eminently marriageable! Everyone would be delighted then that he loved her and she loved him. As it was, her true love must remain a secret for now. And she must take care to keep Mr Brook's proposal secret, too. For if Aunt Linnie found out she would be pressing her to accept such a suitable match.

Everything was really most complicated.

But it was only the beginning.

"That naughty, uncaring girl, how could she do this to me . . . to Miss Prince. Now you, Caroline, I could well understand disappearing about your own affairs. You have so little sensibility for an aunt's cares and worries. But Adele! I expected better behaviour."

118

Bitter Harvest

Aunt Linnie lay on the sofa and pressed a hand to her brow. Her cheeks were flushed. Jane had removed the glass and replaced the sherry bottle, much depleted, in the cupboard before Miss Prince's arrival: Mrs O'Hara had needed something to give her the courage to face Miss Prince's disapproval. Miss Prince sat with a ramrod back and pursed lips, one narrow black boot tapping its impatience on the hearthrug.

"She has probably found something pretty to sketch and forgotten the time," Carrie said soothingly. "Shall I go and look for her?"

"Jane went scarce half an hour back and not a sign of her in the gardens or in those wretched orchid houses – and none of the gardeners had seen her. It is so distressing when Miss Prince has an appointment.

"And," said Miss Prince in a voice to splinter ice. "I am already late by seven minutes."

Jane stood by the half-open kitchen door listening to the ladies and twisting her apron nervously. If only she could catch Miss Carrie's eye. She had to get Miss Carrie on her own. She was afeared of saying what she knew in front of the other ladies. Jane was possessed of A Secret. She knew it must be A Secret because why else would Miss Adele leave a sealed letter on Miss Carrie's pillow with her name written across it? Why should Miss Adele have lied this morning, saying she was going to them glass places where the funny flowers grew, that wasn't half so pretty as roses to her mind, and she'd not gone there at all? What was more, some of her clothes was gone. And the bag she carted her paints about in. Only *they* was put away in a drawer. Jane, who had owned so little in her life, knew to a handkerchief what the ladies possessed. It was her pride to see every garment clean and pressed, laid neatly in its appointed place, guarded from moth by lavender bags. Well, it was a lot more than an 'andkerchief gone from Miss Adele's drawer.

Then there was the matter of Mr O'Hara's actin' funny. Up wi' the lark he was, and down to his breakfast togged up in

119

Anne Goring

his best coat, calling for eggs and kidneys before she'd even cleared out the hearth. She'd scuttled about to do his bidding and he'd sat there, big and beaming and smacking his lips over the kidneys.

"I've a journey to make today," he'd said as he pushed back his chair and belched, his broad hand, its knuckles glinting with gingery hairs, pressed contentedly to his stomach. Then the hand had shot out and fastened on her thin arm. "However," he'd added, his smile widening to show his large teeth, "that is between you and me and the gatepost, Jane. I'm away on a bit of business." He tweaked her arm painfully. "You keep your mouth shut, understand? No telling anyone in this house that its master's away conducting a bit of private business." The pads of his fingers dug into her slight muscles so that she winced. He thrust his face near hers. "I shall know if you've gabbed when I come back, because I shall enquire. And if you have it'll go hard with you." With a last brutal wrench he pushed her away and she had fled for the shelter of her kitchen, hearing him chuckling. Later he'd gone out and she'd peeped out to see him carrying two large leather bags and walking briskly. She hoped fervently that he'd stay away a long time.

When Mrs O'Hara had sent her looking for Miss Adele the gardener's lad, the cheeky one, had called after her, "Lost yer chick, 'ave you, Janie? Well she ain't been up here, cause I'd 've noticed such a natty pair of ankles." There was a burst of coarse laughter from the other lads supposed to be hoeing among the daffodils. Jane had stuck her nose in the air. "You keep your clogs in the muck," she'd answered. "It's where you lot belong. And don't talk about your betters like that."

"Eh, an old Bawdy Georgie's missin' today, an' all."

"Wenchin' it no doubt, wi' that boilin' piece of his," another called, sparking another bout of laughter.

"You want your mouth rinsin' out wi' soapy water," she'd cried, but she'd slowed her retreat as more spicy bits of information were called out over the gracefully nodding daffodils and stiff green spears of budding tulips.

Bitter Harvest

Now Jane absently massaged the purpling bruises on her arm and thought of the man who'd inflicted them. So, he'd a fancy woman had he, down in Manchester. No doubt that was where he'd gone today. Oh, he was a bad 'un. If he never come back it would be too soon. Poor, poor Mrs O'Hara to be treated so. No wonder she drank so heartily of the sherry wine.

She caught her breath. At last, Miss Carrie was looking her way. Frantically she signalled. Miss Carrie raised her brows. Oh, dear, they were all looking . . . No, no, Miss Carrie had caught her drift and was saying something to distract the ladies. Here she was at last!

"I shall ask Jane to bring tea," she was saying. "By the time we have drunk it, I am sure Adele will be returned."

Carrie walked into the kitchen and closed the door. "Is anything wrong, Jane? Such strange faces you were pulling. Oh, and tea if you please. It will perhaps turn away Miss Prince's wrath."

"Miss, oh, Miss." She thrust her hand into the deep pocket of her apron and pulled out the letter. "Miss, this was on your pillow when I went up to do your room – and it's from Miss Adele an 'er clothes is gone . . ."

"Hush now," Miss Carrie said, taking the letter and breaking the seal. "There is no need to have hysterics. There is probably a perfectly sound . . . perfectly . . ." Her voice died.

Jane watched anxiously. Miss Carrie's face went very pink, then paled. Her eyes scanned quickly down the page. At one point she put her hand to her mouth as though to stifle laughter, yet her voice when she spoke held tears. "Jane," she said, "Jane, I do not know whether my sister is a heroine or a foolish child. She has eloped, Jane! Eloped with Mr Elliot Sanderson!"

"Eloped, Miss!" Jane's eyes were like saucers. "But Mr Elliot was to have been married in a few weeks."

"And Miss Prince is waiting in the parlour to take her brother's affianced visiting. And I shall have to walk out there and tell her Adele has run off . . . and for all I know may be married already."

Anne Goring

"It's like a fairy tale," breathed Jane, now that responsibility was shifted onto more capable shoulders beginning to appreciate the drama. "Eh, Mr Elliot's right handsome. An' rich." She clasped her hands ecstatically to her scanty bosom. "He must've fell head over heels wi' Miss Adele and now he's carried her off under the noses of Mr Sanderson and Mr Prince . . ."

"And the rest of us," said Carrie. She put her hand to her forehead. "It is such a shock. I have been so caught up in my own affairs . . . I should have seen the change in her today. She has been so different of late – since her engagement – and this morning she was like her old self."

"She was singing this morning, Miss," put in Jane helpfully. "Ever so prettily. I've not heard her singing for ever so long."

"Singing?" Carrie gave a faint sigh. "Yes, I suppose she would be." Slowly she refolded the letter. "Well, I had better go and face them. It is not a pleasing prospect and I fear, Jane, that the sensibilities of the two ladies are about to be fearfully bruised. Make tea quickly, Jane, and find the smelling salts. I suspect both will be needed."

Then she straightened her shoulders, gave Jane a wry smile and took the letter into the parlour.

Chapter Five

ELLIOT Sanderson's letter was delivered about the time that his horse wandered back to the comfort of its stable. The urchin who had been paid a whole shilling to hand the letter to the housekeeper at that particular time, scuttled away to spend his money, unaware that his mission prevented a hue and cry. Word went quickly from the drawing room to the stable that the hunt for Master Elliot was to be called off. It was all a misunderstanding. Master Elliot was called away unexpectedly. A message was also sent to Miss Linton at the lodge, requesting her to attend at the big house immediately.

Carrie looked at Mrs Sanderson's slashing handwriting and at the almost indecipherable signature. Rage seemed to leap from every jagged letter. Carrie felt sick. She'd already come through one scene. Miss Prince's shock had vented itself in a vituperative outburst that had reduced Aunt Linnie to helpless tears. She had swept off, leaving spite and frustration hanging like a miasma in the parlour. Aunt Lnnie, moaning, had been put to bed and dosed with a sleeping draught.

Carrie left Jane sitting by the bed. "I shall be back as soon as I can," she whispered as her aunt's eyelids fell to cheeks blotched and puffy with weeping.

She braced herself. The Sandersons must be faced. Mr Sanderson, their friend and patron, had always been fond of Adele. He might, just might, be on the side of the runaway lovers.

Mrs Sanderson, however, was quite another matter.

Despite the sunshine glittering on the runnels of water among

123

Anne Goring

the gravel, a cold finger laid itself on her spine. She pulled her cloak more tightly about her throat and dismissed the disloyal wish that Adele might have realised the uncomfortable position in which she placed her family, before she had planned such an unconventional action. Then she smiled wryly. Of course Adele would not think so far ahead. It was not her nature. She was a creature of instinct, of emotion. She was warm and loving and romantic. She would have seen her elopement as an ideal escape from an unpleasant future. She would think nothing of the consequences for other people. She would return expecting, in her innocence, forgiveness. Carrie thought that Mrs Sanderson – whose plans and ambitions were now in ruins, whose cosseted only son was to have made a fashionable and highly suitable marriage – would hardly be prepared to give it.

The housemaid who let her into the house eyed her with curiosity. There was a rustle of starched skirts, the faint echo of excited giggles in the air. Carrie had no doubt that the story of Elliot's strange disappearance was enlivening the servants' day. She kept her back straight, her chin high, as she entered the long, elegant drawing room.

They were by the far window. Mr Sanderson sat in a bow-legged chair. He had a plaid shawl across his knees and another over his shoulders and Carrie's first, shocked, impression was that that he had shrunk to an old, old man. The flesh had melted from his bones, his face was colourless, the skin sagging and lined. He sat hunched and diminished under the huddle of shawls yet he was the first to speak and there was kindness, a touch of the old briskness in his tone.

"Come, my dear. Tell us what you know of this distressing business."

"Very little, sir. Adele did not confide in me. I fear I must have been very unobservant of late. I should have noticed – had some idea . . ."

"You must not blame yourself. These foolish children have outwitted us all. You do not know where they may have gone?"

Bitter Harvest

"No, sir."

"My servants tell me your step-uncle is also absent this morning, without explanation. Do you suppose this has some bearing on the matter?"

Carrie closed her eyes. Why had she not seen it before? She had taken little notice of Jane's whispered confidences, caught up as she was in the greater drama. Now, the bruises on Jane's arm, took on a sinister significance.

She said, "I have never trusted him. He was always sly." She recalled how Adele had seemed, of late, to be closer to him. As though they had had some understanding. "It . . . it would not surprise me if he was involved."

"And you think he will return today?"

"Jane, our maid, said he was wearing his best clothes and carrying bags. I did not think much of it at the time she told me. Uncle George comes and goes as he pleases." She shuddered. "If he has helped them, it is not from goodness of heart but for his own devious ends. I cannot think he would be able to return and face us after this."

"So, we are not further advanced." Miles reached up and patted the long white hand that lay on his shoulder. "Dolly my love, I think we must resign ourselves. I do not condone what Elliot has done. His behaviour is outrageous. To reject Miss Gordon almost at the altar, to cause such upset and heartache, not least to you . . ." He shook his head. "Elliot has his faults, but I thought we had raised him to be a gentleman. I fear his actions today prove otherwise. However, he is over twenty-one. If he has chosen to elope there is little, legally, we can do about it."

Into the silence Mrs Sanderson's voice was quiet and whispery, like snow drifting upon ice. She had stood the while, very still, behind her husband's chair. Her gown flamed around her rigid figure, its colour emphasising the deadly pallor of her face. Her eyes were two blazing holes above her cheekbones as she uttered, "I shall not allow this marriage."

"Dearest it is quite possible that they are already wed." Mr Sanderson's voice was suddenly querulous. His shoulders sagged

Anne Goring

under the weight of the shawls. "And if they are not, tell me, where should we begin to look?"

"They cannot have gone far."

"North, south, east, west, where do we begin?" His fingers rubbed his upper arm as though kneading away some pain there. "Had I been young and fit I would go myself. With half a dozen keen and discreet men to make enquiries with me I might pick up their trail before it's too late. As it is . . ." his words trailed away wearily.

"This is all too much for you, Miles. It is unforgiveable that you should have been tried in this way."

"If there is one thing I have learned over a long life it is to be philosophical over disappointment."

"Disappointment!" The word hissed out. "This will cause the greatest scandal, Miles. Imagine the feelings of the Gordons! We shall never be able to hold our heads up in society again."

"Ah, Dolly, I do understand. You have worked so hard and dreamed so long. Elliot's marriage to Miss Gordon would have been the crown of your achievements. To see your ambition come to nothing is a bitter pill to swallow. Perhaps, my love, you have underestimated Elliot's own desires. Perhaps you have pushed him too hard when it might have been more prudent to give him his head . . ."

"And you think that he has made a wise choice now? This . . . this witless chit of a girl without breeding or background?"

"She is amiable, loving and undoubtedly pretty. And he has no need to marry a fortune. It may turn out better than you think, though she is younger than I would have wished . . ."

"But not too young to marry Mr Prince, a man practically in his dotage." Carrie could not restrain the bitterness in her voice.

Two pairs of eyes fixed upon her. Mr Sanderson's were troubled. "I had quite forgot," he said. "Forgive me, child, but illness makes one self-centred – yet, I remember now, that I was told Adele was agreeable to the marriage." He glanced up at his wife who made a curt dismissive gesture. "Charlotte Dawes," she said, "assured me that all parties were satisfied."

Bitter Harvest

"Except my sister. I do assure you she was made thoroughly miserable by the engagement. It is hardly surprising that she sought to escape."

"So," Mrs Sanderson said, "she was unhappy and set her cap at my son. I knew it. I knew that she must be a schemer."

Goaded, Carrie cried, "Adele is no schemer. It is more the truth that she has been led astray by your son, spoiled as he is and used to having his way in all things. Believe me, madam, I regret this elopement as much as you. But my sister has been badly used and I will not let her become a scapegoat because your son has chosen to escape from your apron strings."

No sooner were the words out than she regretted them. Not because of the outright hate that flashed into Mrs Sanderson's eyes – she did not care a fig for her feelings – but because Mr Sanderson, who was a friend, seemed to shrink down into his chair as though, suddenly, it was all too much for him.

Carrie stepped forward but, weakly, he waved her away. "Dolly," he said, gasping. "Dolly, ring . . . for Cunningham. I . . . I must return to my room. I can talk no more of this." In a few moments he was gone, borne gently out by his valet and a footman, turning his head at the door to whisper painfully, "Let it be, Dolly. We must . . . accept. And forgive . . ."

His words hung upon the air as the door closed. After a moment Carrie said, "I shall take my leave now, Mrs Sanderson. There is nothing more to be said."

"Is there not? I rather think you presume too much Miss Caroline Linton."

With slow deliberate steps Mrs Sanderson swept across the velvety blue Tientsin carpet that muffled her tread so that she seemed to glide like an outraged and avenging spirit. Her handsome face was scarred with the anger she had contained while her husband was present and it took Carrie all her willpower not to flinch.

"You think it is all ended and that sly cat of a sister of yours will be permitted to enter my house as my son's wife? Oh, no, indeed. She may think she has her claws in a fine catch, but I shall never allow it. Never!"

Anne Goring

"You may have no option but to accept. A legal marriage . . ."

"Legal? Some hole-and-corner affair, legal? I shall employ – and I can afford to employ – the best lawyers in the country to untangle this sorry mess. To free my son from this obnoxious trap."

"Let us be clear," said Carrie sharply. "Adele laid no trap for your son. She may have faults but she is neither deceitful nor a fortune-hunter. I know my sister. She is a romantic, a dreamer. She has eloped with your son because she is, or imagines she is, in love with him, and for no other reason."

"Your sister may be the veriest angel, which I doubt, but I shall still deny this marriage."

"Mr Sanderson seems inclined to accept it."

"He is a sick man, far too ill to realise the enormity of what is happening."

"That your pride is hurt? That your society friends will turn their backs on you? Poor reasons, madam, to ruin your son's happiness."

The dark eyes blazed. "How dare you speak so. You chit! You stand there so prim and self-righteous and puffed up with your own cleverness and you know nothing of life. Nothing!"

"I know that I care for my sister and her happiness. I will fight for her as you fight for your son."

"Happiness!" She gave a short, harsh laugh. "What is happiness? You speak of it as though it were something to . . . to be plucked from a tree like a ripe fruit. Something easy and available. Anyone who believes that is a fool." Her glance slid beyond Carrie to the pale spring light falling against the window. "It is a fickle commodity. It comes in rare, brief flashes and sparingly, when it is most unexpected. Mostly, Caroline Linton, as you will find as you grow older, life is a series of blows and kicks and struggles and crises. The gods, the fates – call them what you will – I am convinced, stand apart from this world and delight in seeing ordinary mortals suffer. They watch our plans and ambitions fall to dust and ashes, see us stumble and despair, then spur us on to pick ourselves up and

Bitter Harvest

begin again by tantalising us with dreams of future bliss." The words hissed out between clenched teeth. "But I will not let them win. I will not! I defy them. They have done their damnedest with me but I shall best them yet." The handsome face was haggard in its defiance. Carrie, despite her own anger, felt a stab of admiration for this stubborn, daring woman who flung out such a challenge to the fates.

She spoke quietly. "Mrs Sanderson, whatever you may think, I appreciate your feelings. However your son and my sister feel towards each other they have acted without any regard to the sensibilities of those closest to them. In particular you and Mr Sanderson. And though I cannot say I ever approved of the betrothal arranged between Adele and Mr Prince, both he and Miss Prince must be deeply offended, and with good reason. But please, please, try to understand a little. Adele refused to talk of her engagement, but she was deeply unhappy about it. Perhaps your anger should be directed towards Mrs Dawes who arranged it all, instead of my sister who was only a helpless pawn in the hands of others." For a moment Carrie thought she was at last getting through to this formidable woman for an odd, reflective expression touched her face – yet was quickly gone. "I think Adele was desperate to escape a distasteful marriage. Whatever romantic emotions your son inspired in her heart, doubtless they were given extra impetus by the situation she was in. Perhaps," she said softly, "to your son, too, Mrs Sanderson."

Mrs Sanderson said, with impatience. "Excuses, excuses. You make a good advocate, but I remain unmoved." For all that, some of the heat had gone. Carrie had the impression that the shrewd mind was busy, abstracted.

Pressing her advantage, she pleaded. "Please forgive them. Give them your blessing when they return."

She watched Mrs Sanderson's face hopefully. Only the eyes held expression. They seemed, unexpectedly, to fill with a haunting sadness.

"I cannot," she said in a faint voice. "You do not understand. I cannot allow this marriage." Then, more strongly, anguish

Anne Goring

twisting her words, "I should have learned my lesson long ago. Never give way to sentimental impulse. Never do anything without a good and rational reason or disaster will strike. Oh, God, why did I do it?" The cry was from the heart, ringing out into the pale spaces of the room, remaining unanswered as, slowly, her gaze swung to Carrie. "Impulse took me out that day to see you. Blind, stupid impulse, because of Robert Linton, your father. What a fool I was to ever believe I owed you . . . him . . . anything. What did he do for me, beyond –" The sentence snapped off as her fist came up, knuckling back the words. When she spoke again it was in a small voice. "Get out," she said. "Get out and never come back into this house again."

Carrie went. She did not wait for the maid but tore open the heavy front door and ran down the gravel drive. The memory of the hate spilling from that handsome, anguished face hounded her. A forcible thing, tangible, howling in that quiet voice that was little more than a whisper, her final words echoing in her ears.

"She shall never have him. Not my son. I shall see her in hell first. Hell and beyond!"

It was foolish to believe there would ever be forgiveness for Adele.

The afternoon drew on. The sun having briefly triumphed now retired defeated as fresh battalions of cloud drove up from the west. The dimness in the musty parlour of the cottage deepened to gloom. For the umpteenth time Elliot paced to the small window and twitched back the half-lowered blind.

"How much longer must we wait in this . . . this chicken coop?" he growled. "Your uncle said a short wait and we have been here hours."

"Not so long, dearest," Adele said soothingly. "Pray be patient. I am sure Uncle George will come as quickly as he is able."

Elliot whisked out a handkerchief and held it to his handsome

Bitter Harvest

nose. "Faugh! It would not be so bad if this place did not *smell* like a chicken coop."

Adele giggled. "The old lady does not have much acqaintance with soap and water, but she has done her best to be kind." She indicated the table laid with coarse earthenware, the remains of a chicken pie and loaf. Elliot had merely tasted his portion and abandoned it. She had found it appetising and she was hungry. It was a long time since breakfast and they had had a slow journey through the town and out into the Cheshire countryside. The earlier tension that had knotted her stomach had relaxed as the miles passed and the chance of discovery lessened. Her inborn optimism had bubbled to the surface when the hired equipage had left them at the picturesque half-timbered cottage obscured from the nearby hamlet by great clumps of greening elms. They would never be traced here, not to this isolated spot. Even the less-than-picturesque dinginess of the cottage's interior and the sly obsequiousness of the wrinkled old lady who had obviously had her palm well greased to hide them for a while, could not dim her spirits. In a few hours, she and Elliot would be man and wife. Seeing him restless and displeased only fired her to greater joy. He would never declare it, for it would not become a gentleman to speak of such things, but his impatience for the mysterious delights of the marriage bed must match her own. Once or twice, almost roughly, he had swept her into his arms and kissed her with fierce passion, only to release her with equal abruptness and resume his pacing. "I hate this waiting!"

"Everything has gone smoothly so far," she said.

"I know. I know. But we are not yet far enough away."

She saw the fear behind his displeasure. She went to him and coiled her arms around his neck, trying to instil in him something of her own confidence. "Nothing can go wrong now," she murmured.

He sighed. "I trust not, but one feels so helpless . . . at the mercy of others. And I would never underestimate Mamma. She might have aroused the militia by now. I should not have weakened and penned the note, yet I could not bear it that

131

Anne Goring

Father should think I had come to some harm. His health is so uncertain at present. As for Mamma," there was a hard edge to his voice, "let her worry herself sick. I care not a jot, so long as she leaves me in peace to make my own way."

"Oh, Elliot," Adele rebuked. "You should not speak of your mamma so. This . . . this difference of opinion you have had with her, you will forget and forgive in time. Say nothing now that you will regret later."

Stiffly, he said, "You do not understand the depth of this disagreement." Then, in a despairing way, he added, "Do I seem a bear, my darling? Forgive me, but there are things I cannot talk of regarding Mamma's deviousness. No, do not frown so. It is nothing for you to bother your pretty head about."

"I shall be your wife soon, Elliot. I should be a poor one if I did not wish to share my husband's troubles."

Colour flowed becomingly into her face as she spoke. He stroked the soft curve of her cheek. "You are all that I would wish for in a wife. You are beauty and innocence and gentleness personified. I have always sought for perfection in my orchids, but in you I see that perfection which has always eluded me. To mar your mind with the . . . the despicable events associated with Mamma, would grieve me abominably. When . . . when we are settled together and all this is behind us, then I may be able to talk calmly of it."

The prospect of that vague, rosy future she had imagined, sharpened into clearer detail. She saw the two of them side by side in a sunny room. The windows opened onto brilliant lawns and the sea glittered in the distance. There was a smell of heat and flowers. She heard whispered confidences, felt the clasp of hand on hers. The sense of peace and security wrapped her like a cloak. She did not connect this glowing future with an infancy she could not consciously remember. She only knew that the room, the sunlight, the scents, the loving presence spelled true contentment. With Elliot she would find all this.

As the weather deteriorated the parlour became so dark that

132

Bitter Harvest

Elliot roused the old lady to bring candles. She came, bobbing her ancient curls and wafting such an odour of staleness from her person that he was forced to press his handkerchief to his nose once more. He curtly declined an offer of a glass of parsnip wine and seemed to be on the point of exploding into wrath, when there was the unmistakable sound of a carriage.

In a moment or two Uncle George's bulk filled the small room. His florid face beamed and he was bowing and apologising and helping Adele with her cloak seemingly all at the same time.

"You have been uncommonly long," Elliot said peevishly.

"Ah, I have had much to do," Uncle George cried. "And I fear I would have been a great deal more delayed but for the kindness of a lady of my acquaintance who has not only allowed us the use of her carriage, but takes such an interest in your story that she has insisted on witnessing such a romantic event."

"What lady is this?" Elliot demanded. "You have not spoken to me before of a lady."

"She is reliable," Uncle George assured him. "No need to get upset. Now, come quickly."

He hustled them out into the damp air which smelt extra sweet after the frowsty cottage. Adele's eyes widened when she saw the carriage. The lady must truly be rich.

Adele was not to know that the whole equipage, including the pair of black horses, which but a week ago had been greys, was the legal property of other people and Uncle George was as anxious as Elliot to get away from the environs of Manchester.

They got into the carriage; the blinds were drawn and it was scarcely possible to make out the face of the lady who cried, shrilly, "Why, how charmed I am to meet you. Fie I think it extremely romantic that you elope like this." She flapped an overlarge fan which sent a breeze strongly scented with lavender water wafting round the carriage. She gave a trilling laugh. "Methinks it almost gives me the notion to elope myself with Mr O'Hara, were he not already so devoted to his dear wife."

133

Anne Goring

"Ah, Miss Quick, you do me honour indeed," George replied merrily.

The name touched a chord in Adele's memory. As the carriage clipped away smartly, she said, "Miss Quick is perhaps some relation to the Mr Samuel Quick who is your friend, Uncle George."

"His own sister."

"I had not heard you mention he had a sister."

"I did not know myself. Miss Quick has spent much of her time in county society and has only recently returned north."

Miss Quick nodded her bonnet. It was, Adele saw as her eyes adjusted to the light, excessively ornamented. A monstrous creation of lace and red roses and pink feathers that matched the plumes and rosebuds that cascaded extravagantly down the front of her mantle. Even the hem of her skirt bore a feather trim as though an unfortunate flock of birds had fluttered beneath the flounces and expired. Adele was so overcome that she had to invent a coughing fit to divert her giggles.

"My word, Miss Linton, you must look to that cough," warned Miss Quick in her striving tones.

"Thank you," Adele ventured weakly. "But it is merely a catch in my throat."

What an odd person. Miss Quick neither looked nor sounded like a person of quality. Yet there was this carriage, the glitter of jewels and gold at her wrist and ears. Was she perhaps an actress? An adventuress? Adele had scarcely begun to speculate on this interesting prospect before the carriage stopped and Uncle George said, "Wait here one moment. I shall make sure all is prepared."

Elliot let up the blind to reveal half an acre of leaning tombstones overgrown with weeds encircling a small grey stone chapel. Under the ominous sky the dereliction of the spot struck coldly at Adele. For the first time she felt doubt. The excitement that had buoyed her up all day dissipated, leaving in its place a sickly, frightened feeling.

What was she doing in this carriage with a strange and flashily

Bitter Harvest

dressed woman who, she could see now, was leering at her in a coarse, knowing way? Was she really to be married to this frowning young man who tapped his foot so moodily on the floor? In her panic he seemed a stranger and for a moment it was like it had been during those awful days when she had been betrothed to Mr Prince. As though her real self, shrunk very small, watched her from a distance, deriding her dishevelled hair and the mud on her cloak. As if from afar she saw Uncle George hasten back to the carriage and his smile was a deceit and his flourish as he handed her and the dreadful Miss Quick down the steps, a mockery.

She heard the rusty gate creak on its hinges as their little party straggled through. She saw the old broken flagstones furred with moss at her feet and the shattered slates from the chapel roof littering the rank grass and the voice of that other self laughing in her mind because it was all wrong. Wrong. Even the parson waiting at the chapel door seemed a shambling figure in ill-fitting robes.

Weddings were not like this. Where were the bridesmaids in their pretty gowns, the flowers, the ribbons, the gaiety?

Then, quite suddenly, it was all right again. The chapel door stood open. Candlelight framed the solemn figure of the reverend gentleman and Elliot's arm was about her waist, tightly. He was no longer a stranger. She looked up at him and saw the mingling of nervousness and apprehension that lay behind the moodiness of his expression.

In a low voice that was not quite steady, he said, "Are you quite sure, Adele?" He gestured with one hand, encompassing the decay, the whole grim ambience of the chapel. "This is not what I would have wished for you. It is so much worse than I supposed . . . so gloomy. I had not realised, that is, I would understand if . . . even now, you did not wish to go on . . ."

She said, simply, "I love you Elliot." And smiled. The response reflected in his eyes brought everything into perspective. She looked at Miss Quick, no longer grotesque, but a gay and raffish figure, pulling some of the artificial rosebuds from her

Anne Goring

mantle and pressing them into her hands. "No bride should go to the alter without flowers." Even her voice was less shrill. Uncle George's smile was hearty and encouraging as he boomed, "Come now, no time for nerves you young people." Then, to the parson, "Lead the way, sir."

Yes, it would be all right now.

Just follow the parson who shuffled ahead, wafting back waves of peppermint that mingled with the odour of brandy and damp and ancient dust. Hold hard to Elliot's arm. Ignore the peeling plaster and the wheeling shadows beyond the candle glow and the scuttle of something skittering among the rotting pews. Take your place and listen carefully to the parson's words. Make your responses slowly and clearly. Do not notice the way the parson's hands shake, or the rim of black under his broken nails. Do not listen to Miss Quick whispering in quite another voice, husky and flat-vowelled and common, "Eh, Georgie, she's but a babe-in-arms. Should you have . . . ?" And Uncle George shushing her abruptly to silence.

The ring was on her finger. The words were pronounced. Elliot's cold lips touched her forehead.

It was done. She was no longer Adele Linton but Mrs Elliot Sanderson.

She was safe. She was part of the glowing secure future she had dreamed of. Now it would all begin.

It had been a long, unreal day. The lodge seemed unnaturally quiet as Carrie sat picking at her supper. Aunt Linnie was sleeping upstairs, her hysterics at last calmed by several glasses of sherry. Carrie had watched uneasily as her aunt had sipped greedily at the wine, and when she went to remove the bottle and glass, Aunt Linnie had cried quickly, "No, Caroline, leave it there. I may wake in the night and have need of it," and had given a dramatic sigh and a small belch which she smothered with ladylike dabs at her mouth. "My digestion is ruined by today's events. My stomach is in knots. I shall not bear to lie awake thinking of that ungrateful child and the worry she has

Bitter Harvest

caused me." She had added, fretfully, "And where is George, pray? Has he not returned yet?"

"Not yet, aunt," Carrie had said, and made a silent exit as her aunt began to nod. She knew he would not return, and that he must be involved with Adele and her runaway match. It could not be pure coincidence. Earlier she had gone to his room. His workaday clothes were tossed carelessly about the floor, together with every piece of darned underwear. Drawers stood open and emptied, a gaping hole at the back of the tallboy revealed a compartment that must have concealed some secret. Everything of any value, even the pottery ornaments, had gone.

She went out of the room and closed the door. As the latch fell with a metallic click it had a disturbing finality about it. As though she had closed the door for ever on Uncle George.

Jane had been sent to bed. Carrie stacked her supper dishes on the tray, lit her candle, put out the lamp and all the while her thoughts went tiredly around her head. She saw Adele's face, understood, now, the secret excitement underlying the happy glow in her eyes. She had a fleeting image of Mr Brook talking of marriage. Of Mr Sanderson shrunken and old under an invalidish heap of rugs. She saw Aunt Linnie's face peevish in distress, uncaring for anything but her own peace of mind. And she saw Mrs Sanderson. Once again she felt the fierce, unforgiving passion, saw the scorn in the handsome eyes.

Rain squalled against the window, rattling the panes. A draught set the embers of the fire spitting and bent the candle flame so that her shadow plunged about the walls, like a black being striving to reach her. She shuddered, feeling an echo of a child's fear of empty rooms with dark corners.

Steadying her hand before picking up the candle, Carrie made herself walk with deliberate steps across the parlour and up the narrow stairs, pausing outside her aunt's half-open door to listen for the sound of her noisy breathing. Her own room – hers alone now, no longer Adele's – welcomed her with its faint aroma of lavender-scented linen. The irrational fear had gone. It had been brought on by the late hour and her tiredness. She was

137

achingly exhausted, she realised. Almost too weary to undress. She dropped her clothes to a chair and drew the clean folds of her nightgown over her head.

The blind was not drawn. She went to the window and stood looking at the blackness. Jem, she thought. Jem. He would be asleep now in the darkened cottage, unheeding of the rain against the other familiar noise, that of the river sliding and rippling below. She saw his sleeping face against the pillow, his long limbs sprawled across the bed. She wished she could lie beside him and it was a passionless thought. Just to lie there, to reach out a hand to touch him would be comfort enough. Tomorrow she would contrive to get a message to him. He would come to her as soon as he knew and she would draw strength from him.

Pulling down the blind, Carrie climbed into bed and snuffed out the candle. She lay in the dark holding Jem's image clear in her mind. She explored the hollows of his face, the shadows where his dark lashes curved against his hard cheekbones, the mouth that could be so gentle, the eyes dark blue and clear as seawater under sun. Thinking of him banished all the disquieting thoughts from her head. He filled her heart and her mind. Tomorrow she must contrive to see him. Tomorrow . . .

By the tremulous light of a horn lantern, the man explored the narrow line of foul mud fringing the river. Above, the squalid tenements reared black against the night sky, pierced by frail yellow oblongs where some sat up late. The rain fell in a miserable drizzle, pattering in the ooze around the old man's broken boots and soaking the sacking bag slung across his shoulders. He took no notice of the weather. Rain or fine, summer and winter, he was out. He was a creature of the dark, like the sleek rats that scuttered around him. By day he holed up in a shanty he had fashioned against the wall of a tannery, emerging only to hawk his wares to those as half-witted and impoverished as himself and to replenish his stock with fresh scourings from gutters and ashpits, and the banks of the Irk

Bitter Harvest

and Irwell where they slid oily and foul below the oldest, the most decrepit parts of the town.

Few pickings here tonight though. He mumbled to himself, his long matted beard wagging perilously near the mud as he poked at it with swollen fingers. Nowt but a bent tin spoon and some lengths of rusted wire for his pains. Still, if the rain kept up it would swell the water nicely and a good bit o' flooding might bring all manner of treasures. Once, he remembered, there had been a week of rich rewards. Day after day the Irk had spewed up the scourings of the gardens and cottages along its route, even a human body or two amid the carcasses of dogs and pigs and fowls, some still penned in their coops. Aye, he'd lived well then, only he'd had to fight for pickings. The river's benefice brought out human rats from the alleys, all eager to trespass on what he thought of as his own personal territory. "Rogues, all of 'em," he said aloud. "I mighta bin a rich man but for that thievin' lot."

He clawed at a piece of string, brought it up dripping to the light, shook the worst of the mud off it and tossed it into his sack.

He'd missed a fine body in that last flooding. Some toff who'd fallen in the river, complete with horse. Tangled together, they'd come down the flood, swirlin' and twirlin', just at dusk. He'd had a sight of the fine saddle, the glitter of gold chain across a velvet waistcoat, as handsome a pair o' boots as ever graced a gentleman . . . but they was on him, all them human rats. Some pious busybody called the constable and before he could raise his voice to curse, they was bearin' him off on a board in the direction of t'owd church.

Floodings was good, but floodings was also bad. You 'ad to be so quick, afore fortunes vanished before your eyes to give you vengeful dreams for weeks. Better by far to take what nature give you in the quiet and the dark. Bodies – and bodies was not infrequent along this stretch, bridges being handy for the tossing over of same – was best come upon solitary-like and in the night hours.

Anne Goring

He stopped, holding the lantern aloft, its guttering light stretching into the murk ahead, picking out a white limb against the ooze.

An arm. Undoubtedly an arm. The man's eyes glittered amid the thickets of unkempt hair, but he did not move. He felt an unusual apprehension – almost a superstitious fear – as though his thoughts had conjured up a corpse. But that was instantly swept away by a thrust of avarice and curiosity.

He went about his business in a practised way. The body was young, that of a solidly muscled and heavy young man, half in the water, half draped over a raft of wood, the lid of a crate or some such that kept his head and shoulders from the water. From his position, he had obviously been thrown down from a narrow flight of steps that ended three foot above the river and led up to a warren of little streets. It was not pretty to look upon, being much bruised and caked with dried blood, but he took no mind of that as his fingers nimbly divested it of its clogs and stockings. The pockets of the breeches were empty. A body found in such a place and in such a condition would naturally have been divested of all coin or ornament, not that this body belonged to the gentry. A working man, he guessed. Sensibly clad, a good woollen shirt to his back, cord breeches neatly patched and wi' years of wear in 'em. He roughly straightened one leg that lay at an awkward angle.

The body moaned. He let go of the leg with surprise, then swung the lantern so that the light fell on the swollen and battered face, giving at the same time, a cruel tweak to the nose. "What? You not quite gone then, lad?"

The eyelids flickered open. They blinked, then the dark pupils focused. "Cold . . . cold . . ." The voice was as thin as a babby's.

"Colder still in a minute. Hush up and let a man do 'is work in peace." He cackled at his own wit and ignored the body's groans as he divested it of breeches and shirt. Presently the sounds ceased. Not that it was quite without life. He could hear the breath bubbling in and out of its lips.

Bitter Harvest

He stuffed the clothes into his sack, eyed the darned wool underdrawers and, virtuously, decided to let the body expire in decency. He rubbed his hands. Night had turned out better than expected. In an excess of high spirits he humped the body so that it lay, arms and legs spread, across the raft of wood, then shoved it with his foot into the current, before he hastened off up the steps and lost himself in the shadows.

The raft tilted, then balanced itself. Jem's feet hung into the water, his face was turned up to the rain that mingled with the dried crusts of blood and caused the gash under the matted black hair to weep. The raft bumped through the currents, nudged a wall, swayed dangerously, then swept on more steadily. For a while the huddled black shapes of the town buildings loomed up above, then they became fewer, falling back from the river's edge, and the watermeadows opened out. The sweet smell of wet earth and grass almost overcame the sewer stench of the water. A barn owl flew swift and silent overhead. Somewhere a small rodent screamed and fell quiet as the raft caught an eddy and drifted to the reedy shallows. For a few moments it turned in a slow dance and finally it came to rest against the side of a sturdy rowing boat moored to the shore.

Jem lay in the dark and the rain, spread-eagled, blood trickling in a thin, persistent line through his hair to form a puddle under his neck that rocked gently with the movement of the raft. He saw nothing, heard nothing, felt nothing. The slow trickle of blood was the only indication that he still lived.

And presently even that stopped.

Sally Quick sat propped up in the finest bed she had seen in her life. It was big enough to hold six, a four-poster of immense size, hung about with crimson curtains, fitted with a fat feather mattress and overstuffed pillows. And if the bed curtains were a little dusty and the linen sheets a touch grey and the Turkey carpet distinctly threadbare, she didn't even notice, because the snapping fire in the hearth sent out a warm glow over it all.

Anne Goring

"Oh, Georgie," she had cried when the chambermaid had closed the door behind them. "I never imagined such a room . . . can we afford it?"

"Anything you want, Sal."

"It's like a palace," she said, staring round, then, high spirits welling up, she kicked up her skirts and did a wild dance round the room, flinging herself at last upon the bed, holding her arms out to him, "C'mon lad, let's celebrate."

He had come to her, laughing, but only to pull her to her feet. "Now, now, your ladyship." He sketched a bow. "Plenty of time for goings-on later. Dinner in ten minutes. A fine dinner and plenty of brandy to wash it down, eh? Then in due time we shall retire to our room. That," he added with mock solemnity, "is how respectable married folk behave."

She held up the hand that bore the broad gold band he had placed on it earlier, when they were alone in the carriage, after the old drunk who thought he was still a parson and the silly, pretty young couple had gone.

"You and me need no scraps of paper to show folk," he'd said, "but I got that old fool to write out something." She had looked at the paper he'd put in her hands. He pointed to their names." That's mine, George Wright as I shall be from now, and yours, Sarah Quick – and that's to say we're man and wife, legal." And even if his real wife was still alive, miserable old thing, who was there to know or care? They were together. She had his ring. He'd bought her all these grand new clothes, brought her to this inn. "We shall take it steady. I've to see a man in Market Drayton tomorrow about the carriage and horses. Fetch a nice price, they will. We'll hire something more modest and go where the fancy takes us. The ship doesn't leave for ten days. Plenty of time to get to London and buy all we shall need to set us up in Australia."

It was perfect. Perfect. Except that when he mentioned that far-off place there were no pictures in Sally's head. She could think of London, imagining it like Manchester but bigger and more splendid, but beyond that nothing. She tried to think of

Bitter Harvest

herself on a ship and to imagine the sea, but it was like there was a blank space and a funny uncomfortable empty feeling. So she didn't think that far ahead. She thought only of today and tomorrow. The rest of it could take care of itself. Why should she make herself miserable when she was Mrs George Wright, and taken for a lady?

The dinner was all that George promised. They sat in the low-beamed parlour while the maid scurried back and forth with steaming dishes. She ate lamb so tender it melted at a touch and floury mounds of potatoes and a good wedge of squab pie and a froth of lemony pudding called syllabub that she'd never had the like of in her life, and could only manage the merest crumb of the fat crumbly Cheshire cheese. She was swimmy-headed with the wine she had drunk and the warmth of the room, for the smart dress was tight at the waist and heavy with its frills and flounces, and her shoes pinched. But she wouldn't have been any place else but here in her finery, opposite her Georgie in his new scarlet waistcoat. Every inch the gentleman he was. You could tell that, the easy way he bowed and spoke to the other gents in the parlour. He'd promised her a lady's life and by God it was all happening. She raised her glass. "To us, Georgie," she said happily.

"To us," he answered. "And Australia."

And now, she had thought, they would nod a bit distant, like real gentry, to those still left in the parlour and hurry up to bed as fast as was decent. She was impatient. The wine, the warmth had made her lusty. She'd give Georgie a high old time. A night he wouldn't forget in a hurry. She would have liked to claw him away from that young sporting sort of toff he'd struck up a conversation with. But real ladies didn't act like that. They sat still on hard chairs, without fidgetin' and didn't have naughty thoughts.

Then George turned to her and said, with that smile of his that could charm birds off a tree, sod it, "You wouldn't mind going up by yourself, Sarah, dear?" She choked on a hiccuping giggle. "I'll be up in a little while," he said, wheedling, his eyelid

143

Anne Goring

dropping in a knowing wink. "There's a little matter of a pair of well-matched dogs . . ."

She scarce heard the rest for wanting to shriek her protests at him, but with the toff's eye on her she was forced to keep up with the play-acting, sticking her nose in the air and saying, "Of course, husband, I have no objection. I shall expect you in ten minutes."

"Not a minute more, my precious," he'd said through his lyin' teeth. She knew him too well. He'd be out in that inn yard layin' bets till all hours and swillin' down the brandy without even noticing he was getting drunk. He'd be no use to her tonight.

Up in the bedroom she tore off the dress, kicked off her shoes so hard one hit the bed curtains and sent up a cloud of dust, then flung herself onto the bed and beat her fists against the pillows. After a bit she laughed at herself. George was George. There'd be plenty more nights. Still, tonight was to 'ave bin special. She was wearing a ring and she did have a piece of paper, carefully folded away in her valise, saying that she was his missus. A proper honeymoon it would have been. She climbed into bed and sank back into the luxury of deep feathers. If only he'd come. If only he would. But she could hear the clatter of boots on the cobbles below the window and presently the distant yap and snarl and yelps of dogs tearing each other to bloody shreds. She shuddered. She wasn't much for settin' animals against each other.

The euphoria of the wine was fading. She had a stale, thick taste in her mouth and the beginnings of a headache. She lay amid unaccustomed opulence and began to wish she was back in her own room with her own things about her, poor as they was. She was used to them. There was no play-acting there. She could be Sal Quick who knew everybody in the Meadow and could stand up to the best of 'em. Here, she was a stranger, pretendin' to be something she wasn't, destined for a heathen place she knew nothing about. Even here, in England, she wasn't so sure of herself away from the streets she knew. So what would it be like in Australia? All the greenness had bothered her as they'd

144

Bitter Harvest

driven through the Cheshire countryside. It was so empty save for a few animals. Fields, hedges, dripping trees were all she saw – scarce a living soul and they seemingly lost in all that space, their cottages fleabites on the big green rolling monster that might turn over and chew 'em up.

That funny, hollow feeling was back. Like there was something ahead to be afeared of . . . shadows gathering. She saw that girl's eyes. Adele. As they'd got out of the carriage and walked to that falling-to-bits chapel, she'd seen summat of the sort on *her* face. As if for a minute or two she was mazed and frightened at what was happening, poor little bitch.

"I'm doing her a favour," George had said. "Linnie wants to marry her off to an old man." But George was deep. He was making mischief with them Sandersons as well as thumbing his nose at his spiteful wife. Well, maybe they deserved it, but she still couldn't help feeling sorry for Adele. She was nowt but a babe-in-arms. And such a looker. The lad, too, though anyone with half an eye could see he was a weak reed.

"God help her," she said aloud to the empty room, like she'd said to George earlier. "Poor sods. What'll happen when they find out they're not legally wed but livin' in sin?"

He had shrugged. "Since when have you been troubled by sinning?"

"Well, me, it's different. She's been brought up decent. And she's such a nice little thing." She'd jabbed her finger in his arm. "You never told me that, Georgie."

"Give over, Sal," he'd said mildly, "or I'll be thinking you've developed a conscience, and consciences is mighty uncomfortable to live with."

She'd let it drop, but it didn't stop her thinking. To George it was a big joke, like catching Carter Smith with his breeches down. Aye, and she'd gone along with that, for Carter Smith was was a dirty minded old devil. It seemed like justice to squeeze a few sovereigns out of him, but there again, George hadn't been content with that; he must force Carter Smith to sack Jem at the yard, who, it turned out, was courting the other niece, Carrie.

Anne Goring

Which was something else George hadn't bothered to tell her. She was beginning to realise that she didn't know her George as well as she thought she did.

Sally thumped the pillow into a more comfortable shape and tried to force herself to sleep. But her brain was too lively now. It thought about Jem, who was a polite lad, who always give her the time of day when she visited her gran and didn't indulge in no horseplay like some of the others. She was sorry he'd been sacked. What wrong had he done George? And she liked it even less that two of the dirtiest rogues in the Meadow were involved. And George hadn't been for telling her that, either.

Snivelling, Carter Smith had come creeping round to her room with his cash. George had taken it from him and tossed him his breeches. "I'll keep the boots," he'd said. "Just in case you decide to start blabbing."

"I'll say nothing," Smith had screeched. "Those are me best boots. The wife'll know – what'll I say . . . ?"

"You'll think of something," George had grinned.

"Course you will," she'd teased, slipping to Carter Smith's side and twining an arm round his stringy neck. "A clever man like you."

Then she and George had laughed fit to bust and Carter Smith had backed away, his face turning purple. "I've done everything you told me to," he had wailed. "I got rid of Jem Walker – me best hand carted off by the constable for stealing that he didn't do. It's made me ill, I tell you."

"You should've thought of that before you followed this lady back to her room."

"I fell among thieves, that's what! Led astray I was." Then, wheedling, "Give me back me boots, for pity's sake."

George had smiled. "Get out before I kick you out."

He'd slunk to the door, looked ready to cry, but at the threshold he turned and faced them. He stiffened, and for a moment there seemed a kind of dignity about the little man, despite his red-rimmed eyes and pinched features.

"You might think you're clever the pair of you, making a

Bitter Harvest

man suffer so for acting the fool over a whore. Well, as I've suffered and poor Jem Walker has suffered, so shall you." He raised a quivering finger. "You've hog-tied me, taken my money, and I curse you for it." Spittle gathered at the corner of his mouth. "You'll spend my gold and every sovereign will buy you ill-fortune. I'll be on my knees and praying for it every night. You're tools of the devil and the devil claims his own in time. Damn you to hell, the both of you."

The door slammed behind him and they heard his stumbling footsteps on the stairs.

George shook the jingling bag of coins, grinning. "I'll drink his health in the finest brandy."

"And a double for me," she laughed. "But what's all this about Jem at the yard?"

He told her and she said, a bit sharp, "Did you have to do that? He's not a bad lad and once in the Bailey it's a hard place to get out of."

"Oh, he'll not be there. Rutter'll see to that. Now, come on. Get into your new clothes. We must make haste."

She said in surprise, "Dan Rutter?"

His eyes slid past her. She sensed he'd said more than he'd intended.

"Yes, him," he said, impatient. "Now get on, do. We've the carriage to pick up . . ."

"But he's a dirty villain. Hard and cold as a miser's heart. He'd kill his own mother for the price of a glass o' gin."

"Look, Sal," George said, cool and hard. "I made a little arrangement. Jem Walker's too honest by half. The justices might have believed him and that meant the constabulary poking round Carter Smith's yard. Who knows, they might have got on to us? So I had an agreement with the constable of the watch and with Dan Rutter. Jem'll be put nicely out of the way for a few days until we're well clear." His teeth flashed as he smiled. "Dan'll make sure he's no use to dear Caroline for a bit."

"I still don't think . . ."

Anne Goring

"Thinking is not your strong point, Sal. I'm here to do the thinking from now on." He paused, eyeing her. "Or are you minded to stay. Without me."

"Course not, you bugger," she scoffed. "It's just that you surprise me sometimes, you really do."

He pinched her behind and she yelped and kicked out at him. "Get on then," he ordered, "and stop your nonsense."

In the flurry of getting ready, of putting on her fine lady act, of waving goodbye to her friends who hung out from every door and window in the alley, waving and catcalling, as she and George set off arm in arm, of getting through the afternoon and evening pretending to be what she wasn't, she'd given it no more thought. This was what she wanted. Her and Georgie together. Respectable. Man and wife and a piece of paper and a ring to prove it. It was all a big joke.

Only now, alone, the room lit dully by the embers of a dying fire, it didn't seem funny at all.

The coals slipped in a flurry of warm ash, making a strange cindery shape. A black rimmed, glowing red eye stared right out at her. *Every sovereign will buy you ill-fortune . . . I'll be on my knees and praying for it . . . Damn you to hell.*

Sally clutched the sheets. The old bastard had cursed them, hadn't he? Her and George was poxed before they'd even begun. Superstitious terror coiled dankly in her bowels. She was mesmerised by the glowing red eye in the fire, frightened to look round in case Carter Smith might be lurking in the shadows, pointing telling her to get on back where she belonged.

And like a child looking for comfort, she longed to be back. In her little room, in her own bed, with the smells of the street wafting in through the broken windowpanes and the comforting sounds of squabbling and laughter in the alley below.

Where she belonged.

Her fingers tightened on the sheets. The ring meant nothing. The paper meant nothing. It was false. Like the whole day was false. A daft play she'd taken part in and now the curtain had come down and it was over.

Bitter Harvest

She was out of her element and she must go back to it. And sharpish. Not now, though. Not tonight. She shuddered at the thought of all those fields and woods, black and wet and full of nameless wild things. Tomorrow, in the daylight.

And Georgie? Would he understand? He wouldn't go back, for sure. It was Australia for him. She remembered all the good times they'd had and felt herself torn. Ah, but she needed and wanted him. Yet there was a part of her that called in another direction. Whichever way she went she was going to be hurt.

A loud thump came from beyond the door. She sprang from the bed as George found the latch and staggered into the room. She looked at him flushed with drink, grinning foolishly, and her guts melted. She loved every handsome inch of him, drunk or sober. He was her man.

He burst into bawdy song, swaying before the hearth, and she hunched her shoulder under his arm, half carrying him to the bed, shushing him.

"Behave, you daft lummock! Folk's'll hear."

"Made a killin'. . ." he warbled. "Fine ole time . . . tomorrow buy you . . . new dresh . . ."

"Mebbe tomorrow I shan't be here to wear it! Leavin' me all on me own to get all of a bother. What a way to treat a girl." As she talked she was stripping him of his coat and waistcoat. She swore softly at the state of him. "What did you do, fall in a midden?"

He blinked owlishly. "Fell . . . yesh. Wenter look at the horses . . . met a feller . . . might buy 'em. Money for us, Sal."

"Never mind the money. There's more things in life than shillings . . . like this blood all over your breeches. And they're all torn. 'Ere lift yourself and let me get 'em off."

He yelped as she pulled them roughly from his legs. She frowned, examining his calf. "That's nasty. You must've fell on a nail or summat." There was a deep, oozing gash matted with strawy muck and even when she'd fetched a basin and mopped it clean, she could see dirt still embedded under the skin. "Drunken daftie," she said mildly, dabbing it dry.

Anne Goring

He didn't hear. His head was back on the pillow, his jaw dropped, snoring.

"You're a tough bugger," she said to his insensible body, "but you're going to feel that in the morning. What wi' that and a sore head, you'll be in a right temper." She slipped into bed beside him, drawing the covers over them both. She snuggled against him, and laughed throatily. "I think I'll hang on wi' you for a day or two longer. We'll have us honeymoon first, lad."

Her fears were receding now she was not alone, and it would all look different by daylight. Tomorrow. She'd do nothing hasty. Maybe she would like to see London. She imagined golden spires set against a blue sky and fancy folks tripping about smothered in furs and jewels. She'd be all right wi' Georgie.

She slipped into her usual deep dreamless sleep.

A few miles back on the road the bogus parson, dressed once more in his usual soiled and odorous attire, lay under a dripping hedge, oblivious of the weather. The bottle of gin that had been part of his payment for the charade, had rolled away and lodged in a hawthorn root.

Even cold sober and shaking this afternoon, he had been more concerned with remembering the once familiar phrases and responses of the marriage service, more aware of his body's craving for the drink that would be his when the ceremony was over, than with the young couple he had married.

He neither knew nor cared that in a humble inn scarcely a mile away the false marriage had been ardently consummated. That the two lovers, limbs entwined, slept the healthy, relaxed sleep of the confident young, who knew that the world revolved round their little affairs and that love assuredly overcame every obstacle.

The man who had once been a parson jerked and twitched as the wind shook the hawthorn leaves, sending rivulets of water cascading over his bare head. He whimpered. The rain felt like the crawling of dream creatures over his shrinking flesh. He

Bitter Harvest

opened his eyes to the blackness of night, then, curled like a foetus, he slept again, unaware that his performance that afternoon had been one of the most destructive acts in the whole of his misspent life.

Chapter Six

Mrs Walker hammered at the lodge door, pushed past an astonished Jane and ran into the parlour where Carrie was crumbling a piece of toast and wondering how she was going to break the news to Aunt Linnie that Uncle George seemed to have departed for good.

"Jem didn't come home last night. I were up waitin' . . . something he's never done before. First thing, I was down at the yard. Oh, and he wouldn't do nowt wrong! It's all some mistake!" Her hands twisted into the fringes of her shawl as the incoherent tale poured out, a tale so incredible, that Carrie's first reaction was pure disbelief. ". . . Then the constables come and took him away, but he ran off. Never got to the Bailey. One of the men told me. It was proper quiet down at the yard. None of 'em could believe it of Jem. It were like there'd been a . . . a funeral." She broke into harsh sobs, mopping at her tears with the corner of her apron. She looked like a mourning creature herself. Gaunt, black-skirted and shawled, her eyes bloodshot, her tall bony figure racked as she struggled to overcome her weeping. "I thought he'd have got some word to you."

Carrie rose to her feet. "No," she said faintly. "He did not . . . Mrs Walker, are you sure? Yes, yes, of course you are. Forgive me. I . . . I just cannot take it in. There must be some dreadful misunderstanding."

"That's what I thought. Carter Smith soon put me straight." She drew a shuddering breath. "He could scarce bring hisself to speak to me. Just told me baldly what had happened and said he never wanted to set eyes on Jem, nor any of his family

Anne Goring

and slammed the door of his office in me face. As God is my witness, our Jem had no hand in stealing." Her sunken eyes beseeched Carrie. "You know my lad. You'll speak up for him, won't you? You got friends as'll sort this out. Mr Sanderson's allus been a real gentleman. Will you ask him . . . ?"

A rock seemed to have lodged itself in Carrie's chest. She said, "I fear Mr Sanderson has other worries," and explained about Adele's elopement and how frail Mr Sanderson was, and about Mrs Sanderson's anger and Aunt Linnie's hysterics. It all seemed remote, happening a long time ago.

"Trouble all round," Mrs Walker said. "I shouldn't be bothering you wi' mine. You've enough on your plate. I just thought, knowing how you and Jem felt for each other, he'd have tried to get in touch." She was past diplomacy. She cried out, "I thought you'd be in for a rocky road, the pair o' you, but I never thought there'd be owt like this."

Carrie's hand went to her throat. Mrs Walker knew. They looked at each other in the small silence. Then, slowly, wordlessly Carrie went to her. Arms reached out. Carrie did not know who was comforting whom. She said, quietly, "We shall find him. Go home now, in case he is looking to find you there."

"And you'll send word if you have any news?"

"I will give him until noon. If I have heard nothing by then, I shall leave no stone in Manchester unturned to discover his whereabouts."

"Aye, and I'll help you, lass."

They stood back, smiling a little in acknowledgement of their shared anxiety. Feeling relief that here was someone else who understood, who cared. Despite the difference in years, they each sensed the strength in the other and drew reassurance from it. If their eyes were shadowed with pain and fear, then that must no longer be spoken of. There would be much to do. Jem was in deep trouble. They would need to be courageous for his sake.

Mrs Walker straightened her apron, rearranged her shawl. She was already ashamed of her breakdown, she who had fought

Bitter Harvest

poverty and hardship all her life and kept her dignity through it all. "I'll be off then," she said briskly.

When Carrie had watched her disappear into the drizzle she went and sat by the fire, staring into it so still and silently that Jane grew disturbed and invented little tasks about the parlour so that she could keep an eye on her. Even the rapping of Mrs O'Hara's stick on the bedroom floor above did not rouse her and Jane was forced to touch her shoulder, so that she jumped. To Jane's relief the blank look left her eyes and she said, with her usual composure, "I must face my aunt now and tell her about Uncle George. Perhaps you will brew fresh tea, Jane, and make some toast, very thin, and boil a new egg. Lay the tray carefully and bring it up in about ten minutes. We must do our best to keep her spirits up and," turning away, "our own."

The soft sigh that escaped her seemed to come from some deep source of grief. It lingered after she had left the room. Jane heard her quiet footsteps ascending the stairs. Poor Miss Carrie. Everybody's troubles fell on her shoulders. She'd taken this last bit of upset hard. Jane was shaken, her fantasies up-ended. It wasn't that nice Mr Brook as Miss Carrie had set her heart on, but Mr Walker and him without a penny to his name, and not even his name worth much now, probably. It didn't seem right. Her Miss Carrie deserved nothing but the best, even more so than Miss Adele who'd run off with as rich a lover as ever was in a fairy tale, and even if his ma didn't like it, who could be cross for long with such a pretty lady? No, it would be fine linen sheets and silk dresses and sunshine all the way and good luck to her. But it wasn't fair that Miss Carrie should have anything less. She winced at the sound of a great wail from the bedroom. Especially with her left holdin' the baby so to speak. And she *was* nowt but a big soft baby, Mrs O'Hara, as'd need dandling and coddling.

Jane set about her tasks in the kitchen with fierce concentration. It wasn't her place to pass judgements. She was here to do as she was bid. But even if it would be wrong to speak out, she'd show Miss Carrie as she had a friend by doing what

Anne Goring

she could to help her. She laid the tray with extra care, her thin face taut. She found a bit of wet greenery to arrange in a tiny glass vase. The egg was boiled to the second, the toast crisped a warm brown, the small teapot under its cosy, the china cup and saucer with its matching creamer and sugar bowl laid with mathematical precision on the blue cloth. Mrs O'Hara couldn't but be tempted.

She regarded her efforts, satisfied that in her own small way she was pleasing Miss Carrie and, bracing herself against the tray's weight, made her way up the narrow stairs. Pausing outside the door she set her mouth to a smile. Sobbing noises came from within and the gentle murmur of a soothing voice. What a morning for tears this was! Well, she'd go in with a smile on her face if it killed her. She'd always believed if you thought things was going to happen for the best, then they would. Like back at the Home. She'd always staunchly believed that things'd look up, that someday she wouldn't have to be imprisoned by bare walls and harassed and scolded all day and sleep three to a bed by night, and be made to feel that it was a sin to be hungry and every piece of coarse bread or thin gruel or watery soup doled out by the overseers was to be paid for by unremitting toil.

And look! Here she was, escaped, and belonging to a real family. Oh, it was goin' through a bad patch, but it'd soon right itself. Mrs O'Hara would soon realise that she was better off wi'out her nasty old man. Miss Adele would come back and live in the big house and be happy ever after. Miss Carrie would get over bein' struck on Jem Walker and in due time she'd come to like nice Mr Brook who sent her roses. Then they'd marry and go to live in his house and Miss Carrie would say, "But I can't leave Jane. I treasure her above everything . . ." And off she'd go with 'em, to be chief parlourmaid and have striped frocks for mornings and plain ones for afternoons wi' frilly aprons and caps so she could answer the door to grand folks . . .

Her heart expanded in her narrow chest at such visions. Eh, it'd all come true as true. She'd believe it and it would. Her

Bitter Harvest

smile was no longer forced. She rapped on the door and went in, prepared to let all the affection in her starved little soul, spill over to hearten her dear Miss Carrie.

Edmund Brook said, "You should not have come out in such weather. If you had sent a note I would have come to you this evening."

"I thought it better not to wait. I hoped you would be home at this time."

Carrie had arrived at his house just as the hooter sounded in the factory for the dinner break. Now she sat in his study that smelt of old leather and cigars, and he leaned against the mantelpiece and looked down at her, shaking his head in mock dismay.

"It says much for your tender heart that you turn up on my doorstep soaked through to plead my assistance for a friend, when you have trouble enough of your own."

She could not meet his eyes. It was an impertinence to expect him to help her, yet who else was there? Mr Sanderson . . . Mrs Dawes . . . Mr Prince . . . there was no one with authority who could help her now, except the one person she had no right to turn to.

"If it were for myself I would not ask. Jem has been a . . . a brother to me. Mrs Walker is beside herself with worry. You see, Jem is as honest as the day. It must all be some terrible misunderstanding . . . a joke, perhaps, that has misfired . . ." She spread her hands wide then, because she felt them tremble, replaced them in her lap before he should notice. "It is not easy for a woman to go alone, and my aunt is in such a state, that I dare not leave her for long. But I do understand if you do not wish to be involved. And if this is the case, I would beg, Mr Brook, that you would lend me your carriage and the support of your groom." She loathed the admission of weakness. She wanted nothing more than to sweep into town by herself and tear it apart to find Jem. Cold logic told her that doors would close against a woman alone, however desperate. She had no

Anne Goring

authority. She must swallow her pride and ask for the help which would find Jem the quicker.

"There is no question that you go alone. Angel Meadow is no place for a respectable woman. I have to go into town later. I shall look into it for you."

"I . . . I am indebted."

"I promise nothing," he warned. "If he has run off as you say, it may well be that he is guilty."

"But . . ."

"And if he deliberately seeks to hide himself away in the rookeries, there are a thousand places for a thief to hide. It would be an impossibility to try to trace him."

"Jem is not a thief."

"A poor man is always open to temptation."

For a full, clear moment she hated Edmund Brook. She saw him, a dandy even in his everyday clothes, leaning elegantly against the carved mantelpiece, speaking with all the assurance of his background and position.

She half rose. "If you feel so," she said coldly, "I would not presume . . ."

He waved her back. "I scarcely know the young man. I am prepared to take your word that some injustice has occurred." He went to the desk. "I must have names. His employer, Carter Smith, is the aggrieved party? There were witnesses?" She told him all she knew and he wrote it down. Then the housekeeper entered with a laden tray. She made to refuse the bowl of hot soup and the plate of sandwiches. "Eat," he commanded. "It will warm you through."

He fell to chatting of an exhibition of paintings he was to view, of a comic item he had read in the paper, of trivial happenings at the factory, requiring nothing from her but an occasional murmured comment. She found the soup good and nibbled at a sandwich. He poured coffee into thin old china cups. She sipped it, feeling the warmth creep back into her cold hands and feet. Without realising it she was soothed by the quiet room and the light, pleasant voice.

Bitter Harvest

Presently, he said, "Feeling better? Good. You do look a little less like a bedraggled waif bearing all the cares of the world on your shoulders."

Embarrassed, she understood that his earlier sharpness had been due to concern for her. He had no notion of her feelings for Jem. He thought that he was a mere incidental and unnecessary problem that she had taken upon herself. As though to confirm it, he began, diffidently as though his gentle probing might upset her, to question her about Adele and Elliot, about the reaction of Mr and Miss Prince and the Sandersons. She was glad to lay all the facts before him, to confess her suspicions that her uncle might be involved with the elopement and declare her deep-rooted distrust of him.

"You say he had a friend, a Samuel Quick, living in the town?" He added the name to his list. "While I am about this other business, I will make enquiries about Mr Quick. He may have some clue to your uncle's whereabouts."

"They are probably known about the taverns," she said bitterly. "He never came home drunk, as he used to do when we lived in Smedley, but there was a smell of drink on him often enough."

The mantel clock struck the hour.

"I must go," he said, "but please stay and rest as long as you wish."

"I cannot leave my aunt for any longer."

"Then my carriage is at your disposal." His smile was reassuring, his eyes fond as his glance rested upon her. "Take heart. It will all blow over. In a few weeks you will wonder why you were so worried. It is the way of scandals that they erupt like summer storms and disappear as quickly. I do not doubt that Dorothea Sanderson is even now concocting some tale that will enable her to save face and welcome her son and his bride back to the fold."

Remembering her last encounter with Mrs Sanderson Carrie could not envisage it, but she was grateful for his well-meant optimism. She wanted to believe, heaven knows, that all would be well.

Anne Goring

At the door he said, "And I owe you an apology. You guessed, did you not, that all was not well with your sister's engagement. You begged my help before, and if I had acted then, I might have prevented this elopement and spared you this suffering."

"Oh, no," she said quickly. "In no way are you to blame. How could you be?"

"By default. But then that is my nature." He shrugged ruefully. "I have a fatalistic streak. People think me stronger than I am because I take adversity calmly. Where another might rail and battle against the shocks of life, I have never felt the urge for it. My style is to accept, to bend with the wind, to let things ride. It is the more comfortable way."

"And sometimes the best," Carrie replied, feeling the need to speak out because it cut too close to her own private assessment. "You have achieved much in a quiet way."

"But had I taken up more challenges, spoken out more loudly, what more might I have done?" He paused, did not answer his own question but smiled instead. "It seems I need someone like you to stir me into action. Have no fear, Miss Linton. This commission you have put to me I shall take up with vigour. You shall not find me wanting. I shall call upon you this evening."

Then he was gone, leaving her torn with guilt because she had seen the sparkle in his eyes as he went; because she longed to be honest and open with him and dared not yet speak out. But she would. Soon. When this ridiculous, appalling business about Jem was sorted out. She would tell him frankly of her feelings for Jem. Of how, as soon as she was of age, they would marry. Mr Brook must not be allowed to harbour feelings of a romantic nature longer than necessary. Necessary. She knew with a sinking heart she had succumbed to using someone who was a good, kind friend, for her own ends. He had gone willingly to do her bidding. In the jaunty set of his shoulders, the spring in his walk, she had seen his pleasure in the errand. He was glad to be able to do her a favour, doubtless seeing it as another step towards winning her affection.

160

Bitter Harvest

Carrie buried her face in her hands. She was too numb, too harassed for tears. But she felt, suddenly, desperately tired and strangely grubby as though the troubles of the past two days had rubbed against her and left an indelible stain.

"Are you ill, Miss Linton?" The housekeeper hovered.

"No . . . no. I must go now. Would you fetch my cloak and bonnet?"

She would make it up to him. The need for secrecy was not so strong now. Mrs Dawes, whose nose was properly out of joint, would never cast her influence over Aunt Linnie again. Provided Uncle George, like the proverbial bad penny, did not turn up again, his influence, too, would be removed. When Aunt Linnie recovered from her present distress, she would speak to her quietly, make her see that whatever the objections, she and Jem would be wed, and if her aunt would not give her consent, then they were prepared to wait until she was of age. After all, that was scarcely a year and a half. Scarcely. It seemed an interminable stretch of time. When they had spoken of it, she and Jem, they had known it to be a lengthy enough wait, but bearable. Now it seemed a fantastically diminished prospect.

She put on her cloak, steamily damp from the kitchen fire, knotted her bonnet strings, pulled on her gloves, and went out to the waiting carriage. Whatever happened, she would make it up to Mr Brook for his kindness. She would work for him. Help him with his new school project. Support him in all his philanthropic activities. Provide the spur he needed.

The only thing she could not – would not – do, was marry him.

He hated this northern rain. It came, persistent and needle-fine, from a sky so dense and grey that it seemed the sun would never shine again. He ached for the touch of heat on his back, for the storms of his homeland that would fling lightning and thunder and huge warm, drenching raindrops, then sweep away leaving the land to steam languorously under a blue and brilliant sky. From his shelter Mahmood stared at the green dripping trees

Anne Goring

and knew that this was the day. A sore tightness in his chest, a lightness in his head betokened a return of the ague that would hamper him if he delayed. Besides, there had been the dream.

He had been back on that deserted beach where he had been left to die. The old crone was there. "I wait," she said, "to see you again. You must hurry, for time grows short."

She had crooked a bony finger and from among the oleanders growing in the sand, they came floating through the pink blossoms that remained motionless at their passing. His grandmother. His mother. Fatimah. Their faces were stern, their eyes glittered. They swelled to gigantic figures filling the sky. Their enormous shadows drowned the beach. He cowered at their feet. They did not speak but their voices clamoured in his head.

"Yes!" he cried, fearful. "Yes, it will be today."

When he looked again they were gone. Only the old woman remained and even as he looked at her she changed her shape. She was slender and young and beautiful.

"Fatimah," he whispered.

"Not she," she said. And he saw that the long hair hung loose in thick tumbling curls the colour of straw and her eyes were a lustrous blue. And he understood, as is the way of dreams, that the spirit of Fatimah watched through the window of Adele Linton's eyes and spoke through her mouth, though he could not tell what she said because of the wind that swirled the sand about them and muffled her voice. She held out her arms. As a plea? As a warning? But his feet were rooted and the sand devils danced and the figure shrank and bent and became the crone.

Then he was awake and sweating coldly and hearing the hateful rasp of the sodden trees bending in the wind. But the memory of her sadness, her hands held out to him, remained.

Mahmood had not eaten all day. There was no hunger in him. No need to rob the hen coops of the surrounding farms for eggs. No need to hoard the last few grains of rice. He had thrown them into the springing ferns, then taken out the kris and placed it carefully in his belt. He remade his bundle and squatted beside it. The hours passed and he watched the fine,

Bitter Harvest

cold rain sifting down, collecting into droplets along twigs and leaves, congealing into large pearls that bulged and fell into slow spreading puddles among the grass roots. He was filled, body and mind, with purpose. His spirit was coiled like a cobra, tense, waiting for the moment to strike.

When grey day turned to grey dusk he rose stiffly and kneaded life back into his chilled fingers. He pulled his hat well down and with his hand protectively on the hilt of the kris, he made his ungainly way from the wood.

Dolly Sanderson sat at her writing desk. She'd had it moved to the dressing room that linked her bedroom with Miles's and had spent a painful hour composing a letter to Lady Gordon. Even so, it was very short. The eating of humble pie was alien to her nature. She skimmed impatiently through the placatory phrases. It was unsatisfactory, but it would have to do. Tomorrow she would put the whole matter in the hands of the lawyers. Elliot had said that he had already written to poor Margaret. Heaven knows what impassioned, compromising rubbish he had put on paper. No doubt the injured parties would make the most of it. Expensively. Still, that was of small importance. She would have paid ten times as much for the wedding to have gone ahead.

She sealed the letter and laid it aside. Then she picked up the other, that lay open on the desk. This letter, addressed to her, bore the evidence of travel. She held it to the lamp for the cramped writing was hard to decipher. When she had read it through she leaned her elbows on the desk and put her head in her hands. If she had been a woman prone to tears, this was the moment when she would have given way. Pereira's letter, innocent enough on the surface, held an undertone she alone understood. '. . . *If you would use your influence with your esteemed husband . . . the agent is being tiresomely adamant . . . the land lies idle and I have plans . . . your old property is taken by a vulgar family . . . speaking of days past, I had word of a servant once in your employ . . . I am sure that your esteemed husband and your son would be interested in news of him . . . I*

Anne Goring

trust you will communicate by return mail, my dear madam, that Mr Sanderson will release the land . . .'

It was the last straw. It brought the past rushing back. Everything she had tried to suppress. All the dark, whirling thoughts that she kept closeted away. She saw Pereira's hooded eyes, his smiling pink-wet lips under the pencil moustache . . . *'The person in question will trouble you no further . . . if I should at some future time seek a favour . . .'*

Her mind flew back in time. She was a bride again, excited, standing on deck watching England's coastline fade to a smudge, resolved to make the most of new opportunities and be a good wife to raffish, unreliable Tom, who promised a whole new world. She was a child, amid other children, who danced round her pointing fingers. 'Your ma's a whore', and some adult, a teacher, driving them off and wiping her tears. And another teacher, prunes and prisms, pursing her narrow lips, 'Your mother has met with an accident . . . the carriage overturned. Broke her neck instantly.' Her beautiful, black-haired mamma broken in the dust like a cast-off doll. 'There is no money now for your board with us. You are to be apprenticed.' The milliner's shop, the hours and hours under the skylight. Plumes and feathers. Silk and straw. Winters, summers. All childhood gone, cramped on a hard stool, fingers forever at work. Someone's voice, a man's, 'A girl like you deserves better than that.' Men's eyes, narrowed, greedy, men's hands touching, fondling. Her bewilderment. her fear. Her acceptance. Her realisation that her face, her body, her wits, were weapons.

She would not be used, she would use them. The ones who did not matter. The ones who had signposted her upward struggle. The groping grocer's boy, the ink-stained clerk, the gay and penniless young officer, the tea merchant who had wanted to set her up in a discreet apartment and who had introduced her to Tom. And Tom, who had offered her his name, worthless as it was. Tom, who had left her to cope with the ruins of his shady dealings. Robert Linton who had helped to dig her out of the mess, a cheerful, golden young man, dazzlingly handsome,

Bitter Harvest

always a different girl on his arm. 'I'm off after this. Home for a breath of honest English damp. Who knows, I might find myself a bride! A rosy country miss, not like the spoiled, idle chatterers they import to these latitudes. There's an offer I might take up later. Not here, though. Had enough of islands. Malacca, perhaps.' His wide angelic grin. The warning in his eyes she hadn't wanted to see. Had pretended not to see. That last glimpse of him at the ship's rail. Turning away, knowing his eyes were already on different horizons.

Then Miles, whom Robert Linton – fate? – had brought before her and she had ruthlessly pursued. He was her triumph. She had employed, without remorse, every trick, every artifice she had acquired. He had slipped, a fine fat fish, into her silken net, without even realising she had cast it, for he was in some ways a simple man, despite his shrewdness in business. He adored her as only a lonely man of middle years could. Their whirlwind courtship and marriage had rescued him just as he was beginning to settle for the contented dull routines that would tip him comfortably towards old age.

She had brought youth and all its accompanying energy, ambition, gaiety, selfishness and impulsiveness to the marriage. His gift had been steadiness, devotion and the wealth to satisfy his great generosity. It pleased him to shower her with jewels and clothes. It pleased her to show her dark exotic looks to their best advantage. It was flattering to see the flare of interest in a man's eyes, but never, she had sworn it, would she be unfaithful to Miles. There was too much at stake. From within the secure framework of their marriage she might peep outside and, occasionally, feel the darts of temptation, but she did not succumb. What she had achieved was too precious. She had remained a true and faithful wife to Miles. She had given him a son. She had given him companionship. It had never been, could not possibly have been, love, but it had become a deep quiet affection. All her tremendous devotion was reserved for Elliot. Elliot. She swept to her feet and began a swift tigerish pacing about the small room.

165

Anne Goring

Why, now, after all these comfortable years had her victory turned to ashes? Why was the whole careful framework of her life crumbling like termite-infested wood – hale on the outside, but falling to dust when touched? Like Elliot's ghastly *mésalliance* with that girl whose gilded beauty was so much a reflection of her father's that even after all these years it aroused too much painful sensation. And even Miles, who was the anchor of her life, but even he was lying pitifully frail in the adjoining bedroom.

"He is gravely ill," the doctor had said this afternoon, the sympathy in his expression saying more than his careful words. "His heart is affected."

"But he has ailed for years and always recovered. He has a strong constitution."

"He is an elderly man, remember. Time has taken its toll. Of course, we must always hope for an optimistic outcome, but the slightest excitement or worry now might be fatal. I shall leave you medicine and pills for the pain."

She had looked at Miles's sleeping face on the pillow. Really looked. She saw the nose jutting bony white against the sallow-grey skin, the tinge of blue at the lips, the hollowed cheeks. An old man. She felt the chill of guilt. While she had been so preoccupied with her plans for Elliot, jaunting about the country, her husband had quietly been sliding from her. As she looked, his eyes flickered open. Focusing upon her, he smiled.

"You have a face as long as a fiddle," he murmured. "It is no face to bring to a sickbed. Cheer up, my love. Those two silly children have caused you a lot of distress, but you must be philosophical. It may turn out well enough if we give them our love and support."

Dolly held his dry hand. How like him to be more concerned for her than for himself.

"I have put them quite out of my mind," she lied.

"Good. Then I shall sleep easier." His lids closed on the animation that had briefly made his face seem younger.

This evening she had sent the valet away yawning, dismissed

166

Bitter Harvest

her own maid. She was irritated by their hovering attentions. She would sit with Miles herself tonight. She was too restless to sleep, anyway. She stopped her pacing, snatched up Pereira's letter with all its insinuating reminders, then tossed it impatiently back on the desk. Pereira would have to wait. When Miles was stronger. If he recovered . . . No! She would not think 'if'. It was too easy a trap to slip into. If she had not done this or that . . . if she had not been the daughter of a whore . . . if she had not married Tom . . . if she had not met Robert Linton . . . or Miles. Most of all, if she had not submitted to that moment of weakness and gone to visit Robert's daughters, tried to do something for them . . . everything would be altered.

A sound sent her to Miles's door, but he still slept, his breathing loud and uneven. He would be rousing soon and she must give him the pills the doctor had left and heat him some milk on the spirit stove.

She moved from the door and stopped, her hand leaping to her heart. For a moment she thought crazily that some apparition had appeared to haunt her, as the small ragged figure loped towards her from the door to her bedroom. The lamplight threw a lurching shadow over the wall and, hysterically, she wondered if ghosts had shadows before common sense told her that they most certainly did not and this was an intruder of a more earthly sort.

The figure lifted his head so that the lamplight fell onto the face under the wide-brimmed hat. The voice, when it spoke, was measured.

"Good evening, *mem*," it said. "I have waited long for this meeting. You remember me? I am Mahmood bin Ahmed and I was once the body servant of *Tuan* Elliot in Penang. Ah, I see you do remember."

The scream choked in Dolly's throat.

"No, I do not look pretty, *mem*. I frighten people." He coughed painfully. "Please, look hard at me. See what you have done."

Was she dreaming? Had she fallen asleep at her desk and

167

been gripped by a nightmare conjured up by Pereira's letter? The panicky thudding of her heart was real enough, the pain of her nails biting into her palms. But this grotesque figure with the glittering eye, surely it was a dream spectre. He lunged towards her and caught her wrist. His touch was burning hot and his breath was a ragged wheeze in his chest.

It was Mahmood. He was here, flesh and blood. Shockingly, horribly real.

He turned his head and the smooth unmarked side of his face seemed scarcely altered. She had a fleeting picture of him, lithe, supple-limbed, moving through the green garden at Elliot's side, the two of them laughing at some private joke, both of them careless in their youth and health. Years ago. A lifetime ago. But this ruined creature did not laugh. He spat out his story, Fatimah's story, in foul gutter language, defiling her ears and her senses.

She was a head taller than Mahmood and a strong woman. But she did not struggle. Shock held her immobile. Shock and a dark uncharacteristic flood of guilt and shame that she could not control. It enfeebled her. Her brain seemed incapable of commanding her limbs to throw him off, to reach for the bell pull, to call for help. All she could do was stand there helplessly, paralysed, and listen and imagine what it had been like for him and know that she and Pereira had long ago sowed the seeds of this terrible moment.

His voice droned to silence. The lamp flame guttered, sending shadows leaping dizzily about the room. Her legs were woolly and weak. If he let go of her wrist she would sink to the floor at his feet.

But he did not let go. With a vicious wrench he twisted her arm behind her back, pressing himself close against her. His smell was rank, coming at her in febrile waves. She turned her head, nauseated, and something cold and metallic laid itself against her cheek forcing her head back again.

He held the knife in front of her eyes, speaking now in his own language, his voice rising and falling. An incantation? A

Bitter Harvest

prayer? She caught his sister's name, repeated over and over, but her shaky knowledge of Malay could not untangle the rest of the tumble of words. Her eyes were fixed hypnotically on the kris. She could see the curving flow of the carving on the handle, the finely honed blade that hovered within inches of her face.

Abruptly he broke off. "Now," he said. "Now you die. As Fatimah die."

She understood. It was justice. Crude, savage justice. Almost, almost she welcomed it. The brief thrust. Pain. Oblivion. Everything over. She swayed, mesmerised by the knife, his presence, her guilt. No more anger, sorrow, regret.

Mahmood moved the kris slowly, lovingly. The edge of the blade touched her neck. She saw the exultation on his mutilated face. Pleasure and satisfaction burned in his eyes. He had followed her over continents and seas for this. For him it was consummation of a fearful lust, but it was revenge and not love that had driven him to this deadly ravishment.

The blade caressed her flesh and she felt the warm slither of blood on her neck. She heard her own voice, detached, unemotional. "Mahmood, forgive me. I had not meant any harm to you or your family."

"Be silent!"

"I did it for Elliot. I wanted only the best for him. Everything has been for him. Can you understand a mother's love for her only child? You and Fatimah were taking him from me, leading him down roads I could not follow . . . Forgive a mother's jealousy, Mahmood."

"Fatimah died for this . . . this *love*. I was made a thing of shame."

"The shame is mine."

The knife trembled at her throat.

"You speak too much."

Her head was clearing. The will to survive was surging up. "I had never meant Pereira to do more than take you from the island."

"Pereira!" He ducked his head and spat.

169

Anne Goring

"He cheated me. He cheated you. I should not have trusted him. He preyed upon a mother's distress. My son was attracted to your sister. Should I have allowed that to go on?"

The cry was torn from him. "You killed her!"

"Not I. Pereira." She saw his glance flicker but his hand still held her in a cruel grip, the knife still rested at her throat. "I am a proud woman, Mahmood. I shall not beg for mercy. I shall not struggle. Does that please you? Would you rather I struggled more? If you kill me, will it bring Fatimah back to you? Will it bring your mother, your grandmother to life? Will anything ever be the same again?"

The blade pressed in. She winced, but her eyes were steely. "My blood will be on your hands."

"I do not care. It is right that you should die by this kris."

"Kill me then." Dolly lifted her chin, baring the column of her throat. The kris trembled, red-tipped against the pale skin. She felt his muscles tense for the final thrust. She was quite calm. "Why do you delay? Do you play cat and mouse with me, or does Fatimah's hand hold yours back because she, above everyone, knows that you do wrong."

"No," he cried. "No. My dreams . . . they tell me . . ."

A hoarse cry sawed the air. For a moment, frozen like a tableau, they hung together – the tall woman, the ragged, misshapen man – then they fell apart, the woman turning and running, the man crumbling in defeat. A dancing doll, its strings severed, falling to a corner, forgotten.

"Miles," she cried. "Miles!"

He tottered in the doorway, his hand clawing at the breast of his nightshirt. His mouth was open, his eyes aghast.

"Lean on me! You should not be out of bed. Oh, my dear!"

"That man. The knife . . . I heard . . . voices."

"It is all over. He will do no more harm. Come back to bed."

"The pain . . ."

His whole weight reeled against her. She could not hold him and he slid to his knees. She knelt beside him, supporting his

Bitter Harvest

shoulders, calling his name. His breathing rasped, stopped, rasped again. He moved his head so that he could see into her face. His lips formed her name and his hand lifted as though he would touch her, then dropped back, half uncurled, relaxed upon the thick pile of the carpet.

She left him then, ran to the bell pull, flew back to cover him with a quilt, cradled his head in her lap. She was still sitting so when the valet touched her on the shoulder.

"Come, madam. There is nothing more to be done."

He helped her to a chair. Other servants were gathering, drawn by tragedy. Someone pressed a glass into her hand and she drank, the spirit making her cough but not touching the dizzying violent emptiness in her breast. The world reeled about her full of echoing voices. Hands held her, forced brandy again between her lips.

Miles. Miles.

She summoned strength, pushed away the glass. "I am quite all right. Pray do not treat me as a child." The coldness in her voice reassured her. She was not about to break down in front of the servants.

Mrs Price, dabbing at her cheeks, asked, "What shall we do about this . . . this person, madam?"

Mahmood was alone in the corner, circled by the drawn-back skirts of the maids who looked at him with curious horror.

Dolly looked at him contemptuously. "There is no need to be afraid of him. He is dirty, but quite harmless." She saw his shoulders twitch. She had beaten him. Even before Miles had called out she had already won her victory. He had hesitated too long. The victory was a joyless one. She did not care one jot for him and his vengeance. She flicked her elegant fingers. "Take him away and give him food. Let him sleep in the stables. Anything. Only I do not wish to set eyes on him again."

He went with the men, bowed, limp, and she wondered how she had thought herself in danger from such a poor broken thing.

Presently, when all had been attended to discreetly, she dismissed the servants. There was no point in calling the

Anne Goring

doctor tonight. All the formalities could be attended to first thing in the morning. Miles lay on his bed, calm, at rest. She put her lips to his cold forehead then softly left the room. Crossing the dressing room her foot kicked against something that spun away and hit a chair leg. The kris. Distastefully she picked it up. A rusty stain marred its silvery perfection. She took it into her bedroom, raised the window. The cool night air swept clammily against her face. She threw the kris out and it fell with a rustle and thud into the thick wet shrubbery below. Then she lowered the window, firmly drew the curtains and prepared to begin her mourning in privacy.

Aunt Linnie had insisted on getting up once she knew Mr Brook might call. All day she had lain in her room with the blinds drawn. Sometimes she was racked with sobbing. Sometimes she lay staring at nothing. In between she berated Carrie. "Had I not taken in two motherless girls," she wailed, over and over, "I should have had none of this distress." And, "Once dear George and I were so happy in our little cottage . . ." Time and expediency seemed to have drawn a veil over all that Aunt Linnie had suffered at the hands of her husband. Carrie sat by her aunt's bed and concentrated on her patchwork. Her needle dipped in and out of the cheerful cotton squares. She spoke soothingly when it seemed some answer was required, otherwise she sat in silence, letting the flow of complaint wash past her.

She had explained her absence at noon, speaking lightly. "Poor Mrs Walker was distraught . . . I felt I must do something for her."

"It is as I would have expected," Aunt Linnie sighed. "You care more for the feelings of other people than for those closest to you. You left me alone, but I am of no account, I quite see that."

"Jane sat with you until I returned."

"An ignorant serving girl! But then, youth has no notion of the sufferings of age . . ."

Bitter Harvest

To cut short the catalogue of woe, Carrie said, "Mr Brook is kindly calling this evening to let me know the results of his enquiries. He also promised to try and contact Uncle George's friend, Mr Quick."

Aunt Linnie's head moved sharply on the pillow. For a few seconds Carrie glimpsed, behind the façade of self-pity, real despair.

"Do you think he will have news of George's whereabouts?"

Carrie gently touched the hand that fretted the sheet. "If he finds Mr Quick, maybe so. But, of course, we do not know his address. It may take time."

Aunt Linnie bowed her head. In a quiet voice she said, "I shall get up later. If Mr Brook has news then I must hear it directly from him." Then, quickly, pettishly. "How my head aches. Give me my lavender water. Quickly, now. It is like knives behind my poor eyes."

As soon as the tea tray was removed she insisted that Carrie help her dress in her dullest gown of grey wool. Wreathed about with equally grizzled shawls, she lay on the sofa the picture of melancholia, opening her eyes only to send covert glances at the clock.

Mr Brook arrived as they were beginning to believe he would not come. Aunt Linnie started up as she heard the rap on the door, but had settled back with an expression of profound suffering on her face by the time he came into the room.

"My dear Mrs O'Hara," he said, taking her limp hand. "How are you?"

"Very low," she said in a pale voice.

"A person of your sensibilities is bound to be deeply grieved by all that has happened."

Linnie raised soulful eyes. "You are so understanding Mr Brook."

Carrie thought he was unbearably long-winded over the pleasantries. He took an age to settle himself, to accept a glass of wine, to remark on its quality. He cleared his throat but seemed to be finding it difficult to choose the right words.

Anne Goring

It was Aunt Linnie who finally prompted him. "Well, Mr Brook? What have you to tell us?"

He sighed. "Nothing to your advantage, I regret, ma'am."

"Did you find Mr Quick?"

"I learned something of . . . of the person in question."

"But did you not meet him? Is it likely that you will? Did you discover where he lives?"

Mr Brook emptied his glass and placed it on the table at his side. His expression was troubled. "Mrs O'Hara," he said heavily. "I fear that I must be brutal. There is no such person as Mr Quick. He was a figment of Mr O'Hara's imagination."

"But how can that be!" She had forgotten, momentarily, her role as invalid and raised herself indignantly upright amid the cushions. "George spoke of him often. He was a strange, solitary sort of gentleman . . ."

"Very strange," he said dryly. "Your husband – and believe me it grieves me greatly to have to tell you this, my dear lady – was the frequent and long-standing escort of one Sally Quick, a female of some ill-repute in Angel Meadow. They were a well-known couple about the taverns and yesterday morning they left town together."

"It cannot be." Aunt Linnie's voice was dry as a husk. Her hand trembled at her throat. At that moment, she looked every inch the invalid.

"They hired a boy with a handcart to push their baggage to Deansgate where a closed carriage was waiting for them. This boy, a sharp-eared urchin, heard them talking. Liverpool was mentioned more than once and when Mr O'Hara paid the lad he advised him on the advantages of striking out in a different country where there were opportunities for young people who were prepared to work hard. He said that all he needed to do was to raise the price of a steerage passage to New York or Sydney and a fortune would be in his grasp. He himself was expecting to become rich and successful within the year. Mr O'Hara, I gather, can be a persuasive gentleman. The lad was much impressed." He paused. "It seems from the evidence I

Bitter Harvest

have gathered that your husband is bound for either America or Australia with his paramour. I am deeply sorry."

The silence was long and heavy with the dark visions Mr Brook's words had conjured up. Presently Aunt Linnie, recovering from the initial shock, said in a soft voice, "Thank you, Mr Brook. Thank you for your frankness." There was no play-acting now. No vapours. No tears. "It is best that I know. For certain. You see, I often suspected . . . no, that is too definite . . . I feared that I, that our marriage was not enough to hold him." She smiled, a ghostly little grimace. "I was once considered the pretty one, you know. My sister, Caroline's mamma, was clever, but I had the looks. When George first saw me . . . well, I was different to the poor creature you see before you now, Mr Brook." With a wave of her hand she dismissed his polite protests. "The mirror tells me the truth, only I preferred not to listen. I have lived in a cloud of self-deception these last years. I have pretended to myself that George was as affectionate a husband as any woman could wish for, that we had settled to a . . . comfortable relationship." She raised stricken eyes. "In my heart I always knew this day would come. The bonds that held our marriage together had grown weak. No, no! I play the game still, you see! I will be honest. Apart from the beginning, the very start of our marriage, when I lost our first child, George has despised me." Her voice broke piteously. "It is only surprising that he stayed so long . . ."

Carrie flew to the sofa. She put her arms round her aunt's shoulders, murmuring words of comfort. Aunt Linnie leaned against her, the tears coursing freely down her cheeks.

"You have been a good girl, Caroline," she said brokenly. "I have not meant to be sharp with you, but I always knew that you did not approve of George. That grieved me . . . but you were right."

"Do not speak of it. It is all in the past."

"It is worse than being widowed, do you see that? To lose one's husband to . . . a . . . a strumpet. To know that you have failed, bitterly failed, at the most important task in a

175

Anne Goring

woman's life – marriage, children. It is humiliation of the deepest kind."

"Aunt Linnie, dear, the fault is all his. It was ill-luck that ever brought him to the cottage. You are better without him."

"It would seem so," she said, "yet should he knock at the door now I would take him back. And gladly." The tears had stopped and a look of sad resignation had spread across her face. "It is a weakness I cannot help. Pray, Mr Brook, do not think too badly of me for it."

"Though the subject may be unworthy, such loyalty of affection does you credit, Mrs O'Hara," he said gravely.

"I think I shall retire now, if you will excuse me."

Mr Brook rose as Carrie helped her aunt from the sofa. "And I must be off home. It has been a long day."

Carrie said, "You have gone to a great deal of trouble on our behalf. Thank you for coming, Mr Brook." And then, calmly, as an afterthought, "Did you discover anything of Jem Walker?"

The look on Mr Brook's face as he shook his head caused a bleak sinking in her stomach.

"I was less successful there. There is little more to tell than you know already."

He spoke briefly of his investigations; he did not enlarge on his thoughts or feelings. It was scarcely the time to worry two ladies already under a considerable emotional strain. Caroline, as he had found out, took everyone's troubles to her own tender heart. But there was certainly something odd about the whole business. Carter Smith had not struck him as a man wronged. His bluster, his talk of trust and betrayal, was too loud and prolonged. Under it all there was a false note. He had strutted about his cupboard of an office and Edmund had watched him sharply, noting the fidgeting hands, the glance that never quite met his own. Altogether he seemed to Edmund to be a man trying to justify his action, rather than one who was convinced that the action had been right. But nothing would shift him. In the end he had terminated the interview curtly, pleading an appointment elsewhere. He had scuttled from his office like a trapped animal

Bitter Harvest

making an escape. Edmund had slowly followed him out and, seeing one of the carts coming into the yard, had spoken to the driver. He was a grizzled, rough fellow and cautious.

"I've said me piece to Master an' got a flea in me ear for it," he grumbled.

"He is not here now," Edmund said briskly, "and I assure you that any information will be treated in the strictest confidence."

"It isn't that I know owt, but I speak as I find. I know Jem Walker to be an honest and hard-workin' lad. Allus has been, since he come here as a nipper."

"Then what is your opinion? Was someone playing a prank that went amiss? Did someone bear a grudge?"

"Mebbe. None of us in the yard, though," he said with an aggressive thrust of his chin. " 'Course there was a bit o' grumbling when we knew t'lad was to be made up to overseer, but that died down after a bit. We all agreed on the rightness of it. He has the book-learnin' y'see. The only ones I don't trust are them in there." He jerked his head in the direction of the office.

"The clerk?" He had noticed the man scratching away industriously at his ledgers.

"He wouldn't have t'guts. A toady that one."

"Who else? Can you mean Carter Smith?"

The man folded his arms across his broad chest. "I bin with him man and boy. He's mean as muck and henpecked into the bargain. His missus is a sour old cat who wouldn't give you the dirt from her fingernails, fine church-goin' woman that she is. But wi' airs. Can't live 'ere where the work an' muck is. Must have a better place where the toffs is, out at Broughton. I reckon as mebbe master has overreached hisself. All this talk o' takin' on a new place, making Jem up to overseer – well, either 'im or his missus has decided to cut a few corners."

"I cannot think he would concoct such a disgraceful way of dismissing an employee."

"Save 'im paying wages and writin' a character," he said

Anne Goring

triumphantly. "Savin' ha'pennies is Carter Smith's reason for living."

Edmund shook his head. The man meant well but he was not overly intelligent. Perhaps he needed to remove suspicion from himself and his workmates, or harboured some long-standing grudge against his master. Impossible to tell. Yet he could not rid himself of the suspicion that Carter Smith knew something about the business and was not prepared to tell. And, perhaps, against all opinions, Jem was not as innocent as he had set himself to be.

He said, "Thank you. I shall bear your opinion in mind."

"You'll not say as I've spoken," said the man hastily, obviously wondering if he'd said too much. "I 'as a wife and childer. I'd lose me job . . ."

"You have my word. This is for your help." He produced a coin, watching the eyes brighten. But the man, stubbornly, would not take it. "I only speak me mind because Jem isn't 'ere to speak for hisself."

"Then you may earn the money – and more – for your aid in another matter. You know the district well. Do you know someone called Quick?"

"Sally Quick?" The man threw his head back, roaring with laughter. "Who don't know Sally Quick I'd like to know. Why, her granny lives just here and a right foul-mouthed old critter . . ."

"No, you mistake me, one Samuel Quick. Does this lady have a brother?"

It did not take long to discover that Sally Quick had no male relatives. They visited old Granny Quick in her cubbyhole where she spat the information that Sal, curse her soul had abandoned her and gone to seek her fortune overseas. Later the man, Harry, took Edmund to some of the murkiest taverns and beerhouses in the town. "Don't open your mouth, sir. Let me do the talking. Toffs don't go down well in these parts."

Edmund, wrapped in a musty old greatcoat Harry had given him did not feel at all the ton, but knew the wisdom of the advice. Even

Bitter Harvest

Harry was treated with suspicion and tongues were loosened only when coins were quietly exchanged. When the whole sorry story had been pieced together they retreated thankfully from the stews, Harry scratching himself and remarking cheerfully that you never got away from Angel Meadow without a few fleas for company.

Edmund felt saddened and sickened. Not for himself but because Carrie and her aunt, for so long and so innocently, had been in the company of such a man as George O'Hara. A man who consorted with the dregs of the town. He had seen the painted whores, heard their coarse laughter and lewd jests in the stifling dimness of the low drinking houses. Seen the ageing, diseased ones, creeping like shadows from the alleys. Pitiful and disgusting. Sally Quick, one of this painted evil band, had been O'Hara's companion. O'Hara had taken the taint of wickedness back to his home. That such corruption should have touched Caroline, however lightly, made him shudder. He longed for the day when he could take her under his protection. To love and to cherish.

She was looking at him now with those great grey eyes dark against the pallor of her skin.

"So that is all I know. Harry from the yard will contact me if he hears anything. But to all intents and purposes Jem Walker has disappeared into thin air and I am afraid that the longer he chooses to stay away the blacker the case will seem against him."

Carrie did not speak. He took up his hat and bowed. "I will bid you goodnight. I shall call again tomorrow if it is convenient."

She regarded him steadily. "Of course, Mr Brook. I shall look to see you. And if you bring me news of Jem, then that will make your visit even more welcome, for though you may harbour suspicion of him, I shall never do so. I know he is innocent and I shall go on believing that whatever other people say. Goodnight to you, Mr Brook."

The door closed firmly behind him. He stood out in the windy

Anne Goring

darkness feeling that he had been rebuked. He smiled. She was a child, still, in some ways. She saw life in terms of black and white and not in the indeterminate shades of grey that he had learned was the predominant colour. He hoped for her sake that her trust in Jem Walker was not abused. He could not help but doubt. But even if her loyalty was misplaced, such constancy and trust was something that caused his own admiration of her to grow greater than ever.

Chapter Seven

IT WAS an exceptionally wet season, everyone agreed. April showers had merged into day after day of drizzle and the May flowers, proverbially encouraged, sagged miserably in the gardens of cottage and mansion alike. Rivers and streams swelled and overflowed. Watermeadows became vast shallow lakes. Fledgelings squawked miserably from wet hedges, and carts and carriages bogged down in miry lanes.

There were those who felt that the weeping skies formed a suitable backcloth for events.

Mr and Miss Prince did not mention Adele's name. In fact there was little conversation at all in the tall, cold house that smelt more and more musty with every damp day. Returning from the bank, Mr Prince tended to lock himself away in his study. Miss Prince declared her rheumatics to be most painful, which prevented her from making calls on her friends and declining to see the few who, out of curiosity, were driven to call on her. She allowed herself the luxury of a small fire in her bedroom and comforted herself by making the life of the maid a misery. Mr Prince's clerks at the bank, never the most ebullient of men, grew even more pale and subdued and viewed the looming approach of their employer with the greatest nervousness. The old goat, ever ready to dock wages for the smallest mistake, was more than usually irascible.

Mrs Dawes decided that a change of scene was called for. She busied herself in writing to a cousin in Hertfordshire, harassing the dressmaker over new wardrobes for the girls, overseeing the packing and repacking of every portmanteau

Anne Goring

to her satisfaction. She paused long enough to feel a pang of real emotion over the death of Miles Sanderson, but with one thing and another she was not up to attending upon his wife. Mr Dawes would represent the family at the funeral. She wrote a long and flowery letter to Dorothea mentioning, in the kindest manner, how grieved she was also to hear that Elliot, while away visiting, had been taken very ill. At such a time one's family was the greatest comfort and it was doubly sad that her bereavement had coincided with her son's absence and indisposition.

Such a stupid story to have put about when all the district knew of the scandal! Several embroidered versions had already reached her ears, the most highly coloured hinting that Elliot had got the girl with child and they had fled to the East Indies. For once, Charlotte Dawes had taken no part in these speculations. She listened and tut-tutted and made haste to change the subject. Deep down she was humiliated and enraged. That chit of a girl! Causing such loss of face to so many persons. Most bitter of all her thoughts was the discomfitting one that a girl of doubtful background and upbringing had swept the catch of the district from under the noses of her betters.

It was best not to dwell on it. Best to keep busy and smiling and making plans. After all, there was a regiment of cavalry stationed close to her cousin's home town. They had enlivened the winter season there considerably. One of her girls might easily catch the eyes of some dashing officer. And by the time they returned, all this present unpleasantness would have been forgotten and she would be able to look Miss Prince in the eye again.

It was undeniably appropriate weather for a funeral. Mrs Sanderson's iron composure was admired as she moved, heavily veiled, through the ceremony. Carrie and Aunt Linnie peeped from behind the drawn blinds of the lodge to watch the cortège pass. Mrs Walker joined a respectful knot of people at the cemetery gates. She viewed the black horses, the nodding

Bitter Harvest

plumes, the solemn, rich splendour of it all, and when the last mourner had splashed past, she turned away silently. There was much to do and she was glad of it. There was constant demand for her remedies for aching joints, for sniffles and coughs and fevers. Besides, many of the low-lying cottages were already being encroached upon by the swirling, filthy, debris-laden waters of the Irk. There was always someone begging help to move precious possessions to upper rooms, or livestock to a less vulnerable spot.

If Mahmood knew anything of the funeral it was only in his more lucid moments, when he overheard the grooms gossiping in the stables below. Most of the time he burned and tossed on his bed of hay in the loft where they had put him. Faces came and went through his delirium – the kindly one of the groom who saw to his bodily needs and steadied his head to help him drink, others less so, who came to peer and make comments and wonder about him. He was a source of curiosity to the servants. In his fever he called out to them but he spoke Malay and they laughed at his heathen gibberish. Jane, who had struck up a joking friendship with the gardener's lads, was taken up to look at him. She had never seen anyone so ugly and maimed. She felt sorry for him and roundly told the lads not to make mock of him.

"He don't understand," they jeered. "He's a savage from some foreign place. Anyways, he's not long for this world, is he?"

"More shame on you then for tormentin' him!" She slapped away the stick one of them was poking in Mahmood's ribs. "It isn't Christian to treat 'im as if he was a peepshow. Now let me out of 'ere for I won't stop another minute."

Chastened they followed her down the ladder. In the following days bowls of soup and dainty egg dishes were carried to the stable loft, though the poor heathen was hardly able to swallow at first. But, gradually, he began to pick up.

Jane told Miss Carrie, of course, because she thought this curious bit of news would interest her, she bein' fastened up with Mrs O'Hara who wouldn't let her out of her sight for

Anne Goring

more'n a few minutes. It was Miss Carrie who suggested the titbits but there was something a bit lacking in her kindness, as though she didn't rightly care. And that wasn't like Miss Carrie. Jane knew she was still frettin' because nothing had been heard of Jem Walker. She chatted cheerfully enough with Mrs O'Hara, keeping her amused by the hour, although often she wasn't really listening to Mrs O'Hara's replies, but staring off into space as though her mind was far away. The sparkle was gone from her eyes and there was a sharp, pale look to her that grieved Jane. The only time the sparkle came back was when Mr Brook called – and it wasn't for the right reasons, Jane knew, but because she was hoping Mr Brook would tell her Jem was found. Mr Brook never did and the hopeful look died away as quickly as it had risen.

Still, Jane thought optimistically, Mr Brook was a persistent gentleman. He'd win through in the end. He called most days, even if it were but for a minute or two, and his visits were a bright spot in the long hours. Even when Mrs Walker called she brought nowt but a gloomy face and she didn't stop long and the intervals between her visits grew longer. Jane was glad, for Miss Carrie was always strung-up and restless after she'd gone.

Jane maintained a loyal silence with the gardener's lads who were always on at her for bits of gossip. It wasn't for her to go spreadin' all Miss Carrie's troubles about the district. If only some word would come from Miss Adele that would cheer everybody up. But the postman went by, on up to the big house. As did all the various soberly clad gentlemen. Seeing to Mrs Sanderson's affairs, Miss Carrie said, solicitors and that. But no business gentleman came rapping on their door. Only the rain pattered ceaselessly down the doors and windows in sad, persistent trickles, like tears. Miserable old weather. If summer'd come, if the sun shone a bit, things would look a lot different.

But even Jane's optimism began to be quenched as wet day followed on wet day and summer seemed a long way off.

*   *   *

Bitter Harvest

The young man they called Moses, because they had found him, on his makeshift raft, caught among the reeds, began to take notice of his surroundings. The first thing his eyes focused upon was the slope of the ceiling, then the odd angles of the room itself. An attic, he thought sluggishly, barely furnished but spotless. A patchwork quilt over his legs, rag rugs on the shining bare boards, flowery print curtains at the tiny window. Rain beyond and sparrows squabbling under the overhang of thatch. He could smell lavender from the sheets drawn up to his chin; he rested on a comforting feather bed.

People he did not know came and went: a round, ruddy-faced man in heavy boots, tiptoeing in and making an awkward job of it. A familiar smell. Stables? Horses? And women, the elder, plump but brisk, talking to him all the time she was in the room, even though his head hurt and what she said made no sense. The young one – a servant? – brought trays, helped to feed him. The two women bathed him, dressed his wounds, changed sheets, changed the night shirt he wore, moving him with kindly firmness. He tried not to groan because he learned that this distressed them, but sometimes he could not help it.

It was a dream state, something between sleeping and waking. He was glad to sleep to escape the constant pain that lived with him day and night, but as the pain began to ease he woke more often. It was difficult to speak at first. His lips would not respond and his jaw would not unlock. But presently his strange grunts formed themselves into the shape of words.

He saw this pleased the women. As his head cleared he began to take in the sense of the older one's talk. Her name was Mrs Dalton. The young one, skinny and dark, was their maid Susan. Mr Dalton was a farmer. His land went down to the Irwell and he had found this battered young man one morning washed in among the reeds. He had been carried to the farmhouse on a litter. Mrs Dalton had bright round eyes like a bird's. She looked a bit like a robin with her red cotton pinafore over her brown dress.

Anne Goring

"Tell us about yourself, lad," she coaxed. "What's your name? We can't keep on calling you Moses, can we?"

He tried. He wanted so much to help.

"Can't you remember anything, love?" she asked, disappointed. "How did you come to be in such a case? You was sorely hurt, you know and it's a miracle you're mendin' as well as you are. Well, no matter. It'll come in good time."

It occupied all his waking moments now, this puzzle. As his strength seeped back he realised how strange it was. It gave him a strange, unpleasant sensation in his mind to come up against a blank about his past. Yet there were things he knew. He knew about horses. When farmer Dalton spoke of the two he owned, he immediately understood and could form intelligent questions. And he could read. Mrs Dalton took to sitting of an evening by his bed, proudly reading passages from the Bible to him and verses from the other book she held dear, a volume of poetry. She was a poor scholar, he saw that instinctively and he knew by heart some of the verses she spoke so haltingly. When he completed one of them aloud with her, she was delighted.

"Eh, but you have an education! I said to Tom, I said you was not a bad-spoken lad." She put the books on his bed. "I shall leave these. If you can manage to hold them it'll while away the time till you're on your feet."

So he knew about horses and poetry and he had had some education. It was little comfort. The more his health improved the more he realised his loss. His past was gone. It seemed his life had begun from the moment he had woken in Farmer Dalton's attic.

Moses they had called him and Moses he must remain until his true name was discovered. Until then he must be content to look out at the grey square of sky revealed by his window and wonder where in the world was his true destination.

The newly-weds were the least aware of the weather. They were absorbed in each other, relieved that they were together and no deputation from Elliot's parents interrupted their idyll.

Bitter Harvest

With every day that passed their confidence increased. Elliot, basking in the heady glow of Adele's adoration, began to think of himself as a devilish sort of fellow to have executed such an escapade. He closed his mind firmly to disquieting thoughts of Mamma and Margaret and Mahmood. In time, he knew, Mamma would have to be faced, but he had decided that he was not prepared to return to Manchester for some while yet. He was quite taken with the idea of showing Adele a little of the country first. She was such a responsive little thing, her interest and enthusiasm in all he told her, most gratifying. He was enjoying more and more his role as mentor, guardian, lover, husband, to this beautiful jewel.

Adele, quite simply, was too happy and contented to contemplate anything but a future of continued bliss. They had moved on to Chester where, upon enquiry, they had learned of superior lodgings to be had at the house of a clergyman's widow. The house was in a pleasant sandstone terrace a mere step from the cathedral and the fashionable heart of the city. There were many agreeable entertainments on hand, but they preferred not to stir too far from their cosy first-floor parlour, idling away many hours with plans and speculations and reading aloud to each other from the volumes of verse on the bookshelves, or harmonising their voices in song or giggling over card games. They patronised the shops only that Elliot might shower his bride with pretty gifts – pairs of exquisitely worked gloves and handkerchiefs, lengths of silks and lawns to be made up into modish gowns, ribbons in every possible shade, ear bobs and brooches; anything she admired on their infrequent strolls, he insisted she must have. They were like children, self-absorbed, living for the moment, uncaring of everything beyond their own small world.

One afternoon when the sun made a watery appearance they took a walk along the ancient Roman walls. They exclaimed over the views, stole kisses in the shelter of the guard houses and laughed when a sudden shower wetted them through. Elliot, as a result of his soaking, went down with a sniffle. Adele cosseted

Anne Goring

him. She fetched every remedy known to modern science from the druggist, tenderly rubbed his chest with various revolting substances and asked their landlady ten times a day if she thought the doctor should be called. Their sensible landlady concealed her amusement, for she had taken a sentimental liking to the young couple so obviously in love and new to marriage, and assured her that the cold would likely clear of its own accord. However, seeing the distress of the bride she offered what comfort she could in the way of advice, extra coals for the fire and tempting dishes for the invalid. She also obtained from an acquaintance who ran the reading rooms, back copies of several Manchester and Liverpool papers to divert the somewhat grumpy introspections of Mr Sanderson, who made a fretful patient.

Elliot did not pick up the papers until an evening when his sniffles had eased and he began to feel that he might yet recover. Indeed, with the curtains drawn against the wet evening, the candles lit, a good fire in the grate and a glass of the landlady's excellent hot lemon and rum posset at his elbow, his spirits revived considerably. He settled back in his chair, his slippered feet on the brass fender, occasionally lifting his eyes from the newsprint to meet Adele's loving glance. She sat opposite him working her initials somewhat clumsily on the corner of a handkerchief. Candlelight caressed the curve of her cheek, the silky folds of her pink taffeta gown. He felt an uprush of emotion. The dear, sweet girl. She had brought him such contentment. Three weeks, he thought, we have been man and wife and already I cannot conceive any other existence. How could I ever have imagined I might be happy with Margaret Gordon?

He said, "I think I am feeling considerably improved."

Adele smiled. "Do I make you a good nurse?"

"Above all others," Elliot said fondly. "Still," he added, casually, "I feel we should both be the better for an early night."

She caught his meaning and blushed prettily. "You are too bold, sir," she laughed. Then she left her seat and came to kneel

Bitter Harvest

at his feet, laying her head against his knee. He twined his fingers in her hair and they sat in a contented silence until a knock at the door announced the maid with their supper chocolate and . slices of the landlady's excellent plum cake.

While they ate and drank, Elliot read aloud some amusing items from the Manchester paper. He thought he had heard nothing so pretty or musical as his wife's laughter. Pray God he would always make her happy.

At that moment his father's name sprang out at him from a column of print headed 'Loss of Respected Businessman'.

From one second to the next everything had changed.

They left Chester in a hired carriage early next morning. It had been a harrowing night. Neither of them slept. Adele, bemused by the sudden turn of events, had done her best to comfort Elliot and he had wept against her breast, like a child. He was surprised by the depth of his grief. Papa, it seemed, had always been the less prominent, the less important factor in his life. It was Mamma who made decisions, who swept him along, made her opinions plain and expected him to fall in with whatever scheme she had in mind for his day, month, year. Only now, in the first shock of bereavement, did he realise the full extent of the affection and regard he had for his father. Mingling, too, with natural regret was an undercurrent of guilt. Guilt because he had been a disappointment to his father who had so clearly wanted him to take up the reins of his business but had never forced or pressured him against his natural inclinations; because he had always taken his father for granted; because he had married against the will of his family and to punish Mamma for what she had done to Mahmood. Uneasily he wondered if the shock of the elopement had contributed to his father's death. And, deep down, as their newly acquired and hastily packed trunks were put into the carriage, he recoiled from having to face Mamma.

They were not comfortable feelings to carry through the day and it was no consolation to see the speedwell blue of the sky

Anne Goring

and the brilliant sunshine beyond the carriage windows. Summer had come, but too late.

Adele insisted that they stop at the lodge, but in truth Elliot did not mind the delay. The sight of Beech Place amid its sweep of lawns had set his stomach churning. At least those at the lodge might have some knowledge of Mamma's state of mind. He wished he had Adele's innocent trust. Adele rushed to the lodge door eagerly, sure of her welcome. He did not think he was quite so eager to pound upon his mamma's front door.

It had seemed to Carrie the longest three weeks of her life. Not since her skivvying days had she been confined indoors so much. Several times she had suggested that she might leave her aunt for an hour or two, but any mention of being left alone brought tears. "Pray do not leave me, Carrie. Not yet. I beg you. I . . . I feel so bereft," she would plead in a small, lost voice, that tugged at Carrie's heartstrings. It was as though she saw her niece as the only stable element left to her and she was frightened that this one dependable person would disappear if she let her out of sight.

Carrie could understand this, but it made it no easier to smile and assure Aunt Linnie that of course she would stay. Common sense told her that she herself would be no more likely to discover anything about Jem than Mr Brook or Mrs Walker, but it was galling to be so restricted. The inaction forced upon her made her unbearably restless. She slept badly, going over everything Mr Brook had told her – which was little enough – remembering how Jem had looked the last time she had seen him, trying to think of anything, *anything*, that might give her a clue to the appalling events that had followed. But there was nothing at all. All she clung to through the dark days was her trust in Jem. She knew he was honest. She knew he loved her. Sooner or later some message would come. Tangled up with this worry was her concern for Adele and her very real grief for Mr Sanderson, who had been a friend.

When the knock came and Jane admitted the bridal couple,

190

Bitter Harvest

her first thought was relief. Adele glowed with happiness. Her great violet eyes brimmed with it. After the first joyful moments when the sisters embraced, she stood a little shyly aside and drew Elliot forward.

"You know each other, of course," she said, "but Carrie, dear, I should like you to welcome Elliot, my husband, as a new member of our family."

Dutifully Elliot bent forward to kiss her cheek. "I hope we shall be friends, Caroline," he said. he looked pale and sad, but the look he bestowed on Adele was loving.

"I hope so too," Carrie said, from the heart.

Then, Aunt Linnie, weeping freely clasped them both in her arms and cried, "Oh, but why did you not write? You cannot imagine the distress you have caused us. To know you were safe and well would have been such a comfort." And, quite forgetting her own part in encouraging Adele to become engaged to Mr Prince, "If you had confided in me beforehand, what a great deal of upset you would have avoided, you naughty children."

Adele said lightly, "But Uncle George gave you our letters, did he not? Mine and Elliot's?"

There was a silence. Aunt Linnie looked suddenly stricken. Carrie said, quickly, "Uncle George is no longer here." Briefly she explained the circumstances.

"But he promised!" Adele looked bewildered. "He was to return here and tell you all about our wedding and give you our letters."

"In mine, ma'am, I explained that I should care for Adele," Elliot said, "and you were not on any account to fret about her. The manner of our marriage was hasty but, in the circumstances, necessary. We hope we are forgiven."

Carrie listened to Adele's account of Uncle George's part in the elopement. How well it all fitted! And how like him to arrange everything to cause the maximum nuisance. No wonder he had fled to another country. She wondered with a shiver what other slynesses might be revealed as time went on. He was a man of great deviousness. It would be a long

191

Anne Goring

while before she could feel they had truly seen the back of him.

"We are returned," Elliot was saying, "Because we read only last evening an account of my father's funeral." His voice quivered. "We . . . we had to come." He glanced at Carrie. "I . . . that is, do you know how my mother is?"

"Mrs Sanderson has not been out of the house, I understand, since the funeral." She added carefully, "Before that, well, she was understandably distressed about you and Adele. Perhaps by now . . ."

"She will surely be reconciled to our marriage," Adele said hopefully. "I thought Uncle George would have spoken for us, but no matter." Her eyes widened. "You will accompany us, will you not Carrie, to meet Elliot's mamma."

"I hardly think my presence will improve your case."

"But you are so good with words, whereas I shall be tongue-tied, I know, if Mrs Sanderson is at all sharp."

"You have a husband, now, to speak up for you," Carrie reminded her gently.

Elliot looked uncomfortable. "I trust that Mamma has become reconciled, but all the same, until I see her, I still doubt . . ." He cleared his throat. "Perhaps your support, er, Caroline . . . ?"

They were both such children. Children playing at being grown up, wanting to thrust responsibility at someone else. It was quite exasperating.

"Aunt Linnie does not like to be left," she said, but her aunt let her down shamefully.

"Oh, but this is different," she cried. "Now that I know that Adele is safe and returned to us it has quite raised my spirits. I know you will not be long gone. Pray do not stand back on my account." She was beginning to realise the advantages of this marriage. Once Mrs Sanderson was won round, why, the possibilities were quite pleasing. After all, to be connected to a family of such importance! For the first time since George had gone she allowed herself a small, hopeful, peep into the future. Adele had married money and she, such a generous child, would

192

Bitter Harvest

always be willing to make provision for her aunt, so despicably used. Perhaps her days at the lodge were numbered. She saw herself in a new neighbourhood where there was no need to be constantly reminded of her shame, where no tongues tattled. Friend and adviser, perhaps, to the dear young things, maybe even confidante of Mrs Sanderson. She settled herself on the sofa, her imagination quite diverted.

Carrie, less happily, drove with Elliot and Adele to the house. It had a shuttered look. The low sun chinked light off its blank windows. No maids hovered. The gardeners had long gone home. When Elliot tried the door it was firmly locked. He rang the bell and it seemed an age before they heard the sound of bolts being drawn.

"Mamma has made herself impregnable," Elliot said, attempting a laugh and failing, as the pursed face of the housekeeper appeared. She managed a softening of expression towards Elliot. She ignored the girls, managing to convey with the swish of her skirts that they were of no import whatsoever. "Madam is in the drawing room," she whispered, as though hushed voices had become the rule in this echoing house.

Mrs Sanderson was seated on one of the elegant gilded chairs, a book on her lap. Carrie's first impression was of total frozen composure. Adele leaned closer to Elliot who seemed to have difficulty in finding his voice. Then, awkwardly, he moved forward and kissed Mrs Sanderson on the cheek. "Mamma," he said, and his voice stuttered. "We . . . came as s-soon as we learned the news."

Black, even the rich silk of her high-necked, full-sleeved gown, did not suit her. It deadened the sallow skin and threw dingy shadows upwards revealing thready lines around her mouth, sagging skin under eyes and jaw. In scarlet or emerald she was dramatically handsome. In mourning, sitting straight-backed and motionless she looked like an effigy on a tomb. Only the eyes lived, dark, smouldering, full of unreadable passion.

"So," she said coldly, "you think it a suitable time to come crawling back to your mother's skirts."

Anne Goring

Elliot looked as if he had been struck. "But Papa . . . papa is –"

"Dead. Your father is dead. He died in my arms while you were about your own affairs. You have never cared for anything beyond your own comfort; why should you care now?"

"You have it wrong! I did care – I do!"

"Not enough, seemingly. Do you not realise that by your despicable behaviour you in no small way contributed to your father's death? Do you expect me to welcome you with open arms? The prodigal returned? If you do, you are too naîve by half, my son. And do not look so stricken. You may weep all you like, but it will not bring back the dear, good man who was my husband."

The words came quick and contemptuous and there was an odd timbre to them as though, Carrie thought, they had been rehearsed and this was but the opening salvo in a well-planned manoeuvre.

Elliot recovered after a moment, strove for dignity, stumbled on. "Mamma, I need not have come. It was out of respect for my father. If my presence is so . . . so painful, then I shall not stay. But we had hoped, Adele and I, that you would give us your blessing now that we are married."

"Married?" A swift change of tone. There was amusement in it, mockery. "Married?"

"We have the certificate," Elliot said sullenly. "Adele is my wife, however you may rail against it."

"You are not married."

"Adele had her uncle's consent. I am of age. The marriage was legal. Oh, Mamma, I know your hopes were grievously dashed over Margaret Gordon, but I know I should never have been happy with her. I am sure that once your disappointment is over you will come to love Adele as I do." There was pride and strength in his voice. In this he is sure of himself, Carrie thought thankfully.

Mrs Sanderson's only response was to sweep her dark gaze slowly over Adele, from the knot of ribbon on her bonnet to

Bitter Harvest

the blue flounce visible below the hem of her travelling cloak. She might have been examining a kitchen-maid brought before her for some misdemeanour.

"Your name is Adele Linton," she said after a pause. "Remember that. It will never be Sanderson."

Now it was Elliot's turn to look amused. He put his arm round Adele's waist. "You are too late, Mamma."

"You think so? I should not be so sure, if I were you. Such a runaway, hole-and-corner affair such as you have accomplished is bound to be as full of holes as a leaky bucket. Any half-decent lawyer would make mincemeat of your so-called certificate."

"Then we shall remarry! In . . . in a cathedral, if needs be! With banns called and choirs in attendance and all the flummery necessary. You will not come between us, Mamma, just because I have flown against your wishes for once in my life. And you need not think," he said with a coldness that for once matched his mother's, "that you will dispose of Adele as neatly and cruelly as you once did Mahmood."

"Ah, yes, Mahmood. I wondered if he had been telling you of his . . . his fabrications. Did you not realise that the poor soul has a damaged mind as well as a damaged body? All that cock-and-bull tale is a delusion. As though I should ever do such a thing." Her voice quavered. "How could you believe it of me!"

"He told me . . ."

"His vile accusations could land him in prison, do you know that? As it is he has been stricken with a fever since you left and is being well cared for here. He has every attention. When he is quite recovered I shall pay his passage back to Penang. He will perhaps recover his wits when he is back with his own people. But let us not speak of him. It is your happiness I am concerned with, Elliot." A tenderness, an appeal, had crept into her voice. "Your future happiness is all that I desire. Can you believe that I who have loved and nurtured you since you were put squalling into my arms want to see you throw your life away? Oh, you have been lured by a pretty face. So has many a young man.

Anne Goring

The damage is not irreparable. This so-called marriage is no marriage at all, I assure you."

Elliot's mouth was set in a sullen line. "I want no other but Adele."

Carrie, who had been trying to think of something helpful to say, put in quietly, "Mrs Sanderson, Adele and I have reason to be thankful for your husband's kindness. We know how good a man he was. Surely had he been here now he would have borne no ill-will but would have wished for a reconciliation. Could you not, for his memory, welcome your son and his wife."

"How clever you are." Amusement was back, Flickering in the dark eyes. "They brought you along, did they, to help plead their case? And you are perfectly right. My husband's reactions were precisely as you suggest. Forgive and forget was his policy." She drew in her breath, showing her sharp white teeth. "I do not forgive. As for forgetting, there is much in my life that I should like to erase for ever, but it is impossible."

Dorothea rose to her feet abruptly, the book heedlessly dropping to the carpet. "I have a proposition to make." She took two paces to the fireplace and rested her hand lightly on the mantelpiece, her back to them. "But before that, I must tell you something. A joke in which I play the fool." She spun on her heels, flinging the words out like a challenge. "You remember that time I came to you? That first time? I spoke then of your father, how he helped me to salvage something from the wreck of my first husband's affairs, and I took some worthless pieces of paper with me as my dowry when I married Miles. At least I did not think them worthless, 'then. I thought I had retained interests in several small ventures which it pleased my husband to manage for me and pleased me, too, to hear that they did well and increased in value. It gave me some pride that I had not gone entirely penniless to Miles." She laughed. It had a cold, bitter sound. "It was the profits on my interests that I so philanthropically arranged for you to have, in memory of the regard I had for your father and because I was foolishly moved by your poor circumstances. So Miles arranged it. Only

Bitter Harvest

there never was any money. The companies had foundered years before. Miles, generous and tactful, had fostered the myth of their prosperity, allowing me to keep my pride. So you see, when I came to you with my wonderful scheme, I really had nothing to offer you at all."

Carrie said, stunned, "Are you saying that all this time we have lived on Mr Sanderson's charity?"

"Precisely. He paid your school fees, gave you spending money, paid for your maid, saw that that silly aunt of yours wanted for nothing."

"Why did he have to go through such a pretence? Advising us the best way to invest the money . . . letting us believe we were independent?"

"Would you have been so comfortable in your mind had you known you were dependent on charity? No, of course not. His little charade bolstered your pride, too. To him it was a harmless game. He had been used to handling the reins of a complex business. It came hard to him to return here and let others manage for him. Your affairs were a diversion. He likely wanted you to make good marriages and so secure your own future. Or make some settlement when you came of age – only now he is dead and no one will ever know. But this is no matter . . ."

"How can you say that! We have lived in cloud-cuckoo-land all this while."

Adele ventured, timidly, but clinging to the one relevant thread of the story, "Surely if it pleased Mr Sanderson to look after us so well, should we not be grateful?"

Carrie said, smiling a little sadly, "I shall ever be grateful for what he has done – perhaps more so than I have been in the past. But it is not easy to realise that we have been objects of charity, much as poor Jane in that foundling home, when I thought our means were somehow earned by our papa . . ."

"Ah, yes," Mrs Sanderson said grimly. "Always we come back to Robert Linton. If I had not felt . . . as I did . . . towards him, I should not have wanted to make any grand gesture towards

Anne Goring

his daughters. If I had not had that small income of my own perhaps I might not have bothered . . . though I had a curiosity to see you both. Strange how it comes back to torment me. Had I not visited you, had I let you fend for yourselves, we should not be here now in this dilemma." On a brisker note she went on, "But this proposition. You are penniless now, you realise. I have no intention of paying you anything and I shall expect you to leave the lodge within the week."

Dorothea held up her hand as Elliot began to protest.

"Pray hear me out." To Adele she said, "You have the means to restore your family's fortunes." She took three strides back and forth then halted in front of Adele, standing over her like a black shadow. "I want my son back," she hissed. "If you go away now, without complaint or protest, I am prepared to be generous. I shall find you a suitable property in some fashionable place – the choice is yours: London, Bath, Cheltenham. The deeds will be made out in your name. You may repair there with your aunt and sister. You will receive every quarter the sum of, say, one hundred pounds – enough to keep the three of you comfortably. All I ask is that you decently relinquish all claims to my son, who is all I have left, the only thing truly mine and whom I love beyond anything you would understand."

Adele's face was ashen. She turned to Elliot. "But we love each other. We . . . we are married, Mrs Sanderson. In a chapel . . . with a parson . . . We have lived together, man and wife. How can you ask this terrible thing?"

"And you shall not!" Elliot pushed Adele behind him protectively. "Mamma, what you suggest is monstrous. Adele and her family are my responsibility. I shall care for them all."

"You?" The mocking note was back. "You are helpless as a baby, my son."

"I have my own income."

"Have you? Are you quite sure of that?"

"Wh-what do you mean? I am of age. It is all settled."

One fine-drawn eyebrow arched upwards. "Again your papa has been devious – in your own interests, of course. And in this

Bitter Harvest

case it pleases me greatly. A pity you have taken so much for granted, Elliot. The increase in income when you attained the age of twenty-one no doubt satisfied you, but you are no man of business. There was no visit to the lawyers, no signing of documents. You assumed, poor businessman that you are, that everything was being handled satisfactorily and were content to bury your nose in your precious orchids. Did you not realise that every penny that came to you was on your papa's signature? That, knowing you for a simpleton in business matters, he saw to it that until you were twenty-five – or made a suitable marriage – you could make no independent claim on your finances? He ensured in his will that I should have the final decision on any demands you might make. May I make it plain, that from this moment on you shall not have a penny unless you do as I wish."

There was a disbelieving silence. Carrie thought that she had never liked Elliot so well as when, taking Adele's hand and linking it through his arm, and with a firmness and calmness she had never heard before, he said, "Mamma, I have always respected you, but now I despise you – and will continue to do so for the rest of my life. You say you had no hand in Mahmood's downfall, but listening to the ruthless way you have spoken today –" His voice broke, but he stood erect and handsome, continuing after a moment, "You wish me to make a choice. Very well. I do not choose Papa's money or your company. I choose Adele. Whatever hardships we must face we shall not be disgraced in the way you would disgrace us. Come, my dearest, we shall not stay a moment longer in this house."

They were almost at the door when, with a rustle of silk, Mrs Sanderson was beside them. "Wait!" She opened the door a crack, peeped through, then closed it silently, leaning her back against the panels to bar their exit. "What you force me to say now must not go beyond these walls. Please. Seat yourselves. Give me this little time more."

Carrie had had the sensation all along that Mrs Sanderson had been building for a big moment – this moment – that all

Anne Goring

that had gone before was preliminary skirmishing to test the strength of the opposition. It had all been rehearsed, move by move, smoothly acted out with just the right touches of anger and bravado and pathos. She was ready now for the final assault. She was braced for it and Carrie saw with surprise, she was not invulnerable. For the first time there was apprehension in the bold dark eyes, and the hands clasped tightly in front of her were white at the knuckles. Whatever she had to say now was to be as painful to her as to her listeners. The death lunge would be bloody. Carrie felt her own nerves quiver in anticipation of what she must hear.

"When I have finished," she began quietly, "you will wish I had not started. I offered you a way of escape but you would not take it. So now I must tell you everything. About myself."

She sketched a vivid picture. They all saw the lonely child brought up by strangers while her beautiful mother swept in and out of her life and ended broken in the gutter. They lived with her the years as a milliner, her attempts to haul herself upwards, to find a better way of life and finding that escape in men as her mother had. They went with her on the long voyage to Singapore, they saw her humiliation as her husband plunged into shady enterprises and finally died in debt. It was as much a revelation to Elliot as the girls. His face was a mask of shock.

"I was in sore straits when Tom died," she went on. "it seemed that all my life I had been used by men and used them in turn to fight my way to respectability and ended up worse off than I had been before. It was no wonder that when the first man who helped me without any suggestion of payment in kind, who saw me merely as a female in distress rather than a woman to take advantage of, was the man I fell deeply and hopelessly in love with. That man was Robert Linton."

"Papa!" Adele's eyes were round blue saucers.

"He was not your papa then. He was young and dashing and popular with every woman who set eyes on him. For he was devilishly handsome. You, my dear Adele, are a constant and

200

Bitter Harvest

painful reminder to me of what I lost. Your colouring . . . your eyes. Can you imagine those eyes set in a masculine face? I was not the only one set aquiver by a glance, I assure you."

Dorothea stopped, glancing around as though for a moment she was uncertain of her surroundings, as though she had gone back in time and had almost forgotten where she was. She had not rung for candles and the room was growing heavy with shadows.

"I fell in love with him." She continued laughing harshly. "And he treated me in just the way one should treat a grieving widow. With kindness, with tact, with solicitude. He salvaged what he could from the wreckage of Tom's affairs. I had no way of repaying him, except one." She paused, speaking straight to Carrie, knowing her quick mind had already leaped ahead from the horror dawning in her eyes. "Yes, I seduced him. Out of no motive other than I loved him. I knew he did not love me, but love and lust are close companions. I knew I could arouse him, please him, I had learned the art well and I was a handsome girl. If he was reluctant to shatter the picture of me as a gently reared, sheltered lady – an image I had perfected – once he shared my bed, he lost his illusions with remarkable enthusiasm."

There was a long silence because there was nothing her audience could bring themselves to say. It was beyond their experience. They could only wait for the next revelation.

"We were lovers for exactly eighteen days; I cherished every one of them. His passage home was booked. For him it was a passing liaison. I knew it. Accepted it. He was going home to look for a wife and later he returned to Malacca with your mother. I understand they were devoted. As for me." She spread her hands. It was almost a pleading gesture. "I am a survivor. Adversity brings out my strength. I had already learned that much, young as I was. I am proud too. Pride and a broken heart can be a devastating combination. I determined not to be a poor hapless widow-woman when Robert returned to the East Indies. Even before he left Penang I had my plans. Miles

Anne Goring

had already started to court me. Unwittingly Robert himself had laid the way open." A softness crept into her voice. "Robert did not love me, I knew that. But he cared, and I clung to that crumb of comfort. He cared that I should not be friendless when he was gone. He persuaded Miles Sanderson to meet me. And in him I saw my escape. He had the two things that I had learned were the only things that truly mattered. Money and position."

"And love? What of love?" The words broke helplessly from Carrie.

"Love?" She almost spat the word. "Love brings nothing but heartache and trouble and grief. I have loved but twice in my life. Your father and my son. The result has been anguish in both cases."

"You set your cap at Papa, as you did Robert Linton," Elliot said huskily. "Did he realise . . . ?"

"Perhaps." His mother smiled, softer now. "But for once it was the right thing. Miles adored me and I was a faithful and true wife from the day he put the ring on my finger. Although he was so much older than me, he was an innocent in some ways. I found that very touching. He was so upset when I had that unfortunate accident and tumbled, so precipitating your birth. You were a small and frail baby, which helped to foster the notion that you were born prematurely. Of course, as soon as I had felt the first birth pangs I had arranged a graceful and unobserved fall upon the stairs."

The lance found its mark.

"So that, my son, is why Adele Linton's face haunts my dreams. Would you have had me say nothing, and watch the pair of you spawn idiots, or worse, for my grandchildren?"

She thrust the lance home, twisted it, withdrew the bloody blade.

"I was already with child when I married Miles. Your father, Elliot, was Robert Linton. You are Adele's half-brother. This 'marriage' of yours is an incestuous mockery. Now what have you to say?"

*   *   *

Bitter Harvest

Afterwards, Carrie was to remember Adele's cry, as though agony had welled up in her throat and strangled there. At the time her senses seemed paralysed. Everything around her happened slowly: Mrs Sanderson moving towards her son with outstretched arms; Adele wrenching herself from Elliot, flinging herself from the room, and Elliot going after her but held back by his mother who caught at his coat-tails, spinning him round. Did she speak? Did she cry, "Stay with me, my son. You must not go after her. It is all too late"? Carrie could not properly recall. Adele's scream drummed in her head and she put her hands over her ears to stop the sound of it. Then Elliot was gone too, flinging his mother aside, calling Adele's name.

Mrs Sanderson, thrown against a chair, slid down it, skirts spreading over the pale Tientsin carpet in a black pool. A lock of hair had come uncoiled, her cap was awry. There was a wildness in her face that was frightening. "Fetch him!" she cried. "Fetch him back to me! For God's sake, go!"

By the time Carrie had forced her legs to move and made her way to the front door, the drive was empty. Adele and Elliot had fled.

Mahmood saw Adele.

Dusk lay heavy across the gardens. The sky was a cloth of deepening cobalt, fading to turquoise and rose in the west. Mahmood was shuffling aimlessly down the long gentle slope behind the house when the girl, cloak ballooning behind her, bonnet strings streaming, came full-tilt towards him.

He had begun to take these long, restless walks now that he was over the fever. Heading nowhere, circling, returning to his stable loft, his mind incoherent. He had lived so long with his purpose, to find and destroy the woman who had ruined his family, that now, his mission a failure, there was nothing more to drive him on. He was eaten with shame. He had had her at his mercy – a triumphant moment when he had felt the power of vengeance surging through every muscle, rippling in his hand, his fingers, all the way to the kris . . .

203

Anne Goring

Then it was gone. Even before he saw the stumbling figure of his old master, he had realised his victory was dust and ashes. He could not kill her. It was like the anticipation of a woman, relishing the sinuous twining limbs, the lustful abandon, the animal fragrance, the prospect of thrusting delight . . . and at the moment of entry finding manhood shrivelled. Perhaps he had lived too long with his lust for the woman's death and it had rendered him impotent. He wished the fever had taken him, but it had not. His punishment was to live and remember his shame. He had failed Fatimah and she, too, since that night had never once returned to his dream country. She had gone for ever.

As he watched the girl coming towards him through the dusk, his heart quickened for a moment. Did she come to him now, showing her forgiveness? Then he saw it was not Fatimah but the other one, whose spirit seemed so alike. The girl called Adele, whom *Tuan* Elliot had taken for his bride.

She did not see him. Her eyes were blank, pits of darkness staring at some invisible, terrible, nothingness. She ran as if the terror was at her heels. He heard her breath rasping, the pounding of her feet. Then she had gone past and someone else was shouting. *Tuan* Elliot, tripping on a tussock, sprawling, getting to his feet, limping on. "Help me, Mahmood! Catch her! I am afraid . . ."

They were both after her then and she was as swift as the wind, not pausing. Elliot's wrenched ankle hobbled him; Mahmood ignored all the protesting pains of his crippled body and drove himself after her, but the gap between them widened. She fled away, down the other side of the hill, thistles and brambles ripping at her cloak as she crossed a strip of common land. She lost a slipper but she did not notice, not even when sharp stones sliced into her foot.

In the distance the river lay like a pale ribbon in its water meadows.

Adele watched the girl running. The girl had a stitch, her poor foot was bleeding and the pretty flounces at the hem of her dress

Bitter Harvest

were all torn and muddy. Such a shame, but she knew the girl had to get away. She had to go somewhere safe where nothing nasty could ever get at her again. She had watched the girl like this before. She had seen her when some people she could not remember wanted her to do something not very nice. Something to do with an ugly ring. She had been unhappy then. But so much worse now. Her heart was pounding so much it seemed it would burst from her chest and it was hard to breathe, but she had fairly flown over the stile and into the meadow that was full of deep puddles, and slippery. Two or three times she went headlong – oh, and it was cold and slimy, with the feel of wet clothes against her skin. But she got up again – not so quickly because her foot could hardly bear her weight – and splashed on. The river did not look nice. It was muddy, sliding past very fast and there were branches and bits of wood and – ugh – a dead cat rushing along with it. Adele felt sad for the girl. The water was so filthy and it would not be nice to swallow it and to feel the dead things in it bumping against her. But it was the only way. She did not hesitate long. They were close upon her now, the two pursuers. Their voices were loud.

A little sadly, Adele said goodbye to the girl, and stepped forward.

They were a fraction too late. They saw her standing on the river's edge and somehow found the strength to go faster; they were almost on her when she went in, but the current sucked her down and away. They ran along the rim until they saw her head bob up. She was not far from the bank but too far to reach. Elliot tore off his coat and boots, ran barefoot, keeping pace with that yellow bobbing head. Then, as Adele swirled under for the second time, he dropped into the water and hit out strongly, using the current to steer towards her. He grasped an arm, lost it, gripped her under the chin, wrenching her head back. She spluttered and struggled. The current was devilish. He could feel it dragging at him for all that he was a strong swimmer. He held his breath as they were sucked under, his

Anne Goring

lungs at bursting point when he surfaced. He gulped air, saw Mahmood's face, blurred, above him.

They had driven in towards the bank and Mahmood was reaching down, his fingers tangling in the coils of wet, yellow hair. Elliot fought to keep her against the bank. Mahmood had her cloak, then her shoulder. Inch by inch they forced her up into the muddied grasses and inch by inch Elliot could feel himself weakening.

He was almost spent when other hands took hold of Adele. A man, taking the river path home, had run to them. She was out of the water, a limp sodden bundle, and the hands reached again, took a slippery hold of Elliot's. At that instant a baulk of timber thumped into him, knocking his hold away. He clawed at the timber but it went circling by. He hit the main current which bore him, swiftly and quietly, into the middle of the river. He panicked now, fighting the water, as the cold bit into him.

They ran after him along the bank. For a while the black curls plastered to his head were visible. Then they were lost and the river took him.

Chapter Eight

ON A WARM morning in September, a young woman walked slowly down Hendham Vale peering at the houses. She knocked at the door of one of the terraced cottages and, when there was no response, knocked again, louder. A woman letting herself into the house next door said, "Wantin' Mrs Walker are you? She's over at her daughter's."

"Is it far?"

"Aye, towards Middleton. She's married to a blacksmith, Lilly is. Mrs Walker goes over there a lot, 'er being on t'lonely side since she's been left on her own . . ." She cut herself short on taking a closer look at the stranger and seeing her to be bold and brassy-looking adding, a bit sharpish, "I should come back this afternoon." She closed her door with a bang and firmly drew the bolts, just in case.

Sally heard the bolt go home and almost grinned. Almost. It was a long time since she'd felt like a good belly laugh. So, the mother wasn't in. She'd have to go and search out the other one, Georgie's niece, Carrie. She knew where she lived, wi' Georgie's wife, and it was a good walk. Still, she'd done plenty of that of late. She still remembered with less than affection the long lonely trudge through the country back to Manchester.

She found Beech Place without much trouble, but they'd gone. The woman that lived in the lodge now was a tight-lipped piss-pot. No, she didn't know anything of them, she'd only been here a month. And if Sally didn't get off the premises, she'd call her husband. The likes of her bothering respectable folk!

She was luckier with a gardener who was up a ladder, trimming

Anne Goring

a beech hedge alongside the wall that enclosed the property. He joshed her a bit, good-naturedly, before parting with the advice that they'd moved down Woodlands somewhere and she should ask down there.

The day was golden, hinting of autumn, with the first dead leaves crunching underfoot. The sky was the colour of a dunnock's egg and the sun was hot on her back. She picked blackberries as she went, enjoying the fruity richness on her tongue, tempted to abandon her search, to find a grassy bank somewhere and loll in the sunshine. No. No, she mustn't. She'd promised herself she'd do this. She must try to find them today. She'd been putting it off a bit, knowing that what she had to say wasn't going to please anybody, but better that they did know rather than going on hoping, as they must've done. How Georgie would've laughed if he could've seen her. "Conscience got you, Sal?" he'd say, mebbe giving her a sly pinch on her backside. "Don't do to have a conscience. Better off without it, I'd say."

"I'm only doin' it because Jem Walker was a nice lad," she said aloud, startling a blackbird that had been gorging itself in a blackberry thicket. "He didn't deserve what you did to 'im. I didn't like it a bit when I pieced together all 'is story. You was a vengeful sort o' man, Georgie O'Hara. Besides, I reckon your old missus might like to know what happened to you, you old devil."

As she walked, she wondered what George's missus was like. George had said she was a bad-tempered old stick who had taken to illness in order to spite him. Sal imagined her shrivelled and shrewish and the niece following the same pattern, but bossy with it. Yet the sister had been a little beauty. She'd often wondered how they'd fared, that pretty young couple. Georgie hadn't played fair wi' 'em, giving them that sham wedding. Still, they'd gone off happy enough and without George mebbe they wouldn't have had the guts to run off at all, and anyone wi' eyes could see they was smitten with each other. Still, they was rich. Any difficulties would be smoothed away wi' nice fat gold sovereigns.

Bitter Harvest

The lane twisted down to the road on the valley bottom. The fields were harvest yellow, the river curled placidly through meadows where cows grazed on the stubble. Dust rose like smoke every time a farm wagon passed her. Sally called to one driver, but he shook his head at her query, more concerned with getting a load of timber home dry, than some daft trollop asking questions.

She stopped by a field gate, leaning her elbows on the weather-bleached wood. Perhaps she *was* being too soft. Should she go back home? They might be anywhere, these folks. She didn't have no definite address. It was a bit of a wild-goose chase. There was always another day . . . But the urge was there, to speak of what she knew. The feeling had been growing that somehow she must find Jem Walker's girl and explain. Even as she thought of it she was touched by curiosity and a distant sort of pity for this unknown girl. Even a bit for Georgie's wife.

Sally walked on, hastening her steps when she saw two people ambling towards her on the other side of the road. An odd sort've couple she thought, coming up to them. A little crippled man wearing a broad-brimmed hat pulled well down over his face and a child in a blue muslin dress – no, not a child, though she had drooping wild flowers in her hands and twined in her corn-coloured hair and mucky smudges on her face. All the same, she wasn't no child.

Good Christ! She looked aghast into the smiling face. White teeth against a skin lightly dusted with gold from the sun, big eyes, violet-coloured. She held the flowers out to Sally.

"Have you any flowers?" she asked shyly. "If you have not I shall be happy to give you these." She waved her hand vaguely. "I can pick plenty more to take home."

Sal swallowed, and said hesitantly, "Th-thanks. I mean, no. You keep 'em."

"Do you not like them?" she said, crestfallen. "I thought they were pretty."

"Oh, they are," Sal said quickly.

The girl smiled, quickly restored. "Then I will take them home.

Anne Goring

I may make a picture of them. Elliot likes me to draw pictures. He loves flowers, too. Very special ones, called orchids. Do you know, he once said I was prettier than any flower he knew." She blushed. "We shall be very happy together when we marry."

Sally remembered the broken-down chapel, the pretty couple. Her skin prickled with cold. She said, wonderingly. "You're Adele, aren't you? Do you remember me?"

The fine eyebrows came down. The lovely eyes under them were blank, totally without understanding or intelligence. Slowly, puzzled, she shook her head.

The little man moved. He took Adele's arm, saying gruffly, "We go now to look at the horses." He spoke the King's English but in a funny, foreign way and he was as ugly as sin. Looked as though a carriage wheel had gone over his face. A mean glint in his eye, too.

Sal said quickly, "I was looking for 'er sister and 'er aunt, Mrs O'Hara. I got a message."

He looked at her evilly, but maybe it was just his face and because he was protective of the girl. After a minute he gave her directions. She was glad when they'd shuffled past. She stood there for a while, watching them meandering up the road, the girl stooping now and then to pick a flower or peer into a hedge, the little man hovering, watchful. The sight gave Sally goose pimples. It was something she wouldn't forget in a long time, the vacant-eyed girl and her ugly keeper.

Sally continued on. There was a factory on the river side of the road. She spelled out the letters, lips moving, on the arch over the iron gate: Brook & Son, Dye works. A scatter of houses, some in new red brick, older ones set back in gardens, a turning between tall elms and a short lane with two cottages facing each other. The one on the right the little man had said.

She went through the wicket gate and up a path set with clumps of thyme between the flags so that as she walked, the sweet and pungent scent drifted upwards. She rapped on the door but no one came. She thought, impatiently, is nobody to be in to me today? But the faint sound of voices came to her

Bitter Harvest

and after a moment's hesitation she took the path round the side of the cottage.

Sal was by no means an imaginative woman, but she thought the sight of the three women in the sunlit garden was like a painting she'd once seen in a shop window. It was a picture-framing place and amid all the shapes and sizes of framing displayed was this one, all blue and gold, it was. She'd stood there on this piddling wet day, just gawping. It was of three women sitting in a clearing in some woods, and there were flowers all round them and they were smilin' nice and looking at birds or some such in a bush. It was the sunny glow of it, the happiness of the picture that had caught her eye. Next time she went by, it was gone and she felt quite let down.

The same sort of quiet peace reigned in this garden. A middle-aged lady in black, wearing an elaborate widow's cap sat on a bench by the back door sorting through a basket of fruit. The youngest, a maid probably, in an overlarge apron was standing on a ladder gathering apples from a bent and mossy tree. The other girl, armed with a pair of shears, was trimming a row of raspberry canes. Everything was calm and unhurried in the sunny warmth. The air smelt of apples and the syrupy tang of boiling jam came from the kitchen window. Even the conversation was quiet and the little 'un on the ladder was humming softly as her nimble fingers nipped the apples from the green twigs.

With extra boldness, because she felt uncomfortable to be disturbing them and with such an errand, she said, "I'm lookin' for a Miss Linton. Miss Carrie Linton."

Three pairs of startled eyes fixed on her. The older lady dropped an apple and it fell with a thud to the flags. "Gracious!" she cried, "you startled me!"

Sally felt at a disadvantage. "I knocked," she said overloud, "but nobody came. So I walked round."

The girl who had been tending to the raspberries put down her shears and basket and wiped her hands on her apron. "You wanted me? May I ask who is enquiring?"

211

Anne Goring

She wasn't a bit like Sal expected. She was thin, yes, too much so, perhaps. But pleasant-looking. The eyes was kind and not a bit sharp and she had a nice head of hair on her, the sort that escapes in curls and won't ever lie flat.

"Never mind me name," Sal said abruptly. "I just want to say me piece and go. It's about Jem Walker, that I think you knows of. About what happened some months back."

"You . . . you have news of him?" For a moment, colour and life flooding into her face, she was nearly as pretty as her sister. Then the colour left her, as she watched Sal's face. "Not . . . not good news."

"No. Y'see I knows the villains that was put up to it. I won't name no names, but they're known for violence."

"Put up to it? What do you mean?"

"Somebody paid 'em to do it – to rough 'im up. Someone as bore a grudge an' wanted him – well – got rid of for a bit. But I reckon as 'ow they did their job too well. There's talk . . . I 'eard that they'd seen 'im off. Leastways, I've not been able to find out nothing different."

Her eyes seemed to have sunk into shadow. Her face, ash-white, showed up the dusting of freckles across her nose and cheekbones. Christ, but he must've meant something to her, poor little bitch.

Sal said, awkwardly, "I'm sorry, like. I 'eard as he had folks as was asking of 'im."

"Yes . . . yes." Her voice was whispery dry, like paper rustling. "Best I know. Big haunted grey eyes, pleading. "Are you sure, quite sure, that . . . that he is dead?"

Sal shrugged. "Seems most likely. For 'im not to turn up again . . . they're violent men, as I said."

"But why? Who would want such a terrible thing to happen to Jem?"

Sal could not face those eyes. She half turned away, saying gruffly, "I know nothin' of that. I must be off." Then, "I knew him by sight. He was a decent sort of lad. That was why I come."

212

Bitter Harvest

"Yes. Thank you." Carrie was trying to collect herself, making an effort. "Would you like a cold drink before you go? No . . . wait . . . allow me to give you something for your thoughtfulness in coming."

"I don't want nothing," Sal said harshly. She began to walk away, stopped, flung the information over her shoulder as though it was something she'd just recollected. "Oh, and the other one, Georgie O'Hara, he's dead an all, y'know. For definite that. Was took with the lockjaw. Chester way, I b'lieve."

"When was this?" The girl, Carrie, was coming after her, catching her arm, pulling her round. "Please! Please stop a moment."

Behind her the woman, Georgie's wife, had risen to her feet. Apples rolled everywhere from the overturned basket. "Oh, Caroline," she cried in a wavery voice. "Did she say . . . Is George . . . ?"

Sally faced them squarely. "Look, let me be," she said, taking refuge in anger. "I've told you he's dead. For certain sure dead and buried. They put 'im in a country graveyard. St Michael's it was. An' he's to have a headstone with 'is name on an' all." The last sovereigns had gone on it. After the bumbling pig of a doctor's fees had been paid and the cheating landlord's bill. He'd charged enormous and begrudged the bed Georgie lay on for all his hand was well greased. Didn't like sickness in his inn. Bad for custom. And the man who was to buy the horses, gone off wi 'em without a penny paid. Those days and nights nursing poor Georgie had damn near killed her an' all. The sight of 'is sufferings had been terrible. The fits that arched his body like a bow until his bones snapped. The jaws locked closed, the nostrils standing out, the eyes protruding, the mouth drawn to a ghastly grin. The doctor's indifferent voice, "We must draw the front teeth and get a tube into his stomach. Laudanum gruel might relieve the symptoms. Though I have little hope. These cases are usually fatal." And almost cheerily, "When he fell in the stable yard, it was likely a rusty nail that he cut himself on. That is sufficient to cause the onset of tetanus."

Anne Goring

Worst of all was knowing that Georgie was clear in the head. Every faculty alive to the torture of his body. *Every sovereign will buy you ill-fortune . . . Damn you to hell.* The words had rung a knell in her heart.

His suffering, hers, was in her face, as she said, "It's all done proper. He was buried decent. You can go and see for yourself if you don't believe me."

Carrie stared at her. After a moment she asked, very quietly, "Who are you? You seem to know a great deal."

"I told you no names!"

Carrie took in the bold looks, the scanty red dress, the bright beads hanging round the strong brown throat and dipping to the swell of the full breasts. She said, "You are Sally Quick, aren't you?"

Sal's eyes flicked to Mrs O'Hara. She saw shock and disgust register on the plump face. She'd been daft to come. She'd only made trouble for herself. "So?" she demanded. "What if I am?"

Carrie said, faintly, "And was it . . . was it Uncle George who arranged to have Jem put away?"

The denial came instinctively to Sally's lips, but something in the grey eyes stopped her words. There seemed, suddenly, no point in lying. "Aye," she said. "It were Georgie."

"To spite me. To hurt me in the cruellest possible way. I might have guessed . . ."

"I'll be off," Sally said.

"No! Please stay." She was not angry, but pleading. "We have been in the dark so long."

"There's not much to tell, beyond what I already said. Georgie cut hisself on summat rusty. The doctor said that was what done it."

She told them all she knew, aware of the round eyes of Mrs O'Hara fixed on her. Sad-faced old faggot, soft as duck muck. Not much of the shrew about her, just a pathetic creature wi'out much sense if she guessed right.

When she'd finished, Mrs O'Hara dropped back stiffly onto

214

Bitter Harvest

the bench as though her knees had given way. She said, faintly, "I am glad I know." She touched a trembling hand to her black skirts. "I have worn mourning these past months out of pretence. Now I can genuinely grieve for him."

A laugh bubbled inside, thinking of how Georgie must've gulled this one. Then it faded. He'd gulled everybody, even her in a way, though less than most, and look where it had got him. Six foot down in a graveyard where nobody knew or cared.

She said, "Your sister. I saw her down the road. What's amiss wi' 'er?"

"The man she married drowned," Carrie said flatly. "It . . . has affected her mind."

"They was a pretty couple. I'm right sorry. About everything." She turned away. There was nothing more to be said.

Carrie followed her to the gate. "If there is anything we can do – if you are ever in trouble and we can help . . . Have you any money?"

Sally managed a grin. Her face felt stiff and hard. "I've looked after meself all me life, love. Don't you fret none." She pulled the gate closed between her and Carrie. She felt better with that barrier between them. More herself. For a minute back there she had felt something pulling at her, like there was a hankerin' in her for that quiet garden, the neat cottage. Would she and Georgie ever have had anything like that? No, daft to think on it. She wasn't no well-raised softie. She'd not be content for a minute away from the crowds and the noise and the rough-and-tumble of the streets she knew. All the same . . .

"Summat I'd like to say. Me and Georgie, we was two of a kind, y'know. We was very attached. I . . . I thought a lot of him or I'd never have gone off wi' him else."

Why'd she said that for God's sake? Excusin' herself or summat? She saw the glimmer of understanding, of pity, in Carrie's eyes before she turned and ran down to the dusty road. A smart carriage roared past her, lathered horses sending up a storm of dust. She spat grit angrily and waved her fist at the

215

Anne Goring

coachman. Then she wiped the back of her hand across her face. Mingled with the dust was the dampness of tears.

The carriage sped on. Neither the coachman nor the woman within noticed Sally Quick in her red dress, but half a mile further on there was a fierce rapping to attract the coachman's notice. He reined in his horses, cursing quietly under his breath. Madam needs must get out. Madam must stretch her legs. He helped her down and she snapped up her parasol to protect her complexion and walked back the way they had come. The coachman shook his head and went to soothe the horses. He was a bit tired of Madam's fancies, all the servants were. Shut up in her room seeing nobody for days on end, then emerging only to find fault, sweeping through the house like a thunderstorm, leaving maids in tears and menservants shamed. Then other days, the ones he dreaded, she would ride out in the carriage and he must drive the horses as though the devil was after her and she was fleeing before him. "Faster!" she would cry. "Can you get no more speed out of those nags?" And they the best pair of greys in the district. He'd be glad when she came to her right senses again. If ever she did.

Dorothea Sanderson had seen them sitting under a hedge. She had seen them before in her jauntings. Seen them and passed them by without so much as a flicker of an eyelid. Even now she could not think what impulse possessed her to stop when she had caught sight of that bright head. But stop she must and now she would go and observe them closer.

She had no qualms. The girl was witless but not violent and Mahmood merely her protector. Strange how he had fastened on to the family. Oh, she knew all about them, even if she left the house only to drive round the countryside without any purpose but to quell the agony that boiled up from time to time and would not be contained. When the mood was on her she would cross-question her maid, wanting to ferret out every detail. At other times the girl would only have to mention, unthinkingly, the name of one of them to have her ears soundly boxed. So

Bitter Harvest

Dolly knew that Edmund Brook had taken it upon himself to keep an eye on them, that they lived in one of his properties in a perfectly respectable fashion, Caroline Linton earning the rent by running the school newly set up at the dye works. Indeed Caroline, once her sister was recovered in all but her wits from . . . from the accident . . . had flung herself into good works. The aunt carefully preserved her role as widow. Adele lived in a world of childhood. We all, she thought, have our ways of escape.

Àdele was eating blackberries, picking them and murmuring to herself between times. Her fingers were stained purple from the juice. Mahmood lounged on the grass beside her, seemingly half asleep. But on seeing who approached, he leaped to his feet and stood protectively by his charge.

Dorothea ignored him. She observed Adele, who glanced up smiling. A distant recollection stirred in her memory. A day such as this, hot and sunny. A girl standing on a sandy track, the sun making a nimbus of her hair. A girl whose blossoming beauty had moved her to compassion and ultimately to disaster.

She asked, "How are you Adele?"

"Oh, I am exceedingly well. I do so love the sunshine. Would you like some blackberries? I will pick some for you."

"Thank you, no. Do you know who I am?"

She shook her head, uncaring. "Are you to be my friend? I have many friends. They come and talk to me and I like that."

Mahmood said, surlily, "I think this *mem* not a friend."

"Oh, but yes, Mahmood," Adele pleaded, her lovely face clouded. "I like to be friends with everyone." Then she smiled, holding out her stained hand. "Come. Come and see the horses. There is a dear little foal who has legs like broomsticks." Stained fingers reached out and clasped Dorothea's black gloved hand. Adele led her to the field gate. "See, they are on the far side. What a shame. But they will come in a moment if you wait. I bring them bread every day."

The hand burned hotly through her glove, making her palm sweat. She pulled it free abruptly. "I cannot stay," she said.

217

Anne Goring

What fool's impulse had caused her to stop? What good did it do to stand here pretending to hold a conversation with a simpleton, other than reawakening the pain that she must always fight to keep subdued? She was inflicting hurt upon herself. She could feel the floodgates shift and all the hateful recriminations and regrets begin to seep through.

"Stay a little while," Adele pleaded, then with disarming innocence, "You must be very hot in that heavy grosgrain. Do you not find black a tediously hot colour in the summer?" She tilted her head on one side. "I should have thought scarlet or emerald would suit you better." She smoothed down the crumpled folds of her muslin skirt, "I have a beautiful yellow gauze at home. We are to go to Mr Brook's tonight and I shall wear it then. For I may be asked to sing and you do not know who else may be there. It is quite possible Elliot will be invited too, and I have to look my best for him."

There was a lump like a rock in her throat. Even with the parasol's shade she could feel perspiration spring out along her upper lip.

The lustrous eyes were fringed with absurdly long lashes. They fluttered a little. "Do you live hereabouts? If so, you may know Mr Elliot Sanderson. He is the most handsome young gentleman."

"Be silent!" Dolly could scarcely breathe. Her voice came out raggedly.

Adele giggled. "You are like Carrie. She tells me I should not be so forward, but I cannot deny that I love him and he loves me." She leaned forward, whispering confidentially, "Carrie has a secret, too. She pretends about it, but I see her looking at Jem Walker. Of course, he is a great deal below Aunt Linnie's expectations. He is only a carter's lad, you see, though he has educated himself and has prospects of advancement. I think they would like to be betrothed, but they will have to wait until Jem returns." She looked about her vaguely. "He has gone away, I forget where. He does not seem to visit any more. It makes Carrie very unhappy. But Aunt Linnie has hopes of Mr

Bitter Harvest

Brook. I like Mr Brook. He brings me sugared almonds when he calls and is very complimentary about my paintings. Oh, see!" Her attention was caught by a pair of tortoiseshell butterflies, fluttering along the hedgerow. She was immediately entranced. When the butterflies had danced over the hedge, she looked round again. But the lady in black was walking swiftly away.

Mahmood watched the cloud of dust raised by the carriage and horses disperse. The ways of fate were strange. He had failed to administer the punishment he thought she deserved, but what she suffered – and it was plain to see she suffered – was something far worse than the sudden plunge of a kris. She must live with guilt for the rest of her life.

Adele had returned to her blackberry picking. He touched her arm, calling her by the fond, private name which he used when they were alone. He felt more at peace with himself than he had done for a long time.

"Come," he said, "it is time for home."

She smiled, ever sunny, ever happy. She would never know hatred or misery or betrayal again. He had vowed to protect her always.

"Time for home," he repeated gently. Then in his own tongue, "Time to go, Fatimah, my sister."

Dorothea Sanderson stormed into the house, swept up the stairs, and slammed the door of her room behind her. The sound echoed down the empty corridor. She stood in the middle of her bedroom. Its pale elegant spaces drew away from her; the white lace coverlet on the bed dazzled her eyes with its intricate pattern; the roses on the pink carpet reared up under her feet. She put her hands either side of her temples where the blood throbbed. Was she screaming or was it only in her mind?

The anxious face of her maid swam into view. She waved her out of the room. Then she tore at the neck of the stifling dress, hearing the silk ripping. Buttons flew. The gown was at her feet and she kicked it away. . . . *Scarlet or emerald would suit you . . . I have a beautiful yellow gauze . . .*

219

Anne Goring

Air moved coolly on her bare arms and shoulders. More Slowly now she unbuttoned her low boots and pulled off the fine dark stockings. The carpet was soft under her naked soles. She lay on the bed in her petticoat and chemise staring up at the high white ceiling. . . . *You may know Mr Elliot Sanderson. He is the most handsome young gentleman . . .*

Dorothea had not cried in all these months. She had heard the remarks, 'How well she conducts herself', 'She is very brave'. Not brave, but so borne along by a great tide of anger and hate against all those involved – against herself most of all – that there had been no place for tears. Now, soft at first, they came sliding down her cheeks into the lines and hollows of her flesh, soaking into the pillow beneath her head. Then a storm of weeping, so fierce that the muscles of her stomach grew painful.

She lay there a long time, until there were no tears left. Then quiescent, drained, her limbs heavy, she slipped into a half-slumber. When she started awake she stared round with gritty eyes. She had been dreaming. She had been back in the house in Penang. She had heard Elliot's voice and Mahmood's in the garden under her window. There had been the heavy fragrance of frangipani. Briefly, she had been touched with joy, light and soft as a moth's wing. But the pale room was not the one with the deep verandah overhung with crimson bougainvillea. No bulbuls called their bubbling cries from the yellow hibiscus hedge. She was in a silent room, in a silent house.

Wearily Dorothea crawled from the bed. She poured water into the basin and sluiced her face, pulled on her robe. She caught her reflection in the long mirror. Her eyes were swollen, her hair, winged now with white, straggled down her back. Had this bedraggled, wretched creature ever considered herself handsome? No man would look at her now and lust to take her.

She looked as she felt. Empty. As though she had been in a fever, had come through a crisis and her eyes were opened on a world she must rediscover. Even the room had the unfamiliarity

Bitter Harvest

of long absence. Her glance went round it. She reacquainted herself with every piece of furniture, every costly ornament. She saw the silver tray piled with unopened correspondence. She had ignored it for weeks and impatiently would have dismissed it now except for a faint awakening curiosity. She riffled through the letters. Familiar and unknown hands writing her name and address. Two letters, much travel-stained, in a hand she recognised. She picked them up. By now Pereira would have the news of Miles's death and the importuning letters would stop. Her fingers paused in the act of ripping them in half; she opened them instead, and took them to the window, where she seated herself and began to read.

Much later when the maid cautiously knocked and entered with a tea tray, she found her mistress still sitting in the window seat. The opened letters lay in her lap and her eyes were fixed unseeingly on the view beyond the glass.

If one good thing had come out of all the unhappy events, Carrie thought, as Mr Brooke's carriage took them that evening the short distance to his house, it was the improvement in Aunt Linnie.

There had been a time early on, when she had been deeply worried about her. The tears, the clinging, the growing reliance on the sleep-inducing, numbing effects of the sherry wine, had been distressing to witness. Adele's illness and the removal from the lodge had, unexpectedly, been the saving of her. For some weeks Adele had had to be carefully nursed while she recovered from the physical effects of her near drowning. Aunt Linnie, at first resorting to hysterics when she knew the truth of the affair, had been pressed by Carrie into taking a turn by Adele's bed while she and Jane, with the help of the strange, deformed little man who had taken part in the rescue and now so mysteriously seemed to have attached himself to the household, busied themselves with packing.

Those hours at her niece's bedside had wrought the beginning of a change in Aunt Linnie. Perhaps it was that tending to the

Anne Goring

needs of Adele – who, it soon became clear, would recover physically but whose intelligence was irretrievably lost – took her mind off her own troubles. Perhaps the sudden dramatic change in their fortunes shocked her into reviewing the narrowness of her life. Whatever it was, during those distressing weeks she seemed to take on a new lease of life.

To Carrie, maintaining a calm appearance while privately racked with worry, it was one glimmer of light in a black time. Mr Brook's help had been the other encouragement. Without him their lot would have been difficult indeed. Homeless and rendered practically penniless overnight, with a sick girl to care for, a dependent aunt, not to mention Jane and Mahmood, who seemed also to be her responsibility now, she would have been hard-pressed to cope alone.

Mr Brook had been firm, sweeping aside all her doubts and protestations. he owned a cottage, recently become empty on the death of its elderly tenant. It was theirs for the taking. He would be glad of responsible people taking over the tenancy, for the property had been well cared for and he did not like to see it lie vacant for too long. Besides, the cottage was convenient for the factory and as soon as she felt able to leave her sister he wished her to take over the organisation and running of a scheme dear to his heart, the factory school. She was in no way, he assured her, to think of these as favours. The rent of the cottage would be the same as that of the previous tenant. Her salary at the school would be by mutual agreement, and he could think of no better person to entrust the education of the young operatives.

In the same tactful way he proffered the use of his carriage to transfer them all to the cottage and one of the factory wagons to remove their goods. He also helped to find buyers for most of their better pieces of furniture which must now be sold. It would have been foolish to refuse. It was no time for pride and, truth to tell, it was a relief to have someone take a little of the burden. Carrie told him everything about Adele and Elliot and Mrs Sanderson's terrible revelations. She owed

Bitter Harvest

him that. She owed him, too, one other explanation. When they had become settled at the cottage and Adele had regained her health and Aunt Linnie had begun to revive her old pleasure in gardening – venturing out to supervise Jane's random attacks on the greenery – and when she had taken up her duties at the dye works, then was the time.

It was in the new schoolroom with the rows of varnished forms and tables and her own tall desk and the newly arrived books and slates still to be sorted, that Mr Brook, surveying it with a pleased air, said, "I fancy your pupils will be impressed. You have interviewed them all now? Are there many who know their letters?"

"One or two only. But all are eager."

"Perhaps more to escape their work for an hour," he said, smiling. "I rely on you to impress upon them the importance of learning for its own sake. Would it aid you, if I offered small prizes of books to be earned by the most industrious at the year's end?"

"It would be a spur to them, I am sure. Few come from homes where books could be afforded, even if anyone could read them."

They paced round the converted storeroom while he examined the fresh paintwork, moved a table more to his liking, returned to her desk where he turned over the books she had ordered. "Capital," he said. "Capital. I think it most satisfactory." The sounds of the factory were muted here. She was conscious of his warm, approving gaze, of their aloneness. He said, quietly, "Caroline, I have not spoken before, you have been too troubled. But now, well, you know what is on my mind." His fine musician's fingers rested on her arm, moved down to touch the bones of her wrist beneath the cuff of her plain grey dress. "I . . . I could make things so easy for you, my dear. If you became my wife, you – your family – I should delight in bringing all under my roof to become my family also."

Carrie turned distressed eyes upon him. "Sir, Mr Brook, I beg you not to say any more. You are my friend. I

Anne Goring

respect you, I like you, but as to marriage . . . it is not possible."

"Not possible? Dear Caroline, there are reasons, I understand that must put you against matrimony. Your aunt's unfortunate case, your sister's tragedy. But," humorously, coaxingly, "our circumstances are very different. I have the deepest affection for you, we share the same interests . . ."

"But I do not love you, Mr Brook. My affections are engaged elsewhere!" It was blurted out at last. She rushed on, feeling the colour hot in her cheeks, "I would not hurt you, Mr Brook, for you have been a most loyal and true friend. How I should have managed without your help I do not know, and I fear I have not been as honest with you as I should. But, you see, we could not speak before. We wished to be betrothed but everyone would have tried to stop us. It was a secret. It could not be anything else." She stopped, took a breath, saw the puzzlement on his face. "I do not make myself clear. You see, it is Jem Walker whom I love . . . so dearly . . ." To her horror, her voice would run on no more. She covered her face with her hands. After a while he said, softly, "Ah, that explains much." His touch came on her shoulder, reassuring, comforting. "You have carried a burden heavier than any of us suspected."

His sympathy seemed a greater punishment than his censure would have been.

"I . . . I shall quite understand if you do not wish me to continue in my duties here. I have no right to expect you to keep me in your employ."

"And you have no right to dismiss my friendship so lightly. I have said it before, I can think of no one more suitable for this post. You will be a great success here. That is all you must concentrate on for the present." His voice was non-committal. In control of herself again she looked at him. He smiled, a trifle wistfully. "About . . . the other matter. There is nothing more to be said for the present. I respect your feelings, Caroline, and your honesty. May we remain friends?"

"It is more than I deserve."

Bitter Harvest

He shook his head. "I forced you to reveal your secret. It is I who have invaded your privacy. It is not your fault that I have harboured hopes. And shall continue to do so. I should be less than human if I did not admit it. But I settle now for your friendship."

So it had been agreed. She had felt awkward in his company for a while but he was so unassuming, so tactful, that she found herself relaxing to their old pleasant relationship.

The school prospered. As well as the younger employees, some of the men approached her about learning to read. She found herself taking classes after the men had finished their shifts. On Sundays she went into town to help at the mission Sunday School. Somehow it was an act of faith in Jem. There she felt close to him.

One Sunday, Carrie called at old Miss Blackshaw's house in Strangeways on her way home. The old lady took her to see the dove, fluttering with its fellows around the dovecot, but it was painful to be there, remembering the sunshine, the hopes, of that spring day when she had been there with Jem. She was glad to make her excuses and leave. The Housing Society continued to progress. The gentlemen of the committee insisted that she have a small honorarium for her work in keeping the minutes. She suspected Mr Brook's hand in it but he denied it. It had, he said, been a spontaneous gesture on the part of the other gentlemen who had learned that her circumstances had become reduced.

So the summer passed. She busied herself every hour of the day and only the nights were long and dreary and full of fearful imaginings.

Jane had refused to be dismissed. "You're me family, miss Carrie. All I want is food – and I'll eat little enough. I'll go out and find cleaning to do if you can't manage that!" she had announced tearfully in the beginning. So Jane became more and more her right-hand in the house, looking to Aunt Linnie, seeing that Adele was kept tidily dressed and that Mahmood returned her home for her meals.

Anne Goring

Adele. Sometimes Carrie thought she was the lucky one. It was all gone. All the tragedy, the heartache. Only the shadows of memories remained: of those closest to her, of a few happy events which she relived, over and over. Looking at her now as the carriage drew up to Mr Brook's house – at the perfect face smiling in anticipation, the curls Aunt Linnie had carefully dressed and beribboned, at the soft yellow folds of her gown – Carrie felt tears pain her throat, remembering another occasion when so eagerly they had travelled to Mr Brook's. Then she had seen Elliot sweep Adele to the floor and dance with her and had not known such an innocent occasion was already sown with the seeds of disaster.

They stepped down into the dusk. The air held the fragrance of the warm day, but there was a sharpness in it that spoke of summer's end. A wraith of mist hung among the trees at the end of the garden, like the ghost of old hopes and promises. Did other spirits watch out there? Mr Sanderson, Elliot? Uncle George? Did they know longing and sadness and regret? Was Jem, now, one of their company? She stood still a moment, aware of light falling from the open door, of voices calling greetings. She reached out with her mind beyond the house, beyond the garden, out, out, to the tiny sparkle of stars in the darkening sky. She searched for him, weeping in her heart, but he did not answer. He was gone. *They're known for violence . . . they did their job too well* . . . She had clung to hope all these long months and now, with hope gone, she was adrift in a terrifying emptiness.

"Come, dear," Aunt Linnie called. "The night air is deceptively cool."

"Yes. Of course."

Her cloak brushed against a late-flowering rose. Its petals fell away from the brown heart and scattered. Her heel ground them into the gravel as, unnoticing, she went into Mr Brook's house.

The evening, as all the evenings they had spent at Mr Brook's, was a success. Mr. Wharton of the Housing Society was there,

Bitter Harvest

with his wife and simple but amusing daughters. Mr Brook played for them – a Chopin nocturne, a Beethoven sonata – and accompanied the ladies as they were pressed to sing. Miss Wharton gave a dramatic recitation of her own composing, on the death of a favourite cat, which had the two elder ladies fumbling for their handkerchiefs, and just before supper was announced, everyone joined in several choruses of a popular sea-shanty.

In such company there could be no mention of their caller, one Sally Quick, and the message she had brought. To the Whartons, Aunt Linnie was a respectable widow who accepted with fortitude the results of her niece's accident during the spring floods, when an unfortunate young man had been swept to his death in attempting to rescue her. For Adele they felt nothing but sympathy that one so pretty had become unhinged from the experience. They treated her as they might a pet kitten. They thought it fortunate that her elder sister was a practical and hard-working girl. Of course, she had no looks. She was too thin by half and too pale. Her face was all bones, and even candlelight, so gentle and flattering to the feminine sex, only emphasised the hollows under her cheeks and the dark shadows beneath her eyes. With such haggard looks it was as well she had brains, for it was unlikely any man would give her a second glance. Her destination was obviously to be a support to her family, working as a tutor or governess. It was easy to be kind to her.

As they went into supper Aunt Linnie managed to whisper to Mr Brook of the visitation. "Caroline will tell you all. It is too hurtful . . . such a common person. But we have no need of pretence with you and it is best we know."

So as Mr Brook helped her with her cloak Caroline was forced to speak of that which twisted the knife deeper and deeper into her heart. Jem's probable death . . . Uncle George's last vengeance. "He tainted everything he touched," she said in a low and bitter voice. "He was a wicked man and met a wicked end. I can only see it as justice."

Anne Goring

Mr Brook held her hand too long as he said goodnight. She felt its trembling pressure and saw how his eyes burned. She had lost all hope but he had regained his. He said, softly, "It is not the finish, my dear. Believe me, time will cure everything."

Carrie wanted to cry, Please, no! Your devotion is another burden. Pray, Mr Brook, do not look at me so because it would be easy to give in. To let someone else bear the weight. To lean, to sink into submission, to fill up the void in my life with good works. But it would be second best, Mr Brook, and not fair to you.

She said merely, withdrawing her hand, "Goodnight Mr Brook. Thank you for a pleasant evening." And then turned away to the carriage.

As his body healed, so the realisation came that he was lucky to be alive at all. Poor Moses, Farmer Dalton thought, had been brutally used by some evil persons. "Beaten to a bloody pulp, you was, lad," he said. "Have you still no memory of it?"

He could only shake his head, though, as summer progressed and his body with youth's resilience began the long healing process, he began to have dreams. Nightmares of running on heavy legs through a mire that dragged him down and of pursuing men, gaining on him until he could hear their heavy breath on his neck. He would shout then in a voice that would not raise itself above a whisper and his leaden limbs would not respond to his commands. He would wake sweating and gasping.

Watching the moonlight on the sloping ceiling he would try to probe into the blankness of his past, into the significance of the dream. Who was he? How had he come to be floating in the river, a battered mess? Did he have parents, sisters, brothers, a wife . . . ? No faces or names came to him, only the fear of those faceless men who pounded after him. He did not speak of these dreams to the kindly farmer and his wife. Perhaps it was that he was a fugitive, a man who had done wrong, who might bring disgrace into their simple lives. He did not feel himself a criminal, but how was it possible to be sure? The crack on his

Bitter Harvest

head could be responsible for the blotting out of the memories of some terrible deed or an innocent life.

He stared at himself in the blotchy glass on the attic wall, and it was the strangest sensation of all, to look upon unknown features. At first the livid bruising blurred the face, but as it subsided there was still no recognition. Dark hair, rough cut by Mrs Dalton, hung in ragged locks covering the healing scar that zig-zagged from his scalp onto the right temple. The nose would forever bear a bump on its bridge. A tooth was missing in his lower jaw. Apart from these things he could not think that the face was so much altered from what it would have been. Yet he did not know it.

He had begun to sit outside in the sunshine and a faint tan enlivened the sickroom pallor. He was able to shave the stubble from his chin, but he did not think that it was a face of any particular merit or distinction. He was a tall man and perhaps had been a strong one, though he was kitten-weak now and his palms as soft as a woman's.

Sometimes he took Mrs Dalton's precious books to read. The words of some of the poems had a familiar quality as though he heard a faint echo through the blankness of memory.

> 'Who doth ambition shun
> And loves to live i' th' sun,
> Seeking the food he eats,
> And pleas'd with what he gets,
> Come hither, come hither, come hither.
> Here shall he see
> No enemy
> But winter and rough weather.'

So, what did it prove other than he was a man who read poetry? Was moved by it? Some lines stirred his senses with an inexplicable sensuousness.

Anne Goring

'Love is not love
Which alters when it alteration finds,
Or bends with the remover to remove:
O no! it is an ever-fixed mark,
That looks on tempests and is never shaken.'

But the frustration of trying to fathom who had been the man who
had learned, who had perhaps experienced, the emotions contained in the lines, made him cast the book aside in despair. It was
easier to involve himself in day-to-day happenings about him. To
sit on the bench by the kitchen door shelling peas or paring potatoes for Mrs Dalton or, as his strength grew and he could manage
the sturdy crutches Mr Dalton had fashioned for him, take on
heavier tasks: fetching water from the well, pail by laborious pail,
feeding the pigs, grooming the great shire when he came in from
his day's work in the fields, or harnessing the pony to the trap
when Mrs Dalton went to the Saturday market in Manchester.

It was a small, prosperous farm, the house set on rising land
amid apple and plum orchards with rich watermeadows running
down to the Irwell. "It were me grandfather's and his father's
and his father's afore that," Farmer Dalton told him as they
took a turn round the yard after supper one evening. "It's sad
that I'm the last of the line. We had but two live childer, me
and t'missus, and they both taken from us as babbies. Well,
the Lord gives and the Lord takes away and doubtless He has
his purposes, but it comes hard to think as all this'll some day
go to strangers."

He chewed on the stem of his clay pipe, as they came to the
limit of their evening stroll where the walled lane led from the
farm in the direction of Manchester. The summer dusk lay grey
and heavy over the smokey blur of the town, but the air was sweet
here with the smell of newly turned hay. "Our eldest now, would
have been about your age. Two and twenty summers." Then,
as though his thoughts marked a well-worn route, "I wonder if
you'll ever know the truth of what happened." He cleared his
throat, said gruffly, "Should you not, there'll allus be a place

230

Bitter Harvest

here for you, young Moses. T'missus has taken a shine to you and I'll confess to some similar thoughts on t'matter." He stared in an embarrassed fashion at a tongue of fern growing between the stones of the wall. "The ways of the Lord are mysterious, lad. Perhaps it was meant to be that you was brought to us in such a strange manner, to learn us ways like a book newly writ upon, to be the son to us as never growed up."

Abruptly he began to speak of the weather and how the hay would dry well with another day or two of sun. The matter was not mentioned again.

He was touched by Farmer Dalton's speech. He liked the good people who had cared for him. He liked the hard routine of the days, the quiet Sundays when they drove twice to the nearby Baptist chapel, and the psalms they sang came to his ear like familiar friends. He liked the quiet evenings in the farm kitchen and the early mornings in the waking countryside. It would be easy to slip into their comfortable ways.

Farmer Dalton had initially been enthusiastic in his enquiries about the lad who had been washed up on his land and Mrs Dalton had asked among the market folk in town, but no one had come forward to claim him. "If you was washed down from town, lad," the farmer said comfortably, "well, it's a big place. When you're properly yourself again you must go and ask about." But in the meantime the farm was at its busiest and there was no time for jaunts. Every hand was needed. First for the hay and then the barley and corn. Then the plums and apples were ready and must be picked for market.

He limped still but his leg, carefully set by a retired apothecary who lived nearby and served most of the district in their more serious ailments, mended well. He began to do without crutches. The sun burned his skin gypsy-brown and the good air and plentiful food and hard work restored his body. He slept deep of a night and the nightmares fell away. He began to trouble less about his mysterious past as he fell more and more into the ways of the farm. There were whole spells when he forgot

231

Anne Goring

to probe and ponder. Perhaps that was why, quite suddenly, his memory started to return.

It began with a girl.

The gleaners were in the cornfield. Women and children with sacks and baskets scoured the brown stubble in straggling lines, bent to their task. He was leading the shire out to pasture when a group of women shouted something and they all laughed and looked at him. He was used to their teasing. He had learned that even with his less than handsome looks, he held an attraction for the comely country girls. Perhaps the mystery of his past had something to do with it. It was best to take their banter with a grin and a joke, and as he was speaking, one of the girls straightened up, her hand to the small of her back. She wore a blue dress and brown curly hair was escaping untidily from under her faded sunbonnet.

He stopped in mid-sentence. Something about her stance . . . the blue dress . . . the curve of her arm as she lifted her hand to wipe her forehead.

He saw her plain, not this country girl, but another, turning towards him in her blue gown, her eyes smoky-grey with green lights and she smiled her wide, sweet, loving smile. For him.

A great cry erupted from him, that startled the horse and set the row of bucolic faces agape, "Carrie!"

As abruptly as it had come the image faded. He recovered himself dazedly, led the horse to pasture. He was left with a name, a face that haunted him, and try as he might he could conjure up nothing more. It was as though a door had opened a crack to admit a ray of light and just as sharply closed, leaving him in a darkness that was worse than before, because he was tantalised by that brief glimpse.

It was two days before the door swung open again, wider this time. He was walking through the orchard and the sun was low. It struck through the twisted mossy trunks of the apple trees in slanting bars. The ground was freckled with leaf shadow and, for a moment, he was standing in a lane overhung with trees with the sun striking blue light off snow and she was there

Bitter Harvest

running towards him. She came into his arms and rested her head against his shoulder with a small contented sigh. Carrie. Caroline . . . Linton. Even the sound of her name in his head made his heart leap.

He said nothing to the Daltons, fearing that even to speak of these moments would make them dissolve away like dreams that cannot be caught on waking. But soon the images were coming thick and fast.

One morning he woke and knew his name.

He told the Daltons then. Mrs Dalton, after her first delighted curiosity, fell quiet. "You'll go then," she said. "Aye, I see that you must and it's only right. But I . . . we all shall miss you, lad."

"And I shall miss you. There's no way I shall ever forget your kindness."

He bent and kissed her rough cheek and she gave him a great hug, saying tearfully, "Should things not go right for you in that other place, remember us. There'll allus be a place for thee here."

There were still gaps. He had no recollection of how he had come to be in the river, of the events leading up to it. The manner of his employment still eluded him, though his work had been with horses. He remembered driving a wagon round the town. He remembered his home, his mother, his sister. With aching anticipation he remembered Carrie and their promises to each other. What had this summer brought to her? He had been gone so long. Golden September was half over. They must all believe him dead, surely. He was impatient to be gone, but contained himself, not wishing to upset the Daltons who made gentle attempts to detain him. "I'm short a man this week, lad. Wilt tha stay a day longer and clear that last acre of apples? If tha stays till Saturday we can take thee into town when we go to market . . ."

They left him by the Shambles. Farmer Dalton wrung his hand soundlessly and Mrs Dalton would not leave off hugging him. There was a lump in his own throat. Such good people.

Anne Goring

He owed them his life and how could a debt so profound ever be repaid? He watched them drive off into the press of wagons and carriages, then stood feeling a bewildered stranger in the throng that pushed past him. After the peace of the farm, the town noise was overwhelming. He kept against walls and protected his leg with his stout ash stick. He had forgotten the hardness of paving, the greasiness of cobbles that made walking a hazard.

Jem looked about him as he walked. No familiar face turned his way, but he knew his route almost by instinct. He threaded through the packed thoroughfares. At one busy corner, where crossing sweepers dodged almost beneath carriage wheels to clear a path for the more prosperous-looking ladies and gentlemen in hopes of a ha'penny, a rattling wagon almost caught one urchin unawares. Jem caught his breath, not at the narrowness of the lad's escape, but at the letters on the wagon's side. Carter Smith. Of course! The wagon was gone too fast for him to accost the driver, even had he been able to run. Besides, when he had seen the name he felt the echo of his nightmare fear. It induced an irrational panic, as if he were conspicuous on this street corner and should slink away and hide. He forced himself to stand calmly, savouring his new knowledge. He remembered Carter Smith, sharp-faced, bow-legged, a little man full of his own importance. He could remember the men at the yard, their names ... the horses. Then, blindingly, everything fell into place. His hand tightened on his stick until his knuckles showed white. By God he had it now, the whole lying business. And all these months had gone by while his name was blackened and shamed. What sickening stories had been carried to those he loved? "Carrie," he groaned to himself, "how you must have suffered." Then he realised he had spoken her name aloud, as two startled ladies averted their eyes.

He crossed the road, blinded by anger and pain. He was but a step from the yard and it was in him to go straight there and face Carter Smith ...

But his rage died as quickly as it had risen and cold logic

Bitter Harvest

took its place. It had been so long that another day would scarce make any difference. There were others more important. Besides, if he were to clear his name he must do so with caution and intelligence and not rush into any hot-headed scheme that might land him in deeper trouble.

Jem walked steadily north out of the town. By the time he reached the Eagle & Child where many a time he had tethered or watered the horses, he was dusty and thirsty and his leg had set up a dull throbbing. He barely glanced at the cool dark little doorway. Something stronger than thirst drew him on. The quiet lanes of Crumpsall were shady, fallen leaves lying in russet drifts. His limp was more pronounced now and he leaned heavier on his stick. Then, at last, he was in the lane leading to Beech Place.

I have nothing to offer her he thought. All I have is the five shillings Farmer Dalton pushed into my hand and a set of second-hand clothes. I have no position, no money and a besmirched name. Yet see her I must.

His need overwhelmed all logic and reason.

The last stretch was the hardest. The more he hurried the more the clay-hard ruts slowed him. Once he tripped and was forced to stop until the pain had died to bearable dullness. Gritting his teeth he went on. The small side gate beside the two elaborate ironwork ones, the lodge with a thread of smoke rising from its chimney into the still air, his hand on the knocker. One moment . . . two . . . he would see her.

"Well?" The sharp face above the coarse dark dress was totally unfamiliar. "What's your business?"

"Miss Linton," he began. "Mrs O'Hara . . ."

"Gone," she snapped. "Don't ask me where because I know nothin' of 'em."

She had the door half closed before he recovered enough to thrust it back. "Please," he said. "I have been away. Surely you must have an address."

"Get off me doorstep. I've better things to do."

"It's important. Why did they leave? Where did they go?"

Anne Goring

A child wailed from within the lodge. "Now you see what you've done wi' your knocking and questions! I tell you, I know nowt but that they left in a hurry. Be off!"

The child's screams intensified. The woman slammed the door. Jem stared blankly at the shiny brass knocker and heard her voice screeching inside. If she didn't know, he'd be damned if he'd go before he found out more. Quietly he slipped round the lodge and set off through the gardens.

He came to the glasshouses and looked around for a gardener; he knew one or two of them by sight. They'd tell him. Yes, there was someone inside the glasshouse there. He limped forward as the figure moved to the door. A tall woman dressed in brilliant purple silk swept out and stopped, raising enquiring eyebrows.

"Forgive me, Mrs Sanderson," he said. "I am trespassing."

Dark eyes raked him over coldly. "Really? Then you had best remove yourself. I do not encourage trespassers on my property."

"I . . . that is, Mr Sanderson knows me, ma'am," Jem said quickly. "My mother, too. I did not mean to trespass, but the woman at the lodge was unhelpful and I wished to find out about the people previously there. Mrs O'Hara, ma'am, and her nieces. I thought one of the servants might know of their whereabouts. I . . . I have been away, you see."

Dorothea held in her hands several newly cut flowers. They were strange to him, waxy and pink on long stiff stems. Could they be the orchids Mr Elliot cultivated? He looked from the flowers to her face. That also had a waxy look as though she spent a great deal of time indoors. She was older than he had thought. He had only caught glimpses of her before, but he had thought her a handsome woman. The sunlight showed up the wings of white in her hair and the lines on her face.

She said, expressionless, "You have the advantage of me, young man. Your name?"

"Jem Walker. My mother is known in the district for her nursing. She came often to the lodge to visit Mrs O'Hara."

Bitter Harvest

"Well, well." The dark eyes regarded him with sudden interest.

"If you could tell me where Mrs O'Hara has gone, I would be obliged, ma'am."

"Would you indeed! Or perhaps it would be a younger member of the family you are more curious about. Miss Caroline Linton, for example?"

He felt his cheeks hot. "Miss Linton . . . and Miss Adele are my friends. I have been away . . ."

"On a very sudden errand, I understand. So urgent that you have been unable to communicate with anyone for some months – and with the trifling matter of a theft hanging in abeyance."

So it was all known. A matter of common gossip! He thrust down his anger; he must begin as he meant to go on. He said, meeting her gaze, "I'm an honest man, Mrs Sanderson and I mean to prove it. I don't know the whys and wherefores, but it was a trumped-up case and if you should wish to know where I've been, then ask the good farmer who dragged me from the river where some blackguards left me for dead. I have been without memory of anything until this last week due to this." He thrust back his hair to show the paling scar.

"A lost memory, indeed. How very convenient."

He had begun quietly, but ended almost upon a shout. "I remember everything now and shall clear my name if it takes all of my strength and the rest of my life!"

"How very vehement you are," she said lightly.

"You'd be vehement, ma'am," he said with cold scorn, "if your good reputation was dragged in the mud."

"My good reputation? Ah, would that I had one to preserve."

"I think I had better go."

"On the contrary, I become more interested by the minute. *You* interest me, Jem Walker." She tipped her head to one side, the dark eyes were amused. "You are a handsome young devil, you know. Even when you scowl. I can quite see why Caroline Linton has pined for you these months. Why, if I were younger . . ."

237

Anne Goring

"This conversation," he said, shocked, "is out of place."

"Now you are embarrassed. I do believe you are truly innocent of your own attraction – and that is enough in itself to ensnare the most world-weary of women, such as I am. No, do not turn away."

"I won't stay to listen to such foolishness!"

With a swift rustle of silk she was at his side. Her white hand fastened on his arm. Her voice was changed, harder. "I ask you to stay, Jem Walker. For your own sake. For hers. I want to talk to you."

He was genuinely puzzled. "What can you have to say to me? We have met but five minutes since. What do you want of me, Mrs Sanderson?"

She said, "When you went away I had a husband and a son. They are both gone from me now. Both dead."

"Mr Sanderson? Ma'am, I didn't know . . ."

She looked down at the flowers in her hand. "Do you know anything of orchids? No? They were Elliot's passion, but I fear they have been sadly neglected since he has gone. It is only recently that I have been able to bring myself to visit the glasshouses, but I know nothing of them, and the gardeners are useless."

He said, awkwardly, "I'm sorry."

"For the flowers or for me, Jem Walker?"

"For both, ma'am."

He thought she was a little mad. Unhinged, perhaps, by her double loss.

"The flowers need your sympathy more than I. They are poor dependent things that will keel over if left untended. But I am of stronger stuff. I depend on no one but myself. I am not a young woman, but neither am I in my dotage. I have many years left and I will not drift through them, uselessly fading, with guilt and grief my only companions. I need a purpose to give my life direction. I have already decided upon the direction I will go and it may be that your path will run alongside."

Jem said patiently, "Ma'am, I merely came to find Car . . .

Bitter Harvest

Mrs O'Hara. I have had a long walk and I still feel the effects of my injuries. If you cannot assist me, I beg leave to go."

"I will take you to her. In my carriage. Would that suit?"

"Most kind, but I wouldn't wish –"

"*I* wish, Jem Walker, and I am a woman who takes unkindly to argument. Now, give me your arm. You will walk back with me to the house where you will take some light refreshment while the carriage is put ready. While we are waiting we shall talk. At least, I shall talk and you shall listen. There has been a world of change while you have been absent, none of it for the good, but perhaps something may yet be salvaged." She took up her long skirts in her free hand as they began to walk along the path. "*She* told me scarlet or emerald were my colours and she was right. However, one cannot rush too fast. I shock them already with my purple when I should be in full mourning still. But the wearing of black will not bring the dead back to life or make grief any more bearable. Do you not agree?"

Jem was too bemused and puzzled by this strange, somehow compelling woman, to say anything but yes.

Chapter Nine

CARRIE looked down at the note. The black spiky hand scrawled across the thick paper and she had an odd sense of being cast back in time, of reading another letter that had urged her to return home to meet Mrs Sanderson. She had sensed change, then, and been afraid. She had been right. The elegant lady who had graced the cottage, the bearer of apparently good news, had touched them all with disaster.

Now she was too tired, too numb, to puzzle overmuch at the command. And of course she could not go.

'I beg an Hour of your Time. On receipt of this Note, I would request you to adjourn to your Home where I shall Await you. Pray do not delay. What I have to say to you is of the Utmost Importance . . .'

The gatekeeper had delivered the note to her himself. "Straight away, she said, miss. Take it to 'er right off and tell her it's urgent." He had been impressed by the fine horses, the carriage, by the lady's tone and by the coins she had pressed into his hand. He had scuttled away to do her bidding.

The classroom emptied. The sound of clogs and boots and youthful voices faded. One group had gone. In a short while another would appear for the precious hour of learning Mr Brook had authorised. The room still held the odour of working clothes and poorly washed bodies. She leaned against a window ledge. The sash was raised and the air was cool, though the taint of the dye works lay upon the breeze.

Anne Goring

It was not so much the tiredness of her body that troubled her – though she knew she did too much; filling every minute of the day gave less time to think – but as now, in this rare still moment, she felt the black exhaustion that was deep in her mind. A joylessness of spirit that nothing would move. Neither talk, nor work, nor music, nor laughter. It was a dark compound of pain and despair. From it came uncomfortable visions. The sly smile of Uncle George; Adele's fearful scream and, more terrible, the blank violet eyes that would smile forever on emptiness; Sally Quick's voice, repeating, 'They're men of violence'; a hundred images of Jem. Jem grinning at her, kissing her, touching her so softly with his calloused hands, holding her so tight that he squeezed out her breath . . .

She put her aching forehead to the cold glass. Time, Mr Brook had assured her, cured everything. Was love, then, a disease to be borne and endured until the antidote of distance was acquired? She loved her sister. Would the moment come when she would look upon her without grieving for an intelligence lost? In quite another, more profound way, she loved Jem. Was it merely an infection that would succumb to the passage of years? Perhaps, as in real disease, it depended on the person, some people taking it so badly that they never truly recovered. With others it gave the merest touch of indisposition, soon over, quickly forgotten.

The door creaked open. She straightened herself, put on a calm face. Mr Brook hurried across to her, his expression eager. He found a few moments of every day to visit the schoolroom. He was always courteous, speaking scrupulously of general matters, tactfully avoiding the personal and private. She was grateful for it yet, in a contrary way she found herself wanting to snap impatiently at him sometimes. It would have been untenable to do so. She was too much in his debt and he was too kind. Perhaps the reasons subtly, lay in that.

"Ah, I have found you alone, how pleasant. But you look a touch tired. Do you find your pupils trying? If so, I shall speak to them."

Bitter Harvest

"Not at all. They behave exceedingly well." She made an effort, smiled.

"Good. Then if I might speak of our Housing Society. There is a property we should look at . . ."

She listened, answered, kept her expression interested. He paced as he talked, looking at her from time to time for her approval, nodding, pleased, when she agreed. Her thoughts drifted. She was walking with Jem; his hand enclosed hers, he was talking shyly of his plans . . . their plans. His arms were about her, his mouth bearing down on hers with a demanding pressure that aroused the strangest, most urgent sensations in her body . . .

She jolted back to reality, the saltiness of tears upon her tongue.

". . . So I thought we would visit on Saturday next." He waited for her answer and when it did not come, said, "That would be suitable, would it not? I should wait upon you with the carriage at nine-thirty in the morning."

She said, quietly, "No, Mr Brook."

"Then tell me when, my dear. I can arrange a time convenient to us both."

"No," she repeated. "It would not work, you know."

"I think we are at cross-purposes. I was speaking of the property in Ancoats."

"And I of dependence and gratitude."

He stared at her in puzzlement. "I do not understand."

"No. No, you would not, Mr Brook." She regarded him gravely. "That is why, sir, I could never marry you."

A flush tinted his cheeks. "I was not speaking of marriage, Caroline."

"But it is on your mind, is it not, though you take pains to mention it not at all?"

Edmund said, cautiously, "Since you have raised the matter, then, yes, I will confess it. I have not spoken because I . . . I did not wish to press you."

"Of course you would not. It is your nature to be cautious

Anne Goring

and patient. Or is it, perhaps, as you once told me, because you prefer to blind yourself to unpleasantness and take the easy way? You know that I love someone else, but you find it comforting to believe that I shall soon forget. But I shall not, Mr Brook." Carrie smiled ruefully. "I fear the disease has me well in its grip. I think, perhaps, you will fight off infection better."

"What do you mean, Caroline? You are woefully obtuse."

"In plain words, Mr Brook, I would not offer you second best. It would not be fair to either of us. I will not marry you now, or in the future. I think that is quite plain."

His face blanched. "Jem Walker is dead," he burst out. "Would you bind yourself to a memory? You are too young for that."

"Rather that, sir, than bind myself unwillingly, out of gratitude. Already you have tied knots about me that are hard to break. But broken they must be."

"Caroline! Dear, dear, Caroline, think what you are saying." He stepped closer, pleading. "You speak so much of gratitude. I do not ask for gratitude. It has been my joy to give things to you and my ultimate happiness would be to give you my heart and hand in marriage."

It was the hardest moment. The worst. She steeled herself against the fawn-like devotion in his brown eyes. She drew strength from the clear, quick knowledge that her action was right.

She said, gently, "I shall, of course, stay until you find a replacement for me. I ... I will advertise for employment elsewhere. It might be better for all of us if we got away from environs that hold too many unhappy recollections."

"It will be too hard for you! Consider the life. A poor schoolmarm, a harassed governess to some spoiled brat ..."

"I have made my decision, Mr Brook. I'm sorry."

"Think what your life could be with me!"

"I have done." Impulsively she stepped forward and kissed his cheek, for the first time and the last. "Thank you, Edmund, for

244

Bitter Harvest

all your kindness. Had I not known Jem, had I not experienced, . . . well, no matter. I shall never forget you."

"Caroline." She felt his trembling. He lifted his hands hesitatingly, reached for her, but she slipped from his embrace. From his life.

The letter had crumpled in her fingers. Carrie looked at it blankly for a moment. She had a longing to be out in the air, away from the schoolroom, from the press of thin, odorous bodies who would soon come through the door. Away from the sad brown eyes that pleaded for something she could not give.

Clutching at the excuse, she said, "This note came for me. From Mrs Sanderson who wishes to see me. Perhaps you would allow me to slip home for a short while."

He said again, begging, "Caroline, stay. Let us talk."

But it was too late. It had always been too late. And she was gone.

She found herself running across the cobbled yard, through the gate arch, down the dusty road. Running away? No, from a sudden surge of relief. Her bridges were burned, a decision had been born out of all the doubts of these drifting months. It had been comfortable to slip into the shelter of Mr Brook's protection. But now she had chosen to step away from it, out into a harsher, more challenging climate. And, willy-nilly, those who in turn depended upon her must go too. It would not be easy for them or for her, but she would work for them, fight for them, with a good heart. She had her health, her intelligence, her wits. Above all, she had her self-respect and integrity . . . assets she had felt submerged and in danger. She felt right with herself now, even if a little frightened at the prospect of a future that must be formidable.

The carriage stood in the road. Carrie slowed. The coachman in his smart livery did not even deign to glance at her as she slipped up the turning to the cottage. His pride was dented. Such riff-raff as he was obliged to carry. He'd look for a new place, he would. Only the horses had kept him here this long.

Anne Goring

A madwoman for a mistress, shocking the neighbourhood now in her unsuitable clothes, talking to vagrants in the street and today bringing with her a ragamuffin young man who *he'd* never have let ride outside, let alone on the fine leather upholstery. Aye, things was sadly awry since Master had gone . . .

The front door stood open. She stepped straight into the parlour, blinking at the dimness after the breezy sunshine. The scent of thyme drifted in with her, to mingle with a dusky, subtle perfume she recognised. The room was small and bare. They had early sold their more valuable trinkets. Mrs Sanderson sat bolt upright on one of the two plain chairs either side of the hearth.

"At last. Good day to you, Caroline. Pray seat yourself. I have begged a few moments alone with you first." She was very brisk. Carrie had not spoken to her since that appalling day when Elliot and Adele had returned. She had not wished ever to see her again.

She said, coldly, "I cannot think that we have anything to say to each other."

"On the contrary, there is a great deal. To our mutual advantage, I trust."

"I seem to recall you came before, offering help. It scarcely turned out to our advantage."

"And you mistrust me now. Good. It puts the discussion on a sensible footing. But do sit down or I shall be forced to stand."

Reluctantly, intrigued in spite of herself, Carrie sat. She sensed in the other woman some inner excitement. The bold eyes sparkled, the hands clasped on the handle of a violet silk parasol were taut. Carrie's wariness deepened.

"I must ask you two questions. I want you to answer them honestly. When you have done so I shall lay my cards on the table. First, I understand your aunt entertains hopes of a match between you and Edmund Brook. Are you of the same mind?"

Carrie lifted her chin. "I hardly think it is your business."

Bitter Harvest

"It is. Answer me. Has he proposed?"

"Yes."

"You accepted?"

"No."

"Thank you. Then I take it you still carry a candle for this Jem Walker?"

Carrie felt the familiar pain, mingling with a shock of anger. How dare she! How dare this arrogant woman walk in here and ask such questions! She said furiously, "Mrs Sanderson, get out of this house. Take yourself off! What right have you—?"

"So you love this poor young man whom everyone thinks below your station."

They were both on their feet now, facing each other.

"Yes, yes and yes! How can you ask, knowing that he is gone and the hurt it gives?" Her voice quivered. "You have done so much harm already. Do you take some perverted pleasure in seeing us suffer more?"

"You misunderstand, Caroline." The voice was soft, entreating "I wanted only to be sure. You see, it is my hope that I shall make it possible. No, I run too fast. First you must know what it is I have decided for myself. I am returning to the East Indies. There is nothing for me here, except a life of dull respectability. I have no taste for it. I am a restless and impatient woman. I shall return to Penang. My late husband's interests have been too long neglected and there are outstanding matters to be dealt with." She smiled. "I think I shall make quite a stir. It will be amusing to set the tongues wagging. A woman, in a community where women are even more pampered than they are here, involving herself in commerce. It will be quite a scandal."

"Your plans are no concern of mine, Mrs Sanderson."

"Oh, but they are. You see, I wish to take Adele with me." She paused to allow her words to sink in. "I am rich. I am generous. She shall want for nothing. Her future will be as secure and contented as I can possibly make it."

Carrie stared. Affronted, enraged, she cried, "Do you think

Anne Goring

I could agree to let my sister go with you? You, who have ruined her."

"For that very reason. Without Elliot my life has no purpose. His marriage, his children . . . Oh, how I should have enjoyed watching it all. Living vicariously, true, but how satisfying to see one's child go out into the world." Her voice became laced with bitterness. "I longed for money once. Now I have too much, too late."

"So you wish to take my sister with you as a sop to your conscience."

Dorothea regarded Carrie steadily, the bold eyes shadowed. "She and Mahmood are the only links I have left with my son."

"Mahmood?"

"He has not spoken of it? Yes, he was my son's body servant in Penang, long ago. He shall go with us, of course. He seems, poor creature, to have taken on the role of protector to Adele. I wonder, sometimes, if she reminds him of . . . of someone else. No matter, he will be glad to be away from here before winter." She hesitated, then said slowly. "Your aunt, of course, may choose to come or stay, as she thinks fit. Myself, I would think some small village or county town, where she may soon make friends, would be preferable. I shall bow to her wishes. Your maid seems a sensible girl and quite attached to her. She soon drew her out of the hysterics my proposals had caused. And when she has had time to ponder . . ."

"You mean Aunt Linnie *knows* all this."

"The bones of it. As much as I thought fit. I reserve the whole for you, for the ultimate decision is yours."

"And what plans have you for me, then, Mrs Sanderson?" she asked acidly. "You seem to have everything arranged to your own personal satisfaction."

For once Dorothy Sanderson seemed at a loss. She took a turn about the room, her heavy violet silk skirts swishing. Then she stopped at the small latticed window, staring beyond the

Bitter Harvest

pots of geraniums, to the garden. In a very different voice, low, emotional, she said, "I have known true love once in my life, as I told you. I fell deeply in love with your father, Robert Linton. When he had gone nothing was ever the same again. All that I had of him was Elliot. I think that was why I held Elliot so close – too close. I feared to lose love for a second time, yet in holding too tightly I succeeded in destroying him. If . . . if it is true and deep this love you and Jem Walker have for each other, I would wish you to have every chance."

"But you know how it is," Carrie whispered, very pale. "He is gone, probably done to death."

Slowly, incredibly, Mrs Sanderson was shaking her head. "I want you both to come with me. He seems an intelligent young man and honest. He is old enough to be sensible and young enough to accept challenges. I think he might make me a trustworthy manager in a few years. She paused, said lightly, "With you at his side, how could he go wrong in anything he chose to do?"

"Jem . . . Jem, do you mean –?"

"He is out in the garden, bearing his exile with great fortitude. No, wait!" She caught Carrie's arm. In a hard, brisk voice, she said, "In a few days I shall return for your answer. And remember I do not offer you and Jem any sinecure, Caroline. You will have to work hard. I detest spongers and sycophants. Charity is for those who are unable to help themselves. Your aunt and Adele will never want again, but you must have the chance to make your own way. I am giving you that chance and it is for you – and Jem – to take or refuse it, as you will."

With a crash, the door to the kitchen burst open,

Behind Jem, a row of faces. Aunt Linnie's open-mouthed, Jane's grinning, Adele's dreamy, Mahmood's watchful.

Carrie saw none of them. Her eyes were blinded with tears, her legs weak.

He cried, "The devil take you, Mrs Sanderson! You said you

Anne Goring

would call me when she came. I have waited long enough!" He moved forward, holding out his arms.

Mrs Sanderson stood for a moment, watching them.

Presently, smiling a little, she slipped unnoticed from the room and closed the door softly after her.